The Priestess of Kelvert Part 1

Beneath the Golden Sands

By

Ben Billups

THE PRIESTESS OF KELVERT PART 1 BENEATH THE GOLDEN SANDS

Cover art and maps by Ben Jamar Billups

Published By Ben Jamar Billups

Available on Amazon and booksbybillups.com

ISBN: 978-1-7359482-2-5

Printed in the United States of America

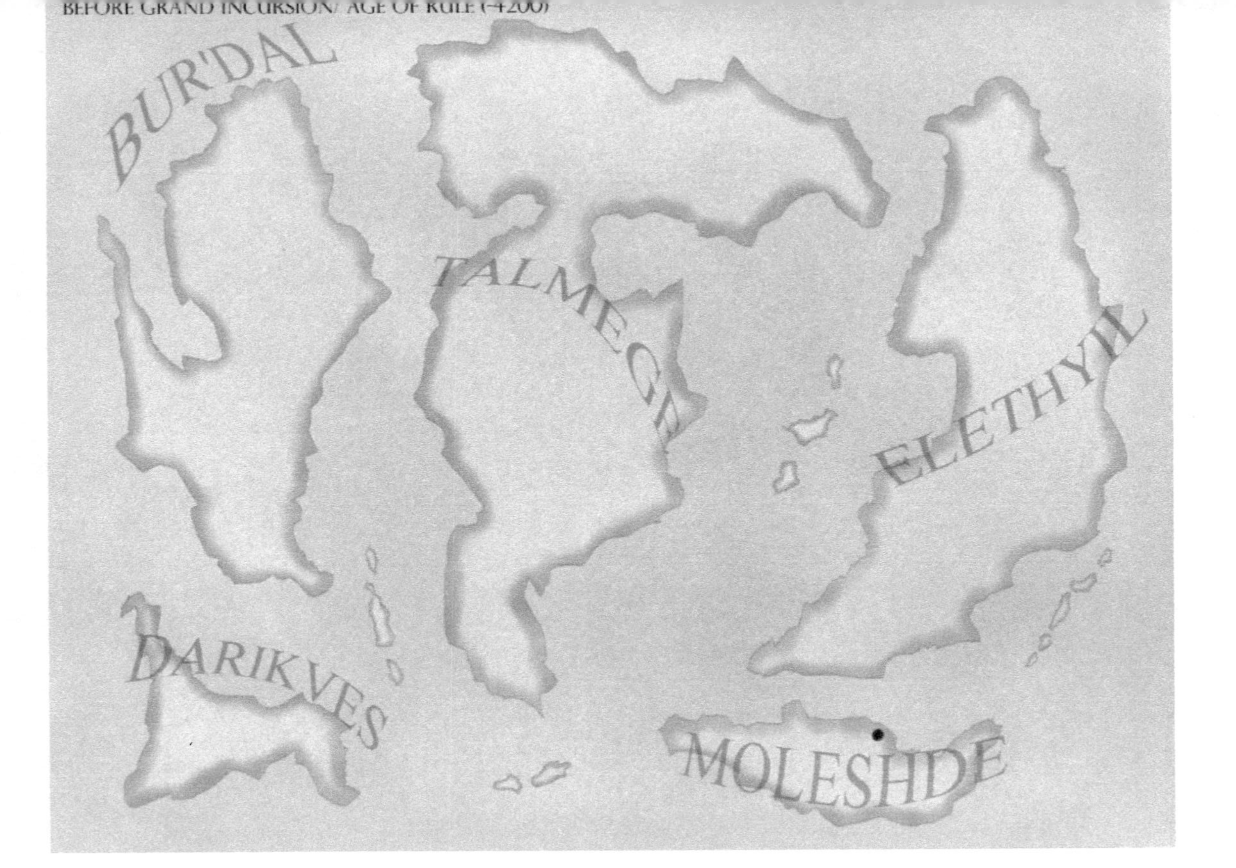

BEFORE GRAND INCURSION/ AGE OF RULE (+200)
BUR'DAL
TALMEGR
ELETHYIL
DARIKVES
MOLESHDE

KELVERT DRYLANDS
LAYOYEM
DAIBOT
ULAI
WAHOP
ALSAC
NAYMO
TUIKON -912 BGI

Table of Contents

Ch. 1 A New Form of Enemy

The sun stood on high, beaming down on the sands. On occasion, something shifted beneath, stirring the flattened surface. Nuyani peered out from beneath her arm for any signs of danger. She found herself sitting on a lone slab of stone sticking out of the sand. She hugged her legs close to her chest. It was the only sense of safety she felt. The only stability that seemed to make sense in her quest. Being exposed to the sun did not help her in the least.

Hot, Nuyani thought as she tried to keep herself cool.

Confident in her speed, she prepared enough rations for a few days into the desert from the drylands. What she did not anticipate were obstacles foreign to her as she had resided in her homeland all her life. The sand was hot and difficult to traverse; a few times, climbing atop the dunes only brought sand slides nearly toppling her in her trek. Worse yet, the terrain was difficult to run along on loose sand in comparison to compact dirt. It had only been ten days into the desert. She felt the weight of exhaustion settling in, her water skins nearly empty, and food rations running low. The towering red cliffs encircling her served as a stark reminder that she was still at the beginning of her journey— their jagged outlines, unyielding and vast, were visible in both the east and west.

Nuyani wiped her brow, loosening several drops of sweat that still remained, to her surprise. She fixed her gaze on the southern horizon and the wide expanse of the desert. Her ember-colored eyes glowed faintly in the light of the sun but remained strong as she looked into the distance. With slow, deep breaths, she tried to find some relief, only to find the air just as hot. Nothing to see. She lowered her head into her arms, shifting her wet, matted hair as a trail of sweat started to descend her bare back and down the crease of her spine. Clothed in runner's wear only added to the issue. Made of red leather from a charge horn, it was a treated attire from a single hooded romper fitted tightly to the wearer with short sleeves and wooden buttons fastened down the front. The brim of the hood was often fitted to the brow to prevent it from blowing back. The arms and legs were covered in wraps and from the hip and shoulder down to the spaces between each digit.

Day in and day out, she had worn the clothing no matter the weather, and for good reason. Her people in the drylands of Kelvert wore the clothing for short periods of time to lure out the same game that they were made from. The charge horns, with their sturdy hides, were easy to lure out for ambush for decent archers to take shots at their necks. Now, however, Nuyani fought the lingering waves of fatigue threatening to make her pass out.

Removing the straps and top half of the clothing, she remained bare-chested, waiting for the breeze aside from two ivory medallions hanging on a leather cord around her neck. Nuyani watched as the two pieces dangled about. One was of a lone fox, a solitary animal that many found fitting for her nature. The other was of a woman engraved into the surface with fine detail, only to be marred by a hasty carving through the neck by one of the new guards within the village. The guard fired an arrow at her as she left into the desert. Seeing it brought a tear to Nuyani's eye as the guilt welled within her.

I had to leave, or the storms won't stop, Nuyani told herself once more. *If I am a priestess, then I must do this for the village and for mother.*

The explanation came again and again, changing with each attempt as Nuyani tried to find what words would quell any anger her village would have for her. To Nuyani, the world had been shifted so drastically that every decision felt as if it would both save and destroy her and the village. Nuyani's thoughts dwelled on the past season. In the beginning, she was an outsider to the village. A sin and demon child marked with strange powers leaving her exiled from her people for a decade because of her eyes. Now, she was named priestess after saving the village by helping to resurrect their god, Kelvert. She had even learned the secrets of their true origin, proving the world was far larger than she could imagine. Nuyani tightened her hug. Her thoughts dwelled not on the victories. She was grateful, but there was one reason they survived. Her mother's spirit had called to her. She had reached out to Nuyani, warning her of the threat that lingered in the desert. Every year, a sandstorm raged from the desert and reached the drylands with such force that the grains of sand could peel flesh from bone and carry large men away like a leaf in a gale. Each year, the storm grew stronger and lasted longer. Learning the origin of her powers from Kelvert, Nuyani was able to cut the storm short.

The storms had a source—a demon, witnessed by another people long before Nuyani's, who had also perished in the desert's unforgiving grasp. Nuyani tried to smile, finding that the demon lands, as her people called the desert, had a fitting name before they knew the whole truth. As she looked out into the desert, Nuyani thought, *I will free you, Mother. I will stop this demon and the creatures plaguing us.* Anger swelled in Nuyani, surprising her that she still had some strength to make a tight fist. Learning her powers and the difference between spirit and magic, Nuyani was warned by Kelvert that the storms harvested the souls and spirits of those slain. It was worse when the first agent of the sealed demon came to attack her. A pale blue spirit of a woman with a shriveled body and hands with long claw-like fingers. Her hair was sparse and floated about. She had sunken voids of black for eyes with only small iridescent glints at the center. Her lowered jaw passed her shoulders as if in a perpetual scream. Nuyani had discovered her powers that same night and first experienced the howls of the spirits that nearly managed to rip her soul from her body.

The reminiscing ceased when Nuyani then felt a ghostly pressure weigh on the side of her body. Like a finger lightly pressing on her skin, she felt the weight not on the surface of her body but on her core. An ethereal sphere that all living beings had what Kelvert had taught her was *edria* (magic). It was both the opposite and byproduct of spirit. The core within her was sensitive to the concentrated pool of *prutosa* (spirit) that was coming toward her. As her core released soundless waves echoing through air, stone, and sand, she felt every grain hitting her skin as if they were pebbles. The softest breeze was a strong gale. The smell of dirt nearly suffocated. The pool of spirit tunneling through the sand below the surface felt more like a pale weight of water compared to normal cup or bowl sizes she sensed in people or normal animals. Though the spirit's pressure was confined to a single point and followed along her core like a compass, she could still feel the slow swirls and sloshing of the prutosa as though it were going to spill out.

Like a single drumbeat, a steady pulse rang from her core. It coursed from the center of her body through her arm and into a bracelet holding a clear crystal bead no bigger than a pebble. A white glimmer flashed on the ground for a moment before the leather thong holding the crystal disappeared, and the small stone was fastened in the round wooden hilt of a curved single-edged blade. Nuyani rose as the trailing sand grew closer.

It stopped at the edge of the stone before sand burst into the air. Nuyani did not hesitate as she delivered a horizontal cleave into the cloud and felt some resistance meeting the end of her blade. Clattering and clicking sounded as a heavy thud landed on the surface. The smell of rotting flesh then filled her nose, causing her to wince in disgust. Nuyani backed away, staying on the stone slab as the dust fell away. Her biggest obstacle and threat to her people was revealed. A parasite came for an eager meal. The creature had a segmented body of dark brown shells with little room for the short thorn-like legs sticking out of the sides, which meant more for burrowing than walking. Their heads had four pincers with points all meeting one another at the center of their mouth, and faded yellow eyes were sitting between each of them. Each one looked as if it were a stone fading in color. From looking at them directly, one could never tell which side was right-side-up for their bodies. All Nuyani knew was that they did not count as living.

The creature's body was halved as yellow pus spilled from the opened end of its body. Yet the creature continued its pursuit as if never struck.

"By the great lord's shine, die," Nuyani hissed as she swung her nimcha and cleaved through the worm's head.

With a final strike, the worm stopped moving and slumped against the edge of the stone slab. Nuyani breathed heavily as she tried to cover her mouth and nose from the smell. For the past ten days, she had encountered dozens of parasites in the desert. She had faced the creatures before. In the drylands, they referred to the parasites as worms for burrowing in the flesh of animals, causing them to grow almost double in size and become walking corpses, ignoring even the fatalist wounds. Those worms were merely the width and size of a man's arm, still grotesque and larger than she had any comfort, but the worms in the desert were nearly twice the length and just as wide as a man. Their bodies did not afford them much speed but allowed them to burrow in the loose sand.

Nuyani's core released another pulse, echoing through the area. Her senses carried on the ethereal beat, spreading out in a sphere for a dozen paces in all directions. She could not feel the presence yet but could hear the rustling of turning sand grow louder and more numerous. She watched her surroundings. More trails started toward Nuyani as though her edria was a beacon calling for the worms. As two more of the creatures sprung from the ground, Nuyani's edria released another pulse through a raised arm and aimed at the worms. The magic erupted from her palm in a fist-sized sphere of blue light before launching forth and crashing through the worm, sending shell and pus to rain on the sands behind it. The next worm then lunged like a spear thrust for her midsection. Nuyani nimbly dodged with a sidestep, almost becoming a blur before her blade came down, cutting through the worm's head.

She then slid her foot to the side, pulling away her tool strap before the slain worm could fall on it. Tied to the simple strap were several sacks and bags of her rations, herbs, daggers, small tools, and poisons she traveled with on most occasions. Throwing the strap over her shoulder, it fell between her breasts, staying in place as she looked to fight the next worm to approach. Reading the pressures of spirit, she anticipated the parasites before they emerged. Stepping onto the sands, Nuyani was forced to dance around the emerging creatures and slash at those she could without giving away her position. She could not afford to be scratched. She did not know if one touch would infect her or if they needed to bite her. Neither answer was appealing as she weaved through the pincers.

However, thirst remained the greater threat as she breathed heavily. Her tongue began to stick to the side of her mouth. Heat rose in her body and slowed her senses, slowed her movements. Nuyani leaned back as a worm she sensed, then saw, lashed out, almost striking her head. She stepped to the side and swung her blade in a circle, cleaving the worm's body in half. It did not kill, but the wound would still slow the creature. Nuyani gave pause as she released another wave of edria through the area. More worms were approaching. Each one pressed on her senses in nearly every direction, all except one. Without hesitation, Nuyani took the lightest path revealed to her. She sprinted forth as clouds of dust rose from her steps, climbing taller than the woman herself.

Nuyani took off toward the south, following the distant hoodoos sitting on the horizon. Her desperate escape proved dire. More pools of prutosa awaken in her presence. Beneath the sands, countless worms stirred and surged with every step she took. Nuyani had outrun them, but they did not retreat. They did not tire. They did not rest. Each passing day magnified their threat as her supplies dwindled, leaving the priestess increasingly vulnerable. Often, her mind wandered to the name she once bore before becoming the Witch of Kelvert—the Witch of the Drylands, the tainted child marked by demons, her speed and piercing eyes standing as proof of that corruption. Now, she understood: these were not curses but gifts, powers given by their god.

Her breathing grew ragged as she made her way toward the stones. If nothing else, the compact ground would force the worms to awkwardly crawl on stone, slowing them drastically and leaving no surprises beneath her. When she reached the stone pillars, Nuyani's eyes widened as she found another solution to her situation. The pillars had several small grooves on their sides, all cut by centuries of wind emitted from the desert center. Nuyani began to climb, going up several stories before she reached an outcrop wide enough for her to sit. She took heavy breaths and turned to lay her back against the shadowed wall. It brought some relief to the day's heat. Nuyani looked down as she saw the worms begin to collect.

"By his shine, now what?" Nuyani wondered, and she looked at the numbers swell from dozens to hundreds. The swarms' incessant clattering reached her ears, leaving her thoughts muddled.

Trying to think of a solution, Nuyani reached for her tool strap and felt one of the sacks from the outside. She searched another, feeling the familiar shape of the contents. When a rounded lump met her probing, she fumbled with the cord and untied the top. Several small boluses of dried leaves and plants were revealed. She reached inside, grabbed one of the boluses with a darker gray tint, and placed it in her mouth. After several bites, the bolus broke apart and became wet. Almost immediately, she could feel the herbs work as her mouth began to salivate as if she were anticipating her favorite meal. The moisture was not a lot, but it helped to clear the mental fog. Nuyani then tried to move her legs over the edge, hoping that losing sight of her would motivate the worms to leave. She groaned at the hopeful thought, knowing the near-mindless creatures would stay down at the base of the pillar, scurrying about until she left or fell.

She looked down at the worms, watching as the increasing waves piled onto one another, attempting to reach her. Each eager parasite merely toppled the last, preventing any true headway, though the fear of them piling up to meet her did come to mind. As Nuyani accessed her situation, she tried to come up with solutions. Though she knew she would need to get down eventually, there was still the climb up. Halfway up the pillar, she saw that the adjacent hoodoo was within reach if she jumped from one top to the other. The only fear that came to mind for her was that of the blood manes. Predators of the sky, they would easily capture her if she were not careful.

As though her thoughts had conjured one of the animals, a wide shadow then sailed over her and down the pillars. Overhead flew one of the animals. A bird's head stuck out of a large mane of feathers with the front legs of a bird and the rear legs of a large feline. Its long brush-ended tail trailed behind. The expanse of the animal's wings was nearly triple the length of its entire body. As its namesake, its entire body was covered in dark red feathers. The animal craned its neck to look at the worms and Nuyani, giving her heart a start. Its large brown eye fixated on her. Though she could move or defend herself with magic, the animal's very strength and size could easily destroy her defenses if she were not careful. Still, a predator that preferred the element of surprise, the blood mane turned away and continued north. Nuyani's heart settled, and her breathing slowed. She remembered being called a demon just as the blood manes and blade jaws were for living in the mountains close to the demon lands. Now, they were merely seen as animals but feared for their strengths and speed.

With the second problem gone, Nuyani then looked down at the worms clamoring at the bottom. Her mind raced to the first one she saw bursting out of the carcass of a charge horn. Creating a sphere of magic to sever the worm's head, she held it over a flame she prepared for cooking. The presence of fire did nothing to bother the skittering head. To her luck, their lack of pain did not mean they were fireproof.

With the thought coming to mind, she then moved to her tools and one of the water skins. She opened the sack containing a crystal, flint stones, and strands of leather and took out the stones and leather. Nuyani then slowly pulled at the drawstring of a water skin, holding it away from her and keeping the opening facing outward. Before her arrival in the drylands, she had collected several bulbs from the death snare. An alluring vegetation in the drylands that had fruit with vibrant colors to attract prey, only for everything in it to poison the prey, killing them or paralyzing them before a serpent-like stalk would move in to bite on the victim and drag them into the center to be consumed. They grew near riversides with their perimeter stalks, all growing the strange yellow fruit, which expanded until they burst, releasing white powder thanks to the water they consumed. The other fruit growing on the stalk sides were berries with dark red cores inside clear membranes that looked like water dew. On contact, thorns would burst from the core to puncture the skin and drain a deadly poison into the victim's body. Even the largest animals fell in minutes to the toxins.

She let the thought go. Nuyani slowly peered into her water skin. The heat had drained much of the water and moisture of the bulbs. With six fully expanded fruits able to sit in the water skin, Nuyani was surprised to see that none had burst beforehand. Two of the bulbs at the top were reduced thinned disks warped by the heat. The next two were half expanded as some of the water still inside the water skin reached them. The last two were fully expanded and ready to burst with a strong enough blow to puncture their tension. Nuyani then removed the half-dried pieces and sat them on the ledge. She then retrieved the flint stones and straps. Looking down at the floor, Nuyani merely saw a jumbled mess of worms mixing and entangling to the point that no one body could be distinguished from another. With a sharp breath, she then lay on the ledge, eyeing the worms. She raised her arm and then pitched the half-dehydrated bulb at the worms. She winced as the awkward throw did not agree with her arm. Pain shot through her shoulder. It proved fruitful, though, as the bulb struck a worm and burst outward with a white powder covering many of the worms. It contrasted with their shells, revealing which and where the powder had landed.

"By his shine…" Nuyani whispered as she moved on to her next step.

Taking up the flint stones, she began striking them over the leather strands. The insistent clicking made her heart race as she looked back at the edge. It was proof the powder did nothing to the creatures. A bleak reminder that they were not living.

Several sparks arched toward the bindings, but Nuyani gritted her teeth even tighter with each failed strike. Not too long before the twentieth strike did the pile began to smolder. She gave a wide smile as the glow of embers matched her eyes. With a few breaths to feed the flame, Nuyani stopped and sat straight. Taking in a sharp breath, she scooped the strands into both of her hands. The flame grew quickly. The burning immediately began nipping at her palms and small fingers. Releasing sharp grunts, she eagerly turned and tossed the strands down to the worms. Nearly throwing herself over, she slipped off the ledge and clung to the crevices once more. She looked down, ready to watch the creatures burn, with a gleeful smile. But the thought faded as the strands descended.

Her eyes widened, and her mouth held open as she saw the gnawing mindless parasites roll and lean away from the burning bundle. *They only think to eat*, Nuyani told herself.

To her luck, so many had gathered at the base of the pillar that she was bound to drop the flames on one of them. The small flame burst on contact, expanding nearly two stories high and two dozen paces outward. Nuyani raised her arm to shield herself from the rising inferno's heat. New beads of sweat arose. She sat back on the ledge. It was a surprise to see the blaze had a great effect on the worms. Whether the powder was needed or not, each worm was lit with flames on contact like a dried brush. They fled in all directions, with many even attempting to put the flames out. Some rolled in the sand. Others burrowed with smoke rising to the surface from the bulges of their tunneling.

No. No. To the sands... No! Nuyani thought as horror covered her face, and she held her hands over her mouth. If they were this self-preserved, what could the worms do?

She let the sudden shock go and remembered her goal. She took up her tools and items in hand. She climbed to the top. Reaching the plateau, Nuyani dashed along the wide space before leaping to the adjacent pillar. Landing on the other side, Nuyani then moved to the opposite end of the hoodoo, where another cluster of pillars all stood. The taller pieces brought both shade and cover as she climbed in between them and found a wider ledge she could lie on more securely.

She peered out and saw several scattered worms still ablaze. The ground was littered with the charred remains of the worms. Smoke continued to rise from beneath the sand, all around the pillars. Nuyani glared at the remains as she fought to ignore the smell of burning rot.

Despite seeing the creatures were smarter, she still gained a victory. A fleeting thought of their easy kindling brought a small mischievous smirk only to disappear. She never learned to conjure flames, but the thought still made her feel strange. Since the start of the season, did she even learn about magic and her powers?? Knowing from visions of

ancient spirits that they could do so much more brought a
shiver to her spine.

With little choice, Nuyani lay down and turned her
body to face the pillar side. Smoke filled her nose as the bolus
was reduced to a pulp, keeping her throat from drying. She
could not afford to move. Not yet, at least. Returning to the top
would expose her to blood manes, and climbing down could
bring the swarms back to trap her there. Worse, the call of sleep
lingered. Her muscles ached. Her hands were burned in a few
spots, and her eyelids felt heavy. Once the cool breeze slipping
through the pillars came and brushed against her bare back, she
succumbed to slumber.

Sleep this time brought a memory to Nuyani. She
found herself in a familiar void of darkness with faint blues in
the distance, each of concentrated edria. Each was in the form
of spheres far beneath the land's surface. She found herself in
edrial form. The surface of her body was nearly transparent,
but looking toward the border or turning portions revealed the
countless waves of edria humming from her center and trailing
over her form. She found herself plunging further into the
darkness along with both her younger brother, a thin boy with a
short afro she had just learned was family in the past season
and only met during his first hunt initiation. He, too, was in a
blue ethereal form, a fade of his body. The ripples of edria were
not so easy to see without focusing on the edge of his arms.
Between them, guiding the two through the darkness, was the

remainder of their god's power. A ball of magic shining bright and as wide as her torso. The three had descended into the land to bridge some of Kelvert's power to the surface.

The same sandstorms raking across the lands were filled with prutosa. They suppressed Kelvert's power with each passing wave. It took the three of them synchronizing their magic to move the sea of edria, which had grown still in the depths of the drylands. It was a strange quality of the forces Nuyani barely understood. Prutosa both flowed and burned, with the amount being more important for spells, while edria beat and hardened to do the same. Both were needed for mortals and life in general, but both had advantages and disadvantages. As her dream continued, she and the others made contact with the blue floor of Edria and concentrated on making the surface vibrate. As it wavered, increasingly bright portions proved they were making headway. Then, plunging into the energy, they willed to move more of it and dragged the line of power to the surface. With some of Kelvert's power in his control, he was able to create barriers to protect the cavern Nuyani lived in during her exile.

A pulse of edria rang from the distance. Nuyani's eyes shot open as she looked toward the south. Nothing was in sight, but she could feel the energy reaching her nonetheless. One source against another felt as if a pattern were ringing over the core, though no audible sound was there. With the memory of the lesson fresh in her mind and a safe place for her vulnerable body, Nuyani then lay on the ledge once more. The sky was tinted in red and violet as the sun set, and the winds rose to a whistle through the pillars. Even the smell of ash and rot had lessened drastically.

Thank the great lord. This should be easy, Nuyani thought as her eyes closed and she concentrated on her core.

At any given time, the core of a living being was constantly humming at a steady pace. This is both to contain one's soul and spirit as well as protect from incoming forces that could damage or corrupt. Though the worms were the closest example of how well those could be circumvented. As she relaxed, Nuyani willed the thrum of her core to move faster until the individual waves melded together. She then tried to mirror her conscience and produce a separate sphere from her body. She had done this twice before, letting her conscience enter a second sphere. But this time, things were proving difficult. As Nuyani concentrated, she tried to maintain the sphere. Several bombarding waves of prutosa washed over the new construct. Nuyani felt as if she were physically trying to lift stones far too heavy for her. The prutosa lingering in the desert proved too thick, and Nuyani grunted as her stamina gave way. The edria returned to her body as her eyes shot open with pain radiating through her body. Nuyani grunted as her fingers were forced to curl, and her stomach clenched, forcing her to sit up. Her eyes widened and closed. She tried to fight the pain. Panic rose as she felt her body inching toward the edge out of her control.

No! Lord Kelvert, no, Nuyani thought as she tried to take some control of her core. With edria so closely linked to the physical realm, its sporadic behavior meant that both her core was about to break and that her muscles would feel every ounce of it. The waves of pain then went away as Nuyani started to regain control of her body. She breathed heavily. Trying to lay flat, her heart gave a start when she felt her leg miss the ledge and dangle over. With most of her body still on stable ground, she remained relatively safe.

After a few more breaths, Nuyani struggled to sit up. She looked out toward the south, wondering how far the waves of edria traveled. Looking at the sun, she wondered if it was worth leaving the ledge at night. She may have rested, but that did not mean she was back to full strength. Instead of wondering, Nuyani put away some of her tools and eventually went down to retrieve the others that fell off the ledge. The smell of burnt flesh returned, growing stronger as she reached the ground. When Nuyani neared the sands, she retrieved her flint stones, her ivory dagger with a fox carved between the blade and hilt, and her crystal. As Nuyani retrieved it, she thought back to when she found it. The piece was a part of Kelvert, though she never knew. She often applied some pressure just by squeezing it, and the crystal would release trailing lights like the glimmer of a river surface before it sucked in or let out anything that was of flesh in the opposite direction of the grip. She managed to kill the charge horn that went after the hunters and passed the stone over one of the beasts. Each one was at least twice the length of a man's height and was as heavy as maybe a dozen or two. Yet despite their size, the palm-sized crystal had taken two in its confines and felt no heavier.

Nuyani then thought back to her attempt of applying magic to it. Feeding a thrum into the stone before allowed her to open a gate into the realm of edria. It was a realm of night with floating spheres of light scattered about like stars, but often, at least a third had lines of white connecting one white light to another.

Putting the crystal away, she ran toward the south, ignoring the charred remains of the worms in passing. The ground still smoked from those buried below. As Nuyani ran along the desert, she wondered what forces could project such magic. She let her mind race with different hopes and possibilities as the cool breeze from the coming night helped to soothe her strained muscles.

The further she traveled across the desert, the stronger and lingering each passing wave seemed. The odd part to Nuyani was that she noticed there was no set rhythm. No pattern to the coming waves. Each one was thick yet seemed to have no true purpose to them as they passed over and through her. She tried to understand the waves and recalled her lessons. Magic was a strange and complicated subject with so many variables determining what spell was conjured. The amount of waves, thickness of the thrum, and sequence were all factors that determined whether one person could conjure fire or move stones. Her own spells were more instinctive from what she was told. Each ability she had was far stronger thanks to the magic Kelvert imparted into her people, but they would never be considered complicated by any means.

Simple barriers and walls were just hardened, magic-fed waves of edria. The same went for the spell bolts and orbs. Even her sense of life and other sources was just the thinnest wave set alone to travel as far as she could reach, waiting for some disturbance in its rhythm. However, with it, she could increase its thickness, which would hinder other cores if it were the intent or make her more sensitive to the pressures and pulses around her. There were different ways of blocking or hiding from any searching pulse. Nuyani remembered when she saw strange river lizards for the first time that were longer than her own body and opened their mouths to wide expanses. It was a shock to her that they easily kept their presence from her even when just a few feet away.

The sun was still on the horizon as Nuyani caught sight of something gleaming in the dark. A jagged piece flickered blue along with several smaller lights of silver. Nuyani wondered what she saw but slid to a stop when she saw there were more dark pieces just on the sand surface surrounding the larger stone. Nuyani then held up her hand and conjured a magic sphere. The blue light shined on the surface of other large crystal shards. Each one was half buried in the sand but looked as though they were broken portions from the same piece. Nuyani then looked at the largest piece. A spike of transparent stone taller than herself with rough sides like a cliff's edge and several cracks. Nuyani released a thrum and found the echo of the wave passing over each but never stirring the concentrated forms of edria.

Moving toward the larger piece, Nuyani carefully stepped around each of the shards. Some were as small as her fist, while others were slightly larger than her head. Placing a hand on the crystal, she remembered the memory Kelvert showed of his defeat. The *haflaj* (angel) had flown from across the land, passing the drylands and heading toward the desert. Following the pressures of spirit that echoed outward, it was Kelvert's nature to fight the demons, the *unflom*. A monster they knew as the false devourer was sealed away in the desert. Yet its lingering power seeped through the cracks of its prison, berating the lands around it for countless miles. So powerful, the creature was able to send waves of prutosa and concentrated beams of spirit directly at Kelvert, sending the haflaj flying backward. His body, made of crystal, began to shatter as the streams broke through the barrier. The angel's body splintered and broke apart mid-flight, fragments of its form scattering across the desert below, before Kelvert was forced to reside in the drylands. A tenth of his strength and size remained. From what she understood, the two opposing beings seldom allowed the other to live alone if they were aware. Opposite in their nature, yet the same. Nuyani wondered if all forms of life came from the vessels created in the realm of spirits (*govtif ved prutosa*). *Then what made them so different? Even her body, though having more matter than either of the other forces, used both ethereal forces to remain alive. Kelvert's own body had a soul to begin with, making her even more concerned with the opposite natures.*

Nuyani took a deep breath as her fingers curled. She placed her forehead on the crystal. *How would I be able to restore you?* Nuyani first wondered. Like the well she helped to make reconnecting Kelvert with the drylands, there had to be a way to reassemble the pieces of Kelvert and bring the deity back. She released a sigh as it merely felt like another arduous mission she did not have an answer for. The suppressive spirit around her was already weakening her, though she went unnoticed by most creatures unless she was too close to the worms.

A ripple and sudden pressure then appeared behind Nuyani. She whirled around and raised her nimcha, ready to swing at anything coming by. A faint silver glint caught her eye. When the light was gone, so was the pressure. A flicker appeared at the corner of her eye but disappeared all the same when Nuyani turned to look. Feeling uneasy, she increased the strength of her thrum, letting the waves radiate from her in all directions. She felt the still thrums of the crystals begin to vibrate and match her own. She could feel the small traces of ripples dance along her core. Something was moving around her. One of the points of pressure grew heavier and just off to her side. Nuyani did not turn but twisted her blade into a vertical circle, cutting toward her side just where she felt the pressure rising.

A yelp rose along with a thud. Nuyani then looked to the side and saw a small man rolling on the ground. Her eyes widened as she looked at him, shielding his body with his arms. Like her, he had dark brown skin and looked to be at least in his mid-forties. He wore a brown tunic and trousers. Those were the only normal things about him. The bewildering part was his larger head in proportion to his body and noticeable with a proper look. The large black eyes that had tints of violet along the sides. His arms and legs grew nearly transparent from the elbows and knees down to the hands and feet. There were several tendrils or streams of prutosa coming from his back in the same purple hue but looked more like a flame burning behind him. The most telling thing about the man, however, was his height was no taller than her hand.

"What are you?" Nuyani asked as she straightened and lowered the nimcha.

"[Don't swing that thing again. I am just trying to talk]," the small man said. Nuyani looked at him, puzzled, as he then lowered his hands and revealed a wide grin.

The air, or reality, seemed to ripple around him. In one moment, he was on the ground. The next, he was lifted into the air. Nuyani could feel the concentration of his spirit propelling him upward. The act reminded Nuyani of her first time moving about as a spirit. Learning to spirit walk, she learned that it required one to direct their flight by burning away prutosa. Yet, as she watched the man smile at her eerily, she did not feel the pressure lessening as he used it. Even more impressive, the smaller man seemed to hold more spirit than what she felt a regular man would.

Comparing quantity, most people had enough for a bowl of water or water skin. The spirits she met could contain as light as a few drops to fill pools of water. Some possessed creatures even had enough spirit equal to a river. Nuyani dropped the blade point to the ground as she looked at the man. She had seen many strange creatures, but not one so small.

"[You must not know what I am]," the man said as he kept his smile and cocked his head a little to the side, and started floating around her in a circle.

"I don't know what you said. Maybe you can help me," Nuyani said as she flicked her wrist, letting lights trail from the crystal in the hilt before the sword twisted and drained inside, leaving the small stone fixed to a leather cord on her wrist. She started to reach for her water skin when a silver flame flickered in the air beside the man. She stopped and blinked as there were now two. Same features in general, there were differences in the faces as the second man was bald compared to head of wiry black hair of the first. *Another group of people,* Nuyani thought, letting caution slip away as she stepped closer.

He too had a mischievous smile on his face but seemed younger than the first. Several more flickering lights came forth with half a dozen more appearing around Nuyani.

Before she could say a single word, the first man then sang in a melodious tone, "[Oh treasure. Mysterious treasure. Desert treasure]." His eyebrows climbed toward the top of his head as he emphasized the last word and started flying in a circle around Nuyani. The others then did the same as they repeated the words. Nuyani did not know what to say as she watched their trailing paths of violet. She felt something weighing on her mind. The urge to sleep grew steadily. Something unnatural. It was not easy for her to feel tired, making her wonder what the reason was. She even felt her core's pulse begin to dull. Giving several blinks to fight the sleep, Nuyani focused and let her thrum race, pushing away the spirit pressing against her will. The song then ended as the men started to laugh instead. Nuyani looked at them for a moment, wondering what was happening.

"What is happening?" she questioned as she tried to reach for her water skin once more. "I'm looking for wa…" her words ended with a yelp as she was pinched on the side of her breast.

As Nuyani guarded, the others howled in amusement. Nuyani swung at him only to catch air. He disappeared in a silver light. With her thrum vibrating faster, she could feel the area shift as if spirits were puncturing through reality. They were teleporting to the other realms. The truth became more obvious as a second ripple of pressure appeared behind her, and the inside of her leg, too high for comfort, was pinched. Nuyani yelped and kicked in a desperate attempt to swat at the man. He escaped unharmed as well. The others began to laugh once more as they encircled her.

Her face went hot as she flicked her wrist, drawing the blade, and started swinging at the points of pressure but catching none of the vulgar fools. Several more pinches interrupted her swing, causing Nuyani to strike the crystal. A loud twang sounded as the blade nearly fell from her grip. With anger and laughter filling her head, she was ready to throw the weapon at them. Though it would do little good. Nuyani then released her thrum, creating a barrier around her that was stronger than normal. The same crystals around her then expanded and strengthened the construct. Though most of the men had fled into the other world, two were struck by the erupting barrier and collapsed within its confines.

Knocked out and at her feet, Nuyani considered stomping on both, even kicking them. Fear stopped her, however, as she felt her size could kill them both. Murder was not something her people ever atoned for. *By the great lord, I will not harm you or forgive you,* Nuyani thought as she walked to the other side of the crystal. Her face felt hot as she covered her chest once more and pulled the tight brim of her hood over her head. So long had she been in danger and desperate, she had forgotten herself. Squeezing into a place between the larger crystal shard and the smaller fragments, Nuyani lay on her side and went to sleep. This time, by her own choice.

Ch. 2 Different Worlds

Nuyani awoke with the distant sound of clicking muffled in her ears. Her eyes shot open. She looked around only to find the barrier she had created still surrounding her. She looked to the source of the noise and found several of the worms scurrying about on the edge of the barrier. With every point of contact, a ripple passed along the surface in an expanding ring as if it were a still pond being disturbed. The worms could not enter. Standing up, Nuyani leaned to look around the shard of edria. To her relief, the little men were no longer there, though the imprints in the sand proved she was not alone. She had never willed the barrier to contain them. Merely wanting her space was enough. Thinking for a moment that the small creatures most likely walked through the barrier before disappearing, Nuyani recalled her experience blocking a barrage of arrows with her shield. It all seemed to depend on intent, which made as much sense as anything else to her. One moment, she could block everything as if she had a physical shield. The next, the barrier could allow only certain things to pass through if she concentrated on the thought alone.

Turning her attention to her settings once more, Nuyani fed another pulse into the crystal. With what took enough energy to make a sphere of edria, the crystal nearly tripled in strength, expanding the barrier into an all-around blast. The push caused their shells to sink into the energy at first before repelling outward violently with smashed shells. A rain of pus and shells struck the sands, making Nuyani wonder what purpose the worms had in trying to reach her through the magic. The event of them fleeing meant there was some sort of mind within them to have a reason. She just did not know what.

Letting the thought go, she then turned to the south and wondered where she could go. Nuyani released the barrier instead and focused the energy into creating a searching wave of edria. The wave echoed outward for miles.

Through the shard, she could feel the presence of the worms just below the sands. Numerous in their groups and all waiting, Nuyani wondered what the creatures were doing out here. Surely, there would have to be a reason for the worms to travel to a remote area with little signs of life. She gritted her teeth as the thought pricked at her.

A pulse then rose and met her path, making Nuyani freeze. Sensing something, she focused her concentration on the sudden thrum. Another pulse then rose. A strange rhythm she did not know proved it to be a spell, which meant another caster and possible water. There were also two sources of edria ringing in the area. Her heart sank as she felt the number of pressures closing in on them and fainting away. She took off running in a mad dash, careless of the crystals around her. With a flick of her wrist, the blade spilled from its confines. It would not help if she were not prepared for the battle, not to mention the worms she would encounter in passing.

The rolling sand dunes started to climb higher as she ran. Being so far away from the crystal, she could no longer feed magic into the shard and was forced to rely mostly on memory. The task proved to grow difficult as she was forced to weave between the dunes. Her heart started to pound, not from the run but from the hills around her infested with the worms. In passing, they stirred either from her presence or from the battle closing by. She could hear the echoes of smashed shells, odd clicking, and a strange caw rising over the sands.

I am close, Nuyani thought as she released a thrum, searching through the sands. She was not alone.

As she rounded one of the dunes, a worm burst from the sands and went to the other side. Nuyani cleaved into the body and began to climb the dune in a wide arch to avoid the excess pus spewing out. She knew the worm was still alive, though she hoped it would at least slow him. The clicking grew louder. Even under her fleeting steps, she could feel the sand shift and turn. A few hard surfaces made her wonder if she stepped on stone or shell. When Nuyani came around the last dune, a bright light illuminated the area. She froze for a moment as she saw a lone man wielding a spear and a strange creature slithering about.

The man looked to be in his late twenties and, from his face, obscured by his dark blue headwrap. He wore a thick overcoat of the same color with sleeves that went down to the elbows and stopped at mid-thigh. Beneath it, he wore a light tan tunic with long sleeves. His forearms were covered with leather arm guards. Around his waist was a large red belt keeping them together. He wore the same light tan trousers with leather shin guards and sandals. He wielded the spear with finesse, but it held a thrum of its own. It had a long, dark wooden shaft with the midsection covered in a white wrap of some kind bearing etchings of strange symbols along its length. At the top was a leaf-shaped spearhead with a red gem at the base between the blade and the neck connecting to the rest.

Changing between lightning strikes and funneling edria, he struck the worms, nearly batting them away as if they were small stones. Their shells fell apart under the strikes.

Nuyani found her mind fixating on the symbols as though she had forgotten them but knew she had never seen them. Aware that there were other gods in the world who commanded the elements, she knew they had such symbols. She remembered one. A seal emblem she needed to either carve or use to stop the false devourer from taking life.

Darting about and crushing the approaching worms was a long-bodied animal Nuyani was certain could be at least the length of four men tall. A large owl's head, wider than her torso, sat at the end of a slender lizard-like body. It had dark brown eyes set on yellow and had a small hooked beak compared to the rest of its head. Though, it seemed to do enough damage, biting through the shell. Even its thin legs with long hooking talons proved powerful enough to crush the parasites in its steps. The end of the creature's tail thinned to a point with an explosion of feathers to fan outward parallel to the ground. Its entire body was covered in both brown and red feathers and scales.

It took her aback as Nuyani saw the man battle. The man struck some of the worms using different elements. Sometimes, using slow orbs of lightning the size of his torso to travel in straight paths before them. Any worms that touched them were halted almost immediately. Other times, he struck using a spell that caused a white surface to appear in the same area, and the worms would stop for a moment as they slowly spread. Delivering another strike, the shell would break away. As the man rounded on two more worms coming at his flank, he fired a simple spell orb, sending the projectile through them with ease. Nuyani wondered why use anything else if that were an option, only to feel the presence of another three burrowing through the sand. Nuyani leaped forward as she felt them approach. The low area between the dunes was already filled with dozens of slain worms as Nuyani stepped into the wet sand.

It made the lunge easier. When the worms revealed themselves, one went for the man's spear as the others went for his body. He erected a barrier, keeping the others at bay as he pulled, trying to remove his weapon from the worm's pincers. Stuck in place, Nuyani created a javelin of magic and sent it through the worm holding his weapon. He then rounded on the other worms, releasing his barrier, and cracked them both over the heads with edria ringing out of his weapon. Now closer, Nuyani could see the sweat dripping from his goatee as he turned to face another section of the wave. Joining in, Nuyani cleaved through the worms or spun out of reach before delivering her own blow. The ground was soon covered in a layer of pus and insect remains, but the constant flow of worms came in all directions.

The large animal wore a saddle with several bags jostling about on their tethers. She had never seen such an animal, but its fierce nature reminded her of the blade jaws. It moved like a raging river of brown and red, washing away the worms that lingered. With a moment's breath, Nuyani gathered herself and returned to the battle. The waves seemed endless as the worms continued to surface. As Nuyani fought, she caught glimpses of the other caster releasing various spells and wondered if she would have better luck using the same. She let the thought go as she wondered why the man was there. Both he and the strange bird remained battling in the same spot. Nuyani wanted to help them escape but found herself stuck in the same mess. Even with her speed and several of the nearby dunes collapsed, she wondered if she could escape without a few scratches. Worse, she was still exposed to their curse-laden stings.

As they battled on, the worms closed in with greater numbers filling the space. Soon, it seemed there was no escape for them. Nuyani hacked through three worms with more to rise from the ground. She glanced at the others and saw the worms scratching at the animal's legs and the caster creating walls of edria as tall as he was, keeping several of the worms at bay before stabbing into the wall. Spearheads took form from the construct and skewered through the worms too eager to move. Though the technique seemed sound, he looked exhausted, and his back was exposed. Seeing this, Nuyani ran toward the man and released a wave of edria. Her concern proved correct as more worms were ready to surface. The man caught a glimpse of her speed, nearly dropping his guard as she approached.

Nuyani created several javelins of edria and sent them through the floor. Her targets died almost immediately. Though the sand did not stir from the projectiles, two of the worm carcasses received punctures as though struck by arrows. A feeling of disgust rose in Nuyani, realizing their difference from the living never ceased. She then created another javelin and arched it around the outside of the man's construct. With a single attack, she managed to kill five more of the creatures. The man breathed heavily as he looked at her. Sweat poured from his face.

"We need to go!" Nuyani said as she pointed outward. He gave her a confused blink before nodding his head.

A wave of pressure then descended on them. Nuyani could feel the encroaching chill creeping into her body. Her core started to dull. The man beside her was gripping his spear with greater fervor and using it to prop himself up. His body began to shake. The animal let out a strange caw that sounded as if calling for help. She did not know what it was, but the sensation reminded her of banshees, violent spirits of women who could steal your soul with their claw-like hands or piercing wails. Their presence alone sent chills through your body. The pressure around them was worse, and it started to affect the caster and his mount. The swarm began to increase. Desperate, Nuyani created a shield encompassing the area and blocking some of the prutosa which lingered around them.

The man then gathered his wits as he looked at the enormous dome of blue light covering the area. Nuyani remained frozen in place as her eyes flared with their ember glow. The owl lizard then stood as well, shaking off the chill. Seeing the animal was okay, the caster then whistled. The animal's small ears twitched at the high-pitched tone and ran toward them. The creature glided beside him, stopping once the saddle was at his side. He then jumped on and released a thrum, calling for the animal's reins. The strands flew to his hand as he gave them a pull, guiding his mount toward Nuyani. Nuyani released the shield and extended her hand, as did the caster. With hands locked, he hoisted her into the saddle as they sped off. Nuyani released another thrum with a shield blocking the worms before their path.

They passed over the fallen worms and the felled sand dunes, burying some of the other bodies. Nuyani was surprised at how smooth the animal's gait was, almost never feeling a single jostle from its steps in a blur. Despite being on the back of the animal, she could hear the ground crumble and the sand shift, sounding more like a waterfall. The animal moved further west as the ground trembled, even through the beast. A thunderous crash sounded behind them. Nuyani moved to look back as the wind rushed through the area. A towering cloud of sand climbed several stories into the sky. More dust clouds rushed outward along the surface. Nuyani's eyes widened as she saw another worm.

Nearly as tall as the same cloud plume, the enormous worm opened and closed its pincers, consuming several of the slain worms before its body tipped forward. The worm then slammed onto the ground, sending a second shockwave and clouds of sand through the area.

"They…They get that big!?" Nuyani asked, not realizing she was gripping the man's collar too tightly. The caster gripped her hand, trying to loosen it. Nuyani looked back and saw the man narrowing his gaze at her as though she were odd. Nuyani raised her hand to her eyes, wondering if that was what he had found strange. A sense of fear rose in her, remembering that her eyes would have earned her an arrow in her back at the beginning of the season. Now, out of the drylands, she did not know if others found her eyes strange. "What?"

The man then said, "[By Do'alc's rain, you can't be from here. Who are you?]" The man then wore a strange smile as if he just heard a strange joke. "[By the gods, thank you.]" Nuyani merely stared at him with a look of bewilderment. Not only were their worms equal to the size, or close, to the visions of the gods, but now there was proof of others and a language she could not understand. The man then pointed further west. "[Let's get to solid ground.]"

It did not take long for them to reach hardened ground several miles away from the plume. When they reached the area, Nuyani transferred the energy she used as a shield to sensory. Surveying their surroundings brought relief when she could not sense any pressure larger than an ant in the solid ground beneath her feet. Despite the distance, she found herself looking back toward the east. The cliffside was now a thin line on the horizon.

The caster, however, was inspecting Nuyani. A strange woman with burning eyes and hooded clothing with short leaves. His eyes started to trail down her legs. Aside from the layers of dirt and dried pus, she had a shapely form. "[Who are you?]" the caster asked.

Nuyani turned around to find a lingering eye following her backside. Quickly turning to face him, she held the nimcha before her as though she were ready to strike. "Don't get any strange ideas."

"[Definitely not from here,]" the man said as he smiled and waved a hand as he stepped back.

The owl lizard then cawed, catching Nuyani's attention and keeping her cautious. Though she was saved by the animal, she was not certain she would not have to battle it as well. Her worries grew however seeing that the man knew more spells. There was an entire language and other gods that powered the forces of the world but, she did not know much about them.

Even her own deity seemed to know a lot about the function but never used the unknown laws of the mortal plane.

The man then smiled as he went on. "[Calm down. Nothing like that,]" the man said as he went to the saddle and unfastened a gourd fixed with a stopper at the top. Nuyani watched him closely but lowered her weapon. He pulled off his head wrap, revealing a head of dreads as freed sweat trailed down his brow. He proceeded to upturn the gourd and poured some of the water into his mouth.

Nuyani lowered the weapon and her glare. "If you are offering water, then why didn't you start with that?" Nuyani asked, feeling annoyed.

The man looked at her once more and noticed the bags tied to strap over her shoulder. He then pointed to one of the water skins. Nuyani looked down and grabbed her nearly empty water skins and saw the man nod his head. She squeezed the bags showing both were nearly empty.

"[Aw. So, you don't have any water. Well, I can help you with that then,]" the man said as he untied another gourd and walked halfway toward her before placing it down halfway between them. "[Please. By rain and cloud, let me show you some hospitality.]" Nuyani relaxed and flicked her wrist, letting the blade pour back into the pebble-sized gem and easing her demeanor.

The animal was now lying down and had a strange gleeful thrum she recognized from other animals in her village, which they called whip necks. Docile animals despite their great height. They had long necks leading to bulbous heads covered in bone with small horns on the top meant to help strike predators. Their fur often grew thick and shed annually, which was still strong enough to make into clothing. Nuyani looked at the large brown eyes of the animal. She smiled and sent a thrum to the animal with a soothing coaxing. The waves edria first met with the animal's one core then brushed around it, pushing away the prutosa that weighed on her core. It was as if both petting the animal and trying to relieve stress. The animal responded with a deep coo she did not expect.

Zonqua laughed as he removed several items from the large bags tied to the saddle. He removed the saddle from its back and placed it on the ground. Nuyani turned the gourd over and took several gulps of water, not letting a single drop fall to the ground before turning back over. Life returned to her as she felt her body's fatigue begin to lessen and cool. She waited and watched as the caster grabbed several bags and rolled tarps before moving to a clear space. He then placed three rugs on the ground, each one red and in rectangular pieces with dark green and yellow symbols stitched into the fabric. He then placed tarps over them, each with holes in the center. Strings attached to the outer edge of the tarps were in loops. He started planting spikes through each of the strands.

Nuyani wondered what he was doing as she held the gourd. The man had an entire camp with him and enough for others.

He's definitely prepared, Nuyani thought as the owl lizard approached, giving Nuyani a start before nuzzling its head into her chest. She chuckled as she held onto the gourd and started petting the animal. Despite the recent battle and desert plane, the animal's feathers gave a sweet aroma like a plant or burnt wood.

She then noticed a bag filled with several small figurines of red stone. Each figurine was of a person or animal. What caught her curiosity were the subtle thrums of edria that lay within them. Each one echoed with a small thrum of energy a little stronger and faster from her blade's gem. *What are those?* Nuyani thought to herself as she saw three copies of a woman figurine. Though it was not so detailed, the woman was in the nude, and her hair streamed to the side, swirling around her extended arm outward. The face was blank, but the body had enough curves to make it obvious what it was supposed to be.

The man then tied the figurines to strands through the small holes before releasing a thrum through each. The energy then doubled in strength and speed through echoing into the tarps. Gusts of wind then rushed forth as the tarps rose. Nuyani looked in awe as shade was set up in a few moments. He then dug out a hole in the center with a simple shovel surprising Nuyani that he would use a simple tool instead of magic but, knowing either could exhaust you may have been a better option.

Once finished, he looked toward Nuyani with a warm smile and gestured to Nuyani to take a seat. "[Please join me at my hearth]," the man then said as he moved back toward one of the other carpets and sat down.

Nuyani waited for the man to sit before slowly moving to her own. She gave a considering look at him. Barely a word was exchanged, and he seemed earnest. The larger animal moved to their own spot, sticking her large head under the tarp and resting. Her eyes widened as she looked at the tarp feeling the lapping currents of wind swirling before the shadow of the tarp. Nuyani crouched and ducked underneath as she felt the cool breeze rush all around her.

By his shine, this is what magic can do? Nuyani thought as she realized most of her use and the visions she was shown by others were mostly of attacks or tools. Technically, this was still a tool, but she never thought of using some form of element in a way that was not conducive to battle. As she sat beneath the tarp, a low thrum emanated from deep within her core, vibrating through the carpet and reaching the small figure nearby. She could feel the differing rhythms within the full pattern of the thrum. Nuyani glowered as she tried to parse one thrum from another, but as edria ran along them in sequence, it was hard to tell when one portion ended and another began. Even more so, she looked at the spear sitting beside the caster and noticed that the symbols before her sat on her mind like a memory evading her grasp. She had never seen them before, at least not before the spirits showed her visions. Yet, they weighed on her mind all the same.

"[You definitely aren't from around here,]" the man said as he removed a log from one of the larger bags on the saddle and placed it in the hole. Nuyani watched him, trying to understand what he was saying as well. There was a strange, familiar cadence to his words and speech, but not one she could work out so soon. "[Zonqua,]" the man said as he placed a hand on his chest. He then turned his palm upward and gestured to the owl lizard. "[Lugna.]" the man said with a smile as he fixed his collar.

"Zonqua. Lugna," Nuyani repeated. She looked at both as she said the names in case there was any correction needed. The large animal gave a soft coo in response to their name. Nuyani did not know if the animal was male or female.

"[I don't know who you are or why you're here, but I don't think I would've escaped that one without your help,]" the man said, shaking his head. He stared at her, fixating on her eyes. Despite the morning sun still brimming over the horizon, her eyes still held a strong glow illuminating her face beneath her hood. Nuyani took another swig of water. "[How will I ask this?]" Zonqua said to himself more than Nuyani. Regaining her attention, he then moved to the saddle and retrieved several rags from another pouch. Nuyani looked at the saddle curiously. With at least two dozen bags of varying sizes and a few boxes fastened to a small shelf behind the seated portion, the man seemed well prepared for his journey in the desert. Once he returned with the rags, he handed one to Nuyani before walking over to Lugna and scratching the side of the animal's head.

He made circles with his hand, and the animal twisted upside down gracefully, sending a sudden wave to ripple down its body. With talons in the air, the man started to clean the animal's legs. Most of the dried pus had hardened now and fell off. Nuyani then looked at her own legs and found most of the pus had hardened as well, leaving small chunks clinging to her shins and, thankfully, no higher than her knee. As though the muck did not exist, the faint scent of rot finally reached her nose, making her grimace.

To the sands, I hope the smell doesn't stay, she thought as she tried to wipe away the excess pus and dirt after dampening the cloth.

With just a few wipes, most of the pus started to come off. *There are other people in this world that look like us and don't,* Nuyani thought, letting her mind wander. She then paused as a detail that first eluded her came forth. "Like us?" she whispered as she looked up at the woman figurine channeling the winds into the tent. Before she realized it, Nuyani felt that the blank face was meant for Do'alc, the goddess of her ancestors.

Her heart began to race, thinking of the possibility that the man before her was somehow another ancestor of the fallen settlement along the coast. With the thought in mind, Nuyani recalled her venture to the settlement and the visions of the spirit. They were a seafaring culture that engaged both in hunting monsters and war. Though her people, who called themselves Kelvertian, named after the guard who led some of the other warriors to protect them, fled through a winding ravine with a path through the mountains molded by the goddess for their escape. It never occurred to her that others may have left through other routes, especially when the attack was so thorough. She took another swig of water before sitting down and thinking of what to ask and how.

When the man was done cleaning the animal's legs, he started back toward his own seat but found Nuyani looking at his spear intently. The red gem fitted within the blade glimmered slightly as she looked, a sign she was transmitting her edria into the weapon.

"[No! You don't want to do that!]" the man called out as he rushed toward her. Nuyani looked back at him, and the glimmer ceased.

She was feeding just enough energy to see if it would retract the weapon like her nimcha. At least, that is what Zonqua thought she was asking when Nuyani lifted her hand, flicked her wrist, and called forth her own blade. With her other hand, she pointed to the gem. It was peculiar to Nuyani that the weapon itself had such a large stone, and it was not meant for storage. Remembering the rings of the three elders in her village, each one held a different power no one could do before normally. The blue ring allowed one to see magic and spirit. The green collected and projected memories or copied them and made them available to the wearer. The violet ring allowed one to heal others though with limits depending on how severe the wound was.

"[You thought that was for storing a weapon? No.]" Zonqua said as he knelt beside her. "[For casting. It's a tegria bisrak edria (forte item of magic).]" Nuyani had little understanding of what the words meant aside from edria but a strange buzz came over her core in hearing the words in that strange language. She could tell which had power and which were a part of the other language from that alone. He then gestured to her blade's gem. "[That is a gaurioxash bisrak edria (retainer item of magic). Really just the crystals, but they have their functions, so it counts.]" Zonqua added more information than he intended, but he felt encouraged to speak with her. An odd person to encounter in the open desert.

Nuyani then looked at the charms that called the winds to elevate the tarps. Pointing at the woman, she repeated, "Gaurioxash bisrak edria?"

Zonqua nodded his head. "[Or just edragaurio (magic retainer).]" Nuyani found it strange. Aware of parts of the name being changed, the same buzz to her core did not resonate. She then pointed to the spear. "[Edrategria (magic forte).]" He then picked up the spear and stood. Pointing the weapon to the ground, he then fed a thrum into the spear, first passing through one of the symbols, changing the rhythm of the thrum; Nuyani tried to read the pattern echoing from the weapon. It gave the same hum as she felt from looking at the symbols. The energy then coursed up the shaft and strengthened force as its speed increased. The thrum burst forth from the tip of the spear as an icicle formed and shot forth as if it were an arrow. It struck the ground at an angle, first kicking up dirt before causing a small perimeter around it to ice over and cause other small spikes to form around it. "[Like that.]"

Nuyani stood. She looked at the weapon with eyebrows climbing to the top of her head. *I must try that,* she thought as she released a thrum echoing toward the symbol and seeing how the rhythm was shaped. When the returning wave of edria met her core, Nuyani hastened her thrum to meet the rhythm and released the wave as she would a sphere of edria. The palm of her hand grew cold and released a sphere of ice the size comparable to orbs of edria. It sailed several paces before descending as it pitched and struck the ground, where it tumbled over, growing dirtier with each turnover. With her thrum echoing around her, she became more sensitive to her surroundings and could feel the air around her become dryer and hotter than before in an instant.

Nuyani cheered, seeing she was able to at least recreate the spell, though not as fast or in the same shape as the casters. She looked at him and saw the man staring at the ice ball with eyes just as wide, but he was petrified. "Zonqua?" Nuyani said as she waited for a response.

When he finally looked at her, he then said, "[Jornoxarra (Elemental). You are a jornoxarra.]" His voice was calm as he turned and looked at Nuyani. A smile crept over his face as he looked at her. Nuyani smiled back as she studied the strange thrum coming from her thoughts of the new word.

"[I must know. Where'd you come from? This isn't someplace for you to be by yourself.]" Zonqua questioned whether that statement had any real weight to it when she saved him, but he had his own reasons.

Nuyani smiled back but broke away as she knelt for a moment to point at the figurine. "Is that Do'alc?"

"Do'alc? [How'd you…]" The man's expression then changed to one of concern as he glared at her. "[Are you some runaway highborn looking for a thrill?]" Nuyani did not understand the sudden change and gripped the nimcha tightly. Well-traveled, Zonqua had met many people, both foolish and intelligent. Meeting some lost and foolish woman out in the desert in over her head was not unlikely, and one of the many traits attributed to some of the highborns was their prowess in magic or spirit, making them great assets to the kingdoms.

Releasing her grip, Nuyani stood and looked at the man squarely in the eyes. She did not know what his anger was from and meeting aggression with aggression never worked out. That was a lesson she learned when there were disputes between villagers in the drylands. "Why are you mad? Do you not like or know who Do'alc is? Did I call it the wrong name?"

Zonqua said nothing as he looked her over. She was using the name of their goddess and yet wore nothing like what he had seen anyone dawn. Her clothes were strange and made of leather. With water in her system, she was able to handle the heat as easily as he did. The blade was also a giveaway that she was different, as its bulbous handle seemed out of place. "Where in Tuikon are you from?" Nuyani just looked at him. Her lips grew flat, showing a horizontal line, which was evidence of her annoyance. "Fine. You… Where?" The man kept his words simple as he pointed at her, then turned south and gestured with a wide sweep of his hands from the south to the west.

He turned around and found the same annoyed expression added as she pointed toward the cliffs northeast of where they stayed. The man blinked several times and looked toward the direction. That would explain her strange entrance or at least prove it. But for what reason? His eyes narrowed as he pursed his lips, pointing at her once more before pointing to the ground.

By his grace, Nuyani thought in annoyance as she gritted her teeth and let her thrum race. In her palm, she recreated her home on the cliffs from the outside in a small blue construct. A cavern entrance on the side of the cliffs was visible. There were shrubs and bushes growing everywhere in the dirt. She even added a recreation of a blood mane flying over the cliffs to add scale.

Zonqua then placed a hand on his head before gesturing for her to sit on her carpet. "[Let's try again]." Nuyani blinked but saw that he was calm and did what she thought he was asking. Lugna was now asleep on her tarp. When Nuyani sat down, she saw Zonqua move toward the saddle once more. "[Not a highborn but still has a mark of a jornoxarra. She doesn't even know basic spells. Either way, she is an odd one.]" The man mumbled to himself as he rummaged through his bags. A capable caster but so isolated, she did not know how to handle magic or even about the language, yet she knew about the goddess. There was a missing piece, but seeing the construct she created meant they had a way to communicate.

He returned to his seat with two rings on his fingers. Nuyani looked at the man, wondering what else he would show her. The man then fed a thrum into a ring with a small gem in a copper band. The thrum increased before a construct formed in the space between them. He showed both Nuyani and himself speaking to one another as an example. *Why does he need a ring?* Nuyani wondered. She then sent a thrum toward him and the ring, seeing that his strength was much weaker compared to hers, but Nuyani remembered that her gifts were from Kelvert's own energy. She started to wonder what gifts the god and goddess Do'alm and Do'alc granted besides storms.

The man then pointed to Nuyani and then to the ground. "[Why are you here?]" Nuyani looked at him, pausing for a moment before creating another construct, this time in a circle with a display from her point of view instead of making constructs. In shades of blue, she showed the first three days of the season, from her first encounter and defeat of banshees to the attack of animals infested with the worms. She went over her mother's warning and protection of the village and her travel to a settlement abandoned centuries ago. Zonqua looked with wide eyes at the display. The wreckage of buildings and older styles of construction were clear evidence that people fled in different directions. Nuyani then showed her second encounter with a spirit with a sober mind, and it was from a small girl who had died due to the palace roof collapsing. Her soul trapped in a bracelet; she was more whole than others. Through contact with her, the vision changed slightly to show the city long ago under attack as various beings of different sizes and shapes attacked the settlement. The warriors put up a good fight, but the invaders were out for blood and easily took many or died trying. As chaos unfolded around them, two towering beings were doing battle at the ocean side. It was Do'alm fighting with a red-cloaked tree being with a hood up and an androgynous mask worn on it but something shining through the eyes. It was the same attire as the smaller invaders.

Once the vision was done of the spirit, it continued to visions of her travel through the city. Several weapons were found in storage, along with a useful dagger of sorts. Nuyani managed to collect many of them in a bag and kept one separate for herself. It proved a good choice as she found herself followed by another animal. It was a blade jaw. A large feline of knotted muscle with two curving fangs, often as long as a human forearm or more. This one, however, was several stories taller. The chase and scramble afterward were desperate and telling as the creature refused to die. Drowned, struck with bolts of edria, sliced, and then chased through the same ravine.

"(The older ones,)" the man muttered as he looked on. Nuyani heard him but continued since the words were gibberish to her to begin with. The vision then showed how she managed to run into the same hunters who first tried to fire arrows at her after saving their lives. Now they were, but the same attire she was wearing was resisting arrows. Zonqua gave her a look and now felt that maybe it was a good thing she wore something so sturdy. That and the fact that she was alive from all that happened and with her own village attacking her. It made him wonder what sin she committed for such ire. He adjusted his collar, still in place.

The vision continued with the sudden protection of the same hunters and opened into darkness before lines of lights and several scattered dots appeared. Nuyani was then pulled to another point and did not wake until she was sitting before a blue floating flame the size of a fist and a boy no older than fourteen, from what Zonqua could tell. It was the same boy who tried to stab her. He, too, seemed to have a glow about his eyes from her perspective. The vision continued showing the hidden city along with the origin of the storms, the dive for her god's sealed and stilled magic, and learning to control her powers, and the travel into the desert with spirit and memory.

It was baffling to Zonqua how much occurred as she traveled. There were the strange animals she encountered along the way. Although they were normal to her. The sequence continued with a meeting with the hunters, defending them from both corrupted animals and the sudden storm and the eventual travel in spirit with her and a man that he wondered if it were her father. Nuyani had left out the parts of Kelvert's memories where she had left the village and the murder of her mother. In the second travel to the desert center, it showed Nuyani and her father, Sutama, a large man with a salt and peppered beard and stern eyes to match any warrior, coming to free her mother. The parents, in spirit, had reunited and ended the storm.

It was your people, Zonqua thought as his brow furrowed.

The vision went from her perspective saving the village in a projection of edria to her saving the village after running once the storm was gone. When the battle was over, she had brought the entire village to her home, or they would come along. Neither truly mattered to Nuyani.

Zonqua looked at her with a glare, giving her a sense that she had somehow insulted him. She furrowed her own brow in confusion. What reason would he have to be mad at her? Her feed of edria was silenced as she studied him. The man then scratched his head and used one of the rings to create his own pool of edria for a vision. The image showed several squared buildings, much like the architecture from the old settlement, with several trees around them. The trees bent and moved in one direction for a while. Nuyani wondered what his point was until she saw one of the trees uproot itself, and the far corner of one of the huts had small bricks falling off. Those that remained were being scarred by the wind. Looking further back. Nuyani could see the sky shimmering away, pulling apart as if it were flames burning through the center of a paper. More sand and dust covered the area, hiding several buildings in the winds.

The vision he showed then returned to the same platform of sorts where the false devourer lay, and the spirits howled. He looked at her with the same accusative glare.

"Y…You're blaming me? What is that? By the great lord's will, are you blaming a storm on me?" Nuyani questioned, now leaning forward on her legs as she looked at him with narrowed eyes.

Zonqua then showed her the remains of another city from a high ridge. The trees were blown down. Small huts were torn apart. Several of the larger buildings' roofs collapsed. The more she looked, the more detail of the destruction appeared. She could see other animals and people strewn across the ground. Nuyani thought it was merely a moment in time, until the thick wall surrounding the city collapsed onto the nearby buildings following the same direction as the trees.

"Is that what the storm did to all of you?" Nuyani questioned as she looked on. She and her people were miles away, and the storms shook the cavern. What happened to those so close by? The thought made Nuyani shiver, believing the cavern would collapse on them. So, in this place, there was plenty of life to see, or as Nuyani considered, what cities and planes would be protected. The city on display then showed a massive crystal in the center. Nuyani remembered such stones were meant to protect but the only time she had seen them was when the strange tree titan consumed them.

The woman stood and crossed her arms as she looked at him and said, "No. I came here to stop that from happening again or any other sandstorm from reaching my village." It was obvious she did not agree. "Help me, and I will prevent it from harming your land, too." Nuyani then created another construct with simple figures of people and a cylindrical platform fading the further down one looked. The blue lights then grew brighter as Nuyani animated a wall or shield covering up the platform.

A wave of brighter light then rose from the top and expanded as if it were meant to be the storm. The layer of edria she placed over it held but suppressed the sudden blast.

This time, Zonqua looked at her, confused as to what she meant. "[You plan to stop the storms?]" his demeanor eased to one of curiosity. That would be an interesting feat to accomplish. For centuries long and before, the storms had burst from the center and made it harder for anyone to survive in Tuikon. "[What will you do to stop it?]" The man sat back, propping himself up on an arm behind him, the other over a bent knee, and the last leg lying on the ground. "[What can you do to stop it?]" Zonqua let the question resonate through his mind as he thought of all the details of the vision. The memory of Nuyani flying through the sky with a mountain-sized crystal and the young boy gave him a few ideas. From what he was shown, Nuyani had as much connection to the foreign deity as she had to Do'alm and Do'alc. She helped the angel to draw its power. He looked up at Nuyani, his mouth gaping and eyes as wide as he could manage. Nuyani narrowed her eyes once more and started to lean back from the man. "[You might have a chance to do so.]"

"I don't know what you are saying." Nuyani sighed as she looked at the man with a more annoyed expression. Her eyebrows rose and furrowed as she saw the caster rise from his seat with the same bewildered expression and move toward the saddle once more. This time, he removed a sack from its bindings and sped toward Nuyani, clutching the bag in both arms. "What are you doing?" Nuyani looked at him as if he had gone mad and stepped back, not wanting to collide with the man.

He rummaged through the sack for a moment while looking at Nuyani with eagerness. Zonqua's hand then rose with a stone pinched between his index finger and thumb. It was a small, clear crystal fragment. Nuyani could feel the dulled thrum within his grasp. "You have a crystal. Why are you showing me this?" Nuyani gave a shrug of her shoulders.

"I cannot move this without great effort." Zonqua shook the shard, emphasizing each word with a bob. The man then fed a thrum resonating from his core, through his arm, and into the shard. The crystal took a moment to even show a dull gloom of white light. Zonqua's thrum increased and moved faster. The edria started to stir within the crystal, making the light a little brighter. He then redirected the thrum from the crystal to his ring. With twice the speed and strength, he directed the amplified thrum to the crystal. The light was as bright as a sphere of edria. Nuyani felt the thrum and noticed something peculiar to it. Though both resonated, the rhythm within the fast hum of Zonqua did not match the pattern that lay within the crystal. With enough speed and repetition amongst the waves, a few would inevitably stir the edria. But altogether, Zonqua was fighting the flow and putting in more work than needed.

Perspiration rose on his brow once more, and he stopped after a while. The light died out, and the thrum seemed as still as it had been before. He then held the stone out in his palm toward Nuyani. She looked at the man and then back at the shard before picking it up. *Why do you have a collection of these?* Nuyani wanted to question but went along with the same experiment. The caster nodded his head and stood back. She, too, released a thrum and fed it into the shard. With little effort, her own thrum matched the crystal's, and it was as bright as a fire. Nuyani winced as her little effort started to blind her.

"[That is it]." Zonqua's enthusiasm rose as he clapped one palm against the fist clutching the sack. This is what he meant.

Nuyani then stepped forward, glaring at the man as she held up the crystal between her and Zonqua. Only a hand's breadth away from his face, she then asked, "Why do you have these? You can't even use them."

Zonqua wore a strange look of confidence. He was certain of something. The man then dropped the bag on the floor, releasing a muffled plop. He then turned his palm toward it and released a sphere of edria. The crystals all activated, creating barriers that repelled the projectile. In a cascade, the energy passed to the other crystals closer to the bottom, making the sight of blue spheres frothing through the sack and ground as if they had never been there. When the initial wave was gone, their thrums returned to their still state. Nuyani then looked from the sack to the man. She found him creating a construct of a city once more with dozens of buildings, walls all around it, farmland on the outskirts, and a tower with a large crystal in the center. All around the city and farms lay a dome rippling as if something was touching it. He then changed the view to one of the brick walls, showing the mortar contained small chunks of shards as well. "That's how you defended against the storms?" Nuyani lowered her hand. "You're using Lord Kelvert's magic to protect your land." The concept took Nuyani aback. With her people so isolated, she did not know what to expect from the demon lands. A different deity was worshipped, yet it brought the same outcome.

The man's face grew serious as he looked at her and nodded his head. "I will help you." He then recreated the false devourer's prison and showed the large crystal shards placed at the edges.

"You want to help me. Thank you." Nuyani then gave a nod in return.

Ch. 3 Scars from Sand

The group waited in the same spot for the remainder of the day. Using the day for rest, Nuyani got to learn more about the desert through shared constructs. She learned that the desert had been divided for a few years into six different lands, all vying to reunite the desert into one empire once more but as the ruling party. The recent storm, however, changed things so drastically that the people dealt with more active war in the last season than they had in the past decade. It was odd to see how little distance Nuyani had covered since her time entering the desert. With ten days and confidence in her speed, she managed to reach the outside corner of the desert. The trek was not easy, she could admit, but that did not mean the same thing when she saw a sixth of the distance crossed.

'By the great lord, let me get there before next year's storm. It was also strange to learn that there were bits and pieces in the language they both understood. Though the words were few and had different meanings from what she understood. "To the sands" was a good example of the same meaning, but different words, such as the latter saying, were shorter, seeming to modify the word sand with an action instead of a location. What was also weird were the different attires that Nuyani saw the other women wear in Tuikon. Most wore skirts or dresses with long sleeves and embroidered sashes. Most had strange pieces connected to their sashes with a ceramic-looking material of a small disk bearing the sign of Do'alm and Do'alc. The men's clothing was not much different aside from wearing robes and trousers often. Both wore sandals as usual, but the warriors themselves wore boots instead. It was odd to Nuyani that such garments would be worn in the desert.

They seemed too hot to be worn, covering all the feet and half of the shin.

It was a small glimpse of what city life was like in a quick construct Zonqua showed. Nuyani remembered looking at the map and seeing where they were going next. Though they were on the far outskirts of any kingdom or territory, they were still a few days' ride from any city. She tried to imagine being in such a busy place. The village, even before her exile in the drylands, felt cramped at times, but the larger cities looked worse. The first city to reach, just south of them, was a place called Turu, a part of the land called Daibot. She imagined herself amongst the crowd of people as she saw in the other memories. Her hand started to tremble for some reason. The thought of the buildings toppling or so many animals looking to eat swarming the city at once made Nuyani feel a strange unease about visiting them. Feeling uncertain whether she was scared or excited, she took a breath to steady herself.

By his shine, there will be a way, Nuyani thought as her fears continued to climb. She had seen the worms before, and some cities were being desolated despite having defenses.

It was another weird thing to learn some of the history of both the people who lived in the desert and the worms' changes. For centuries, some of the boats that escaped had rounded the entire map of the continent they lived on, were captured by other ruling races, and were used like cattle. It was strange to see such forces moving about in the desert. According to the stories that Zonqua showed, there were lizard people called kymacs and snake women called vorjecoudya (people of Vorjeo), with the top half as human while the bottom remained a long tail starting at the hip. Their glares could freeze men to stone. Then there were udrogxalc (dwarves). All three ruled the area both above and below amongst the others. A strange turn of events occurred when the same beings with odd abilities could resist the worms, which were taken out by the same humans. They were enslaved, finding that a man or woman like her people were more vulnerable to the disease.

It reminded Nuyani that there were also worms that had changed. The creatures were more often created by the same parasitic touch as before, but the difference now was that they were either older and grew with so much mass that they outgrew their host or were people cursed by the layers of prutosa flowing from the center. There was more to all of it. Some people worshipped the god and goddess. Some only cared for one or the other. Some people worshipped the sandstorms, claiming them to be the new form of the storm gods. It made as much sense in comparison as it sounded crazy. It was not much of a leap as Nuyani saw some of the city statues and constructs showing depictions of both gods with two other forms that held the same name.

It made Nuyani wonder if that meant that the bodies of the gods that perished in the past were just one copy of their forms. Wondering only helped to pass the time as she looked toward the ground. There was much to learn, and she barely had an idea of what to do. Zonqua retrieved a piece of wood and some bags filled with food. Nuyani found herself snacking on some strips of jerky as she tried to fire ice into the ground and create the same nest of spikes as he did. Instead, she managed to create more ice balls faster than her first attempt. They rolled off to the side before beginning to melt. Nuyani stopped using the spell after some time as she was plagued with dizziness and her throat growing dry. It was clear to her that the spell was taking water from her body and not just the air. A quick swig gourd, and she felt a little better than before.

As Nuyani rested, Zonqua saw to his spear. Cleaning the blade, he, too, had learned a few things about her clothing. She had removed the leather strands and straps that normally covered her arms and legs, not something he'd complain about, but the material was strong and flexible. The variety of animals they used gave them plenty of goods and tools to make. Learning about the dagger and its meaning for the hunters was another matter all in itself. Her ivory dagger with a lone fox was a unique symbol meant for her as a solitary animal, while hunting parties had various other animals to represent the regions they occupied. His brow rose at the thought of a simple village still had some complexity to it with different groups. He also learned that the two medallions around her neck were to honor her new role as a religious figure amongst her people. The same fox was on an ivory piece, and the other was a woman silhouette turning to the side, but this one had an ugly mark carved through the neck. He did not pry, but when Nuyani showed them, a pained smile came to her face. There was also the crystal. It allowed Nuyani to store things once living, just like the gem at the end of her blade stored the blade itself, but here in Tuikon, it did not work. It would not budge.

A small chuckle rose from the man, too soft for Nuyani to hear. *This land hinders you so much yet is relying on your god more than we realize,* Zonqua thought as he looked on. When the spearhead was clean of any pus or dirt, he then wiped away the grime on the shaft. Not much work was needed, but it did well to let time pass and get his thoughts in order. Despite their meeting and a new purpose, Zonqua had to find a way to get more crystals for Nuyani to use and see. But to get more edria when the cities needed them, and were even his trade, made things difficult. While foraging the desert was not the safest choice, it was the best he had. Zonqua fixed his collar once more. The shift in his shoulder made Nuyani look. It was odd to see such a habit. She looked at him for a bit more before returning her attention to what she could do with magic.

After some time, the night finally fell. In the hearth, Zonqua burned a log with a sweet aroma that was treated with oils and had a strange ability to produce a barrier as they slept. It was never something Nuyani thought could happen, but it was welcomed in the same way. Sleep came to her easily, especially with the comfort of the figure calling wind into the tarp. Nuyani then felt the prayers of her village. The slow current of spirit flowed into her, bringing whispers of pleas and the voices of the various people in her village. Instinctively, she redirected the energy to enter the medallions. She had controlled the flow of prutosa of others before. It was exhilarating to the spirit, but if you stayed in that pool too long or did not have a way to keep your conscience separate, it would eventually change you.

Nuyani then rose as the faint whispers took over her thoughts, and she found her eyes watering. There were many prayers coming to her. She felt the longing, fear, skepticism, and anger of those who prayed. The confusion of others was hard to bear at times, but Nuyani often held strong and remembered that their prayers were also thanks. They often came with the love, admiration, and joy of their lives as well, even pride and comfort in some. When the pour of prutosa had ended, Nuyani lay once again and looked at the burning log. She closed her eyes and fell asleep thinking of their travels for the next day.

The next day, Nuyani awoke as the sun peeked over the cliffside. She rubbed her eyes and took a moment to let her sight settle. She looked at the sunrise and noticed the top of the dunes may have held a golden glow. That did not mean the same for the areas around them. The compact dirt instead held the violet hues of the sun's light, slowly growing brighter. She then turned toward the northeast, facing the demon gate's general direction. With her right hand on her breast, she then turned her left palm to the sky. Closing her eyes, she then began her prayer. "As I gaze upon the dawn, may your light guide me. Under your glow, I am protected. Under your glow, I will protect. I will aid my kin. I will aid my home. As day ends, I follow the will of your gleam even through night." As the final words rose, Nuyani found her own spirit swirling in a torrent, leading to a pour rising from her core through her raised hand. The prutosa freed streamed from her body toward the Northeast. It was merely a fraction of the pool of energy she had, but it would soon be replenished throughout the day. Something Kelvert had taught them was that souls required spirit and would draw the force from the soul realm to collect around it.

Nuyani lowered her hand and sighed as she thought of home. Normally, her thoughts were always available and open to Kelvert. Speaking through waves of edria, their minds were connected. Here in the desert, it was just another lost sense she had to do without. When she stood, Nuyani found Zonqua looking at her with a curious expression. He did not seem to be judging her and went about his business breaking down the camp once she was done. Nuyani helped to do the same, first seeing how he used his thrum to still the ring of edria from the small figurines. It required no more force than it did to activate them. She, in turn, did the same to her tarp figurine and caught it in her hand. It was odd to Nuyani how simple it was to use.

Returning to the task, she soon gathered the tarps, carpet, and hooks all together and handed them to Zonqua. When they were put away, he buried the fire pit and carried the saddle to Lugna. The animal lay on the sand, waiting for the weight to settle before standing so Zonqua had room to tie the strands in place. Nuyani looked at the leather piece and wondered if she could make such a thing on her own. The leather was worn but still looked sturdy. There were several spots of dried blood staining the light brown color. She started to wonder about the man's past as she noticed he fixed his collar once again. *What is he hiding?* Nuyani questioned as she watched the man for a moment. She then released a thrum and sent the wave coursing through toward him. Which not only showed the core in his stomach but, the weaker echo in his neck.

The man then stopped and looked back at her as his second ring, a small clear gem in an iron band, lit up. His brows furrowed but softened. He seemed annoyed mostly but somewhat offended. Nuyani looked at the ground and then back at him as she dawdled forward. She then gestured to the man's neck with a finger. Zonqua said nothing to the woman but slowly shook his head. Nuyani sighed as he turned away.

He removed a strange light-yellow fruit the size of a fist and tossed it a few inches in front of Lugna. With a swift chomp, the animal bit through fruit gushing with juices and let it fall to the ground. Like a normal bird, Lugna began to peck at it vigorously to take up every chunk.

Once Lugna was done eating, Zonqua jumped into the saddle and ordered her to lower her body. Nuyani then climbed on, and the three left. Her heart began to flutter. A faint thought emerged as they spent the hours traversing the land. Though she had never been to a settlement that was living, the thought of the sudden chaos befalling each started to sink in. She saw the destruction of three settlements in a matter of days. The ruins of their ancestors. The silent tome of the (dwarves). Finally, the village was destroyed by the last storm. It did not take long for Nuyani to realize she was no longer following the destruction but might be ahead of it. She might even prevent it. The thoughts swimming through her mind were a comparison she felt was both foolish and necessary. If she could save one or many of the massive settlements, then compared to the village, it would be a simple task. Nuyani gripped the edge of the saddle as she looked over the horizon.

As they rode on, Nuyani's eyes widened as her heart hammered away. She looked to the south as the horizon grew dark. Clouds of dust rose into the sky as they headed toward them. Nuyani's body shook. The wind grew stronger. When the grains of sand started to nip at Nuyani's ears, she flinched. Zonqua seemed not to notice until she was burying her forehead in the man's back. *It's a simple storm, right? Just a normal sandstorm. We will be fine,* Nuyani thought. Zonqua covered his face but found it unnecessary. Nuyani had created a barrier around them, but with her will in trying to block out the sand and winds, she and he started to slide off the saddle. The pulling weight made Lugna stop and look back as the sphere of edria cut even into the ground beneath their feet.

"[Nuyani! Calm yourself,]" Zonqua called. Lugna's eyes widened. The animal gave a shrieking caw. When Zonqua turned in the saddle, he clutched Nuyani's shoulders. She tried to remain small as the winds rushed about them. "[Nuyani! It's not the storm. The season is over,]" Zonqua said. It did not matter if there was a language barrier. The softness in his tone reassured Nuyani as she tried to sit straight and look into the surrounding clouds. Even as she looked ahead at the darkness around them, her mind flickered to the hunter she could not save. The storm pushed his body to the edge of her defense and slowly pulled the man apart, pulling and turning flesh into a mush of blood and sand as his body was forced upward. A shutter traveled through Nuyani's back, but she let the fear go and focused on what she was able to do. With a shift in concentration, Nuyani willed the sphere to guard against the sands. A circular gash in the ground appeared as they moved forward, only for the ground to descend by a few inches from the displacement.

Lugna crouched low and cawed in protest at the collapsing ground. "[Do'alm's breath, how are you able to move so much? You must be a jornoxarra.]" Zonqua said under his breath as he turned back in the saddle and took up the reins. It was clear that Nuyani was keeping the sands at bay. The clouds parted over her construct, making small ripples appear on the surface as if it were a river berated by rain.

They moved at a slower pace now. Following only the beaten path of what compact road remained in the desert. It was an odd thing to Nuyani, but she had already seen that the desert was not all desert. Tuikon had areas of regular dirt, which meant fewer worms as well. The same comfort came to her at the thought of following such a path. Nuyani did begin to wonder what made the worms strong enough to burrow through sand but not the dirt. Could they eventually do so? None of the possibilities seemed to sit well with her, and their threat started to grow. *Can they transform from the animals instead of just infesting them?* She let the thoughts go when they saw a set of stones on the side that were made of fallen brick and mortar. The stone was red, but it was only evident from a fallen wall that showed it was surrounded by a brown shell.

Zonqua gave a nod, seeing it was a clear sign they had either reached a village or were on the proper path to one. The group continued until evidence of another wall came to them. Nuyani felt strange in the area. Though she could not sense their surroundings with the barrier erected, she did feel the concentration of prutosa grow heavier around them. Before either had the faintest clue, they saw the corner of a home pass through the barrier. Charred portions of the building were smoldering, then lit with the little air it was provided. Nuyani narrowed the sphere around them, letting the wall pass through the barrier. Only the faint silhouette of the building remained.

The caster then pulled on the reins, stopping Lugna. He looked around and tried to peer beyond the defense. It was not easy with her dim light contrasting the darkness of the normal sandstorm. He gave a crack of the reins and led Lugna toward the sides. Nuyani was not certain what his plan was, but she felt that he was searching for something. In response, she let the barrier return to a sphere. Zonqua pulled on the reins, signaling that Lugna should stop. The caster began to look around, trying to make out the faint forms beyond the dome.

Nuyani started to fidget in her seat as she looked at the man, wondering what he was doing. She then tapped him on the shoulder. When the man turned enough to see her out of the corner of his eye, Zonqua saw her inquisitive expression. He then used his ring and created a construct of a worm burrowing in a hut. Then, two figures came in and killed the worm before resting. Nuyani did not like the thought of staying inside someone's home but there was fire. That meant trouble and she could not feel the presence of anyone around them. Nuyani then looked at the edge of her defense and shivered. A body lay on the ground motionless. Zonqua studied Nuyani's reaction. She was starting to understand what it meant. The village had been abandoned.

They stopped at another hut mostly because its size would even allow Lugna to pass through the front. Nuyani studied the structure, seeing the bigger difference between her home and other settlements. Though they were not truly round or squared, the buildings most retained flat tops. They still had the same rectangular windows as the others, and the passage had double doors. It was odd to Nuyani, but she never considered that buildings could have multiple floors. Once they closed the door behind them, Zonqua released a thrum, passing through the area. It was released from the ring instead of his own core. Nuyani looked at him for a moment, wondering if there was anything there. She felt the urge to release a thrum and search as well but instead readied her own thrum for an attack if it were needed. It was peculiar to Nuyani how different but similar the building was to her village.

Mostly built with tents lower than ground level, the floors were covered in carpeting, and underneath were foundations, not only to keep storms from blowing them away but to keep any burrowing pests from entering.

The home they had entered had several rugs covering the floor, each with intricate designs. Several cushions sat strewn about the first room. It was not a large room, making Lugna duck so low even the saddle was close to scraping the ceiling. They sat down on the carpets and listened to the whistling wind of the sandstorm. Zonqua created a wisp of light cutting through the dark. He looked around and tried to see what was available for them. Nuyani looked at the man with a glare as she started moving from the first room to the others.

We need to get food, Zonqua thought as he pulled a lid off a large urn and looked through the dried figs and nuts. His brow furrowed as he wondered what purpose someone would mix the two. If the figs ever caught a disease or aren't clean, you only have a better chance of getting sick. He closed the lid and instead went to the other urns, looking for something to eat or drink. It mattered little, though. He began to wonder why nothing was taken. There were not even signs that people lived in such a place aside from the food. The longer he looked about, the layers of dirt collected in the corners far more than a recent storm would bring. Instead of dwelling on the lack of care, he wondered what goods might still be there. He walked past the entry and saw Nuyani's eyes glowing in the dim room, looking at him. Zonqua was not certain, but he had a feeling she was glaring at him. The glow made it difficult to tell. He then fixed his collar once more as he moved on.

Also, a change of clothes for her, Zonqua thought as he moved to the next room.

What is he doing back there? Nuyani wondered. Both could tell worms were not there, if ever, nor people.

Nuyani then wondered what happened to the people. The room's light grew brighter from the cracks beneath the doors, and the wind died down. With the storm passing, Nuyani moved to the front entrance and went outside. To her dismay, the first village was not a pretty sight. There were animals and people on the ground, some half chewed or swelling. Others were on fire or had been. Many of the smaller buildings had their roofs collapsed, and the ground had several holes wide enough for a man to crawl through. Nuyani breathed heavily as she looked at the death around her. It was happening again. Aside from her own home, until the storm came, each settlement she saw had been destroyed. Thanking Kelvert for his gift, Nuyani wondered about the next village.

She moved into the street, looking at all that remained. Smoke billowed into the air and more bodies. Nuyani released a thrum through the area, trying to find some form of life. She turned to look further down the road and saw a different animal than she had before. Its hay-brown fur looked clean aside from the rim of its mouth, which was covered in blood. Nuyani compared it to a fox but taller, much more muscular, and seemingly aggressive. The animal stared at her with a strange intensity, which Nuyani had not expected.

"By his shine," she mouthed as the thrum of the animal faded from her senses. The animal lowered its head and stared at Nuyani. Its leaf-shaped ears pointed to the sky. Nuyani retrieved a stone knife from its sheath as she looked at the animal. The animal began to stalk forward, staying low.

Before it could take a few steps, a loud caw then sounded as Lugna bound forth between Nuyani and the animal. The smaller beast did not yelp or whine but ran in a different direction. Zonqua soon came after with his spear in hand.

"[What happened]?" Zonqua looked Nuyani up and down, trying to see any signs of harm. She did not need to know what he said to understand a question. Creating a construct, Nuyani showed the animal that ran. "[Wild hound?]" His demeanor relaxed, though he still looked about. "[They're not safe to be around but, they aren't the worst things to see.]" Zonqua chuckled as he lifted his arm and showed a dark brown garment along with two arm guards in hand. They were like his but smaller.

Nuyani took them in her hands as he passed them over. Lugna then came back to the two and nuzzled their head into Nuyani's shoulder. Returning her weapon to its sheath, which Zonqua noticed, she started to pet the animal. Nuyani released a soothing thrum to the animal. She then looked at the man and held up the clothing he brought.

Zonqua pointed his finger to his left wrist. Gesturing to her bracelet, he then made a motion of putting on the leather armor. He then pointed to the brown garment and made a motion of wrapping it around his own waist. Nuyani narrowed her eyes at him. She shook her head. "To the sands with this thing. It's too hot." She then held her arm out toward him, waiting for the man to take them back. "Besides, I'm not taking someone else's belongings."

"[Just take them.]" Zonqua stared at her almost as intensely as the animal that ran off. Nuyani shook her head. "[No. You will need them.]"

"Why are you giving me these?" Nuyani started glaring at the man. Zonqua then showed two different scenarios through constructs. The first was a woman with revealing legs walking by until she was pulled through a doorway by a larger man. The other was a woman wielding a blade-like hers but with a rectangular handle instead, and two men held the woman down as a third cut off her hand.

"By his shine?" Nuyani said before dropping the items and placing her hand on Zonqua's brow. She released a thrum letting the edria radiate from her core, through her arm, and into the man's head. There she stayed, waiting for him to let her through. Zonqua's eyes widened as he felt the energy waiting at the border of his mind. He looked at Nuyani, surprised by the energy she displayed. If she wanted, the natural barriers of his core and spirit could have been shattered with little trouble. The biggest shock to Zonqua, however, was her ability or some understanding to access memories. The rhythm was natural and did not hinder his own core.

"[Alright. If you want to see,]" Zonqua stated as he focused on his thoughts and allowed his own magic to shape the memory. Nuyani's own thrum followed the pattern replicating the visage in her mind.

With a tug on his collar, Zonqua was standing amongst a crowd of people, all looking toward a raised wooden platform with men wearing similar attire as his. The biggest differences were their dark blue clothing and yellow or green sashes worn diagonally over their chest. Each of the warriors had their blades in sheaths at their sides and had loose leather boots instead of sandals. There were at least a dozen of them, with a few people gagged and tied up on the platform. An older looking man with a long face and longer beard was yelling to the crowd about the deeds of each person.

The man then pointed to the woman and presented a nimcha with a squared handle and gem fitted into the end. She did not notice the chopping block at first but saw another man standing near it with an axe in hand. Its crescent blade looked heavy, making her wonder if it took an effort even for the larger guard to swing. He pointed at the woman as he held her, but all Nuyani could do was make out the names Do'alm and Do'alc. The guards holding her dragged the woman to a block heavily stained with blood and forced the woman to extend her arm over it. She yelled and kicked at the floor as they forced her to kneel. The man continued shouting until he continued to repeat the name of the storm god. Nuyani's heart was racing as she saw the man wielding the axe raise it and bring the blade down on her wrist with a heavy thud. The limb went flying, with blood rushing from both ends. The woman screamed louder than ever as the guards released their hold on her. The woman rolled on the stage in her own blood as she clenched the limb.

Nuyani shuttered as the lead warrior with a yellow sash shouted to the crowd and lifted the nimcha overhead. Nuyani felt sick and wanted to break the connection but stopped when she remembered that there were two points he was trying to make. With the second starting, the vision of an open night sky above the rising stone walls came forth. Zonqua was smoking something as he sat on a cushion. Dim lights from torches lit the area, and a sweet aroma filled it. There were other guests moving about the area as well. Men were wearing rings and bracelets along with long robes and trousers bearing symbols with bright colors and intricate designs.

Contrasting the men were women wearing nearly nothing. The few gems they wore were glistening and had gold or silver bands holding them. Most of their hair was covered and put into braids or hair tails, ornated with the same golds. Each of them stood, moved, or talked, trying to lure men with lust. Zonqua's attention then turned to one of the doorways in a darker section of the hall, where a woman left with another large man kissing more affectionately than she felt was appropriate for public display. Before the two took three steps, a larger, well-built man then grabbed her arm and pulled the girl through the same doorway. The first person merely smiled as he was approached by someone serving drinks. Nuyani tried to piece together the lesson until she saw how open the women's attire was. Either the clothing was so thin that the dark skin was easily seen contrasting with the bright colors, or cuts in the fabric showed enough leg that it made little sense for the women to wear them. Nuyani even felt what she wore was more appropriate than the others.

Nuyani saw his point and pulled away from Zonqua before ending the visage altogether. She looked down at the ground as she wondered what she should expect from a larger city. Questions piled up. Were women seen as so little in value to others? What did a weapon really mean to the people, and why was Zonqua so calm about her wielding a blade? He had to be hiding something. What was under his collar that made him so cautious? It was a bad habit that would create more alarms than could go unnoticed.

Nuyani looked up at Zonqua for a moment, seeing an expecting expression on his face. He knew that it would disturb her. Even his constructs were merely human silhouettes and not so detailed. Zonqua then pointed to the leather arm guards and clawed at the air, signaling that Nuyani would give the armor back. Once she did, He moved them to one side and gestured for her to wear the skirt. As Nuyani did so, Zonqua started to look at the armor pieces. Fixing the garment around her waist, she found it paired with another sash. Quickly fixing the skirt in place, she watched as Zonqua started cutting into the inside of the leather. She felt a strange warp of energy looking at the symbols carved into the arm guards. When he finished, he then pointed at Nuyani's bracelet.

You want the blade? Nuyani thought as she narrowed her eyes. Seeing her reluctance, he sighed and fixed a half smile as he took out a leather piece and wrapped it around his own wrist. 'You are trying to hide it?'

Curious, she extended her arm to the man. Unraveling the strap, he started to wrap her wrist, keeping the distant edge looser than the rest but still overlapping to hide the crystal. Keeping the band from overlapping too much, he then gestured for her to put the arm guards on. Once she had done so, Nuyani found that it fitted comfortably on her arms without cutting off circulation. The leather piece had enough of a lip to cover the back of her hands and elbows. She rotated both and moved about in general twists and turns. Her arms remained mobile. When she was done, Nuyani flicked her wrist and called forth

the blade. Without a nick or snag, the nimcha came forth
smoothly.

She looked up and gave a satisfied nod. "By his shine,
thank you," Nuyani said.

Zonqua nodded his head, and the two mounted Lugna
and rode off. Nuyani then felt a faint hum off to the side. When
she looked, she expected the animal she had seen earlier, but
she found not one but at least ten of the animals peeking
around the corner. They stared at her as if considering whether
to give chase. It reminded her too much of the river lizards that
Nuyani had faced in the ravine. It sent a chill through her. They
made it feel as though there was only one of them instead of a
full pack.

They left the village and passed a stone foundation
surrounded by more crystal shards. Off to the side was a larger
hole compared to the others. Nuyani wondered what could face
a crystal as the energy stored within seemed even stronger than
her own core. They rushed toward the south. In their travel,
they found more villages burnt and abandoned. Things grew
dangerous as one of the few lying between them, and Giode
had people who were fed on by worms. They clicked and
trotted about going from one place to another, but they had
some difficulty getting their meals. Nuyani leaped into the
fight, eager to kill them, as she saw one of the creatures
sticking out of a child's body.

By his will, I will stop this plague, Nuyani thought as
she cleaved through the worm and body. Zonqua stopped and
shook for a moment, realizing she had managed to attack it but
felt ashamed. She hugged herself, trying to keep herself from

shaking. It worked, but it did not stop the tears from coming. Each child taken and each life lost felt heavy and unfair. Now, she was in the desert and had a way to solve the problem. Zonqua came to her side and placed a hand on her shoulder. Nuyani looked forward in surprise and turned so he would not see her that way.

I'm a priestess. He gave me the gift. I need to help the others, Nuyani reminded herself.

It did not work as her knees started to feel weak, and the shuttering returned. Zonqua looked at Nuyani with surprise, seeing her break down. Releasing a thrum, he created a barrier pushing through both of them. Nuyani then stopped shaking and felt a sudden pressure sitting on her core. She looked to the side, looking at some of the spirits of those slain. Bloody gashes showed on the flesh, bleeding as if they had just been made. *I was possessed?* Nuyani thought in disbelief. Each spirit glared at her as though the blame was her doing.

"[Do'alm's grace, I didn't think spirits would show so soon,]" the man said. He then used his spear and shot a line of edria from the tip through the specters. Blue sparks rose from the spirit, and Nuyani felt the soul ascend. Gritting her teeth, she stood straight and ran for the next specter. This time, her core reverberated to the point of becoming unmoved by the outside forces. She cleaved through two more apparitions before turning around and thinking of attacking some of the far-off worms. She went after the pests in fury, while Zonqua defended himself on occasion but focused on lighting any bodies he saw on fire.

After burning all the infested, the two quickly rode off, making their way to Giode. Nuyani used a cloth she took from one of the burning homes to wipe the blade clean. Though she did not like the idea, feeling it was close to grave robbing, it mattered little when her efforts were to help the living. She then thought about the sentiment. *I am a priestess,* Nuyani thought. What was that supposed to mean now? Her thoughts went back to her home and the other villagers. There was much she did not know yet and needed to learn as soon as she could. Fear then crept forth as the thought of the larger worm making its way toward the north. She wondered if it could burrow through stone. She let the thought go, knowing that there were others stronger than her in the village. When she turned around, Nuyani saw Zonqua looking at her as well.

She wondered why but then remembered he had just prevented her from collapsing. "Thank you," the woman said with a nod of her head.

Zonqua blinked several times. She was not certain he understood but tried to keep her tone friendly and positive to convey something.

If you thanked me then... the man gave his head a nod and looked forward. His thoughts dwelled on her eyes and strange attire. How was he going to explain her origin to anyone and keep himself safe. It was an arduous predicament to begin with but now it seemed he would have to tell her more about his situation.

In the distance, another sandstorm raced across the desert. This time, Nuyani fought the urge to flinch and overcommit to a barrier. Instead, she created a defense that allowed them to see but block out the grains. It was difficult to see further than a few dozen paces, but the fallen pieces of stone were all the proof they needed to be heading in the right direction. Worse yet, there was evidence that the city was visited by the worms as smoke billowed through the grains and collected on the outside of her barrier. The dark cloud streamed away, with the winds never growing too dark to obscure their view of the area. Stone pillars and homes remained in silhouettes in the distance, but the beaten path led the group through the outer section of the city.

They only stopped when they found the gate to the city closed. Zonqua then looked at the walls and guided Lugna to walk parallel to the structures. Nuyani furrowed her brow as she wondered why he had stopped. Before she could ask, he tightened his grip on the reins and pulled Nuyani's arms around his waist. Nuyani did not fight, seeing that there was a purpose in his actions. Lugna seemed to understand what she was about to be instructed to do. The caster then cracked the reins as Lugna lowered her body before dashing forward and up the wall. As if it were merely ground, they were up and over within a moment and with little turbulence. Nuyani felt uneasy at the shift of orientation, only to look about and see that the city was facing many of the same problems as the villages.

Zonqua had given her a spare ring earlier with a clear gem sitting on an iron band. With it, she was able to redirect some of her thrums to different spells. Maintaining the barrier, she fed a thrum into the ring to send a searching thrum for any present worms or living. Her brow climbed higher as she felt the prutosa of the area was thicker than ever. Amongst the rubble and homes were dozens of pressures, all moving about and keeping calm flows within their confines. They had yet to

notice them despite the amount of magic they were using.
When they were finally on the other side of the wall, Nuyani
found herself clinging to Zonqua tighter than she expected.
When he turned or tried to, she broke off. He looked back and
found her in awe and petting the animal's side. Before they
went deeper into the city, Nuyani looked back at the wall.
There, she could see the shards all placed in the mortar. Each
brick was at least twice as thick as her torso.

With a defense like this, how could it fall? Nuyani
wondered.

They traveled down the road as the sandstorm
continued. There were countless bodies of people and livestock
scattered on the floor. Several turnovers or smashed kiosks
littered the area. Nuyani felt several pressures growing heavier
toward her left. She placed a hand on Zonqua's arm, gaining
his attention. She then pointed in the direction of several
alleyways before showing the construct of a worm. With a
second crack of the reins, Lugna was directed to climb the next
building, which was mostly intact. When they did, clattering on
stone echoed from the hall before two dozen worms appeared
and scattered about. Each one started searching. Nuyani
lessened the barrier to evade their notice, and the group began
riding along the roofs. It did not help with smoke and sand
filling the air. The sun in the distance remained a dim light in
the sky.
When Nuyani tapped his arm, she signaled that they
were free of the worms for the time being. Descending from
the roof tops, the sandstorm began to cease. The area cleared in
moments showing more of the damage that took place. Nuyani
covered her mouth as they saw a wide trench filled with debris
on a lower level of ground. Several collapsed buildings filled

the space along with the tower Zonqua had shown before. Half buried in the rubble was a large crystal shard with metal and stone surrounding it.

"By his shine…" Nuyani said. The amount of soul and spirit lingering in the area created a river of pressure she felt could swallow them whole. She clenched her fist and looked about, trying to see if there was any space not marred by the creatures' chaos. They saw several worms amongst the rubble. Each one seemed to be spewing pus onto the stones. Before she could ask why, the group moved on, following a trail of carts, clothing, and other items. There were more victims of the worms along the path. With so many lives lost Nuyani's stomach turned. The same question arose as she thought about the threats that occurred. The possibility of all that happened. *How long until the village is attacked?* Nuyani wondered.

With so much going on, Nuyani started to pray to Kelvert, wishing the village was safe. She could feel the flow of her spirit flowing toward the north. Distant ripples in the energy showed that even her own spirit was being bombarded by the desert's oppressive spirit. Even so, she persisted letting her own spirit push through on until she could no longer feel her influence on the energy, or if it were being swept away.

Making their way to the other side of the city, they followed the trail of debris and footsteps left behind those Zonqua was certain were heading to Turu. Nuyani looked on occasion at the worms scouring the ground below. She was grateful the normal ones were only able to burrow and walk the ground. Their claws did not allow them to scale any building, but with the change in their make, she wondered if that would remain an obstacle for long.

Ch. 4 Wounds of Survivors

They scaled the outer wall once more on the opposite side of Giode. Though the gatehouse was open, it had more bodies and worms feasting on them. The sight made Nuyani look away. The worms were too large to burrow through them but instead used their pincers to hold and crush whatever piece of flesh they could before turning their heads to the sky and letting the remains fall in. Happy to leave the dead city, they were on the road once more, following the tracks of wheels and footsteps.

Despite hours of the day passing and the winds carrying sand, the evidence of the city's departure remained obvious as scores of bodies and discarded goods remained behind. Two bodies of a large man and an old woman were seen on the side, but evidence of their deaths came from their necks, hacked almost all the way through. Second blood stains revealed wounds of the worms that may have been hidden. Nuyani did not like the thought but saw Zonqua light them on fire all the same. She looked at him abashed for a moment but remembered that those wounds could mean they were infested. It did not sit well with her at how quick he was to dispose of them. They were once living. Pushing the thought out of her head, she focused on their travel instead.

Several hours had passed as they traveled. More lost items and thousands of tracks all proved that they were heading in the right direction. Nuyani kept her senses strong, even synchronizing her thoughts with those of others to increase her range. The lone whisper of the wind only reminded Nuyani that there was little life around them. They continued down the path until a strange plume of smoke rose into the air. Unlike black fumes, the clouds were green.

"[We are close,]" Zonqua said as he snapped the reins, directing Lugna to run. The owl lizard ran faster, using their connection to run faster than before. It was an odd thought to Nuyani, but it seemed that animals had as much ability to control Edria as she did. The thought of a blood mane moving faster with magic made her wince. She then studied the plume as it contrasted the scene before them. At the top, it dispersed easily in its expansion, but at the bottom, the plume was thick and dark. As they grew closer, they noticed small dust clouds rising from the ground and several moving square structures. Nuyani focused her eyes and saw that they were carriages. Though she had seen a few small wagons in the visions she was shown, she had never seen any structure that moved or stood on wheels.

Focusing her attention on the people before them, Nuyani noticed the carriages stopped moving and several thrums radiating from the caravan. *Do they think we are a threat?* Nuyani wondered. *How did they notice us already?* She then noticed Zonqua lifting his spear into the air and a simple thrum radiating overhead. She looked up and saw a bright orb of light almost as blinding as the sun. She looked away just as a horn blew. 'If we are signaling, do they see us as a threat?'

Her answer soon came as a group of riders on their own owl lizards were riding toward them. Nuyani watched in awe as their bodies slithered like snakes over the ground with their legs in a near blur. They kept their heads level with little rise or fall. Nuyani wondered how well hunters would do shooting arrows from their backs instead. Concern gripped her, however, as the signal she released was then transferred to a barrier. It did not take long for the riders to come into view. Like Zonqua, they all had blue tunics with long sleeves and dark green trousers, but over them, they wore chain mail that went below their waist and half their arms. They wore leather guards over their shins and forearms. Instead of sandals, each of them wore boots. Around their waists were sashes or belts holding blades and small bags. Some even had small daggers for secondary weapons.

Seeing other owl lizards, Nuyani noticed the differences between Lugna and the others. Some were the same dark brown and red as Lugna, with a few seeming thicker in their bodies and limbs. Some had longer bodies and nearly white feathers and scales but were a light khaki color. The remaining were dark, a darker khaki with hints of red in their feathers, matching more of the sand around them.

Zonqua lowered his spear and stopped Lugna. Despite his calm demeanor, both Nuyani and Lugna were prepared for a fight. She readied her thrum, letting the vibrant energy radiate through her body as Lugna began to crouch as if ready to pounce. When the soldiers were only a few dozen paces away, they ran in a circle around them, kicking up dust as they did so. Nuyani could feel the thrum radiating from them. They, too, had spears with gems housed in the base of their blades, but Zonqua's looked more ornate compared to theirs, with their lighter color on the shafts seeming worn and no carvings of instant spells or leather wraps for easier grips. The party only stopped after a few rotations, with half of them pointing their spears at them and the other half keeping an eye out for their surroundings.

Nuyani met their hardened gazes with her own, and Zonqua gave her a look for a moment that seemed to tell her to stay calm. He looked back at the others as some of the men parted, letting in another warrior with a yellow sash across his torso from shoulder to waist. Unlike most of them, he was an older man with more gray than black in his beard and had a narrow build smaller than some of the others, but his stare seemed as commanding and absolute as her father, Sutama. Nuyani still felt that small sense of fear from years of her exile. She did all she could not to release a bolt at him as he approached.

"[Search for wounds]," the man said as he looked at one of the other warriors. One of the other warriors then moved ahead on his mount as Zonqua raised his arms and looked to Nuyani to do the same. She mirrored his movements slowly but was still feeling the urge to fight. Lugna seemed to echo the sentiment but eased only a little, with Zonqua releasing a thrum to coax their mount. With eyes fixed on another version of her with more bulk than Lugna, Nuyani wondered what was wrong. "[Where are you two coming from?]" the man then said.

"[From North of Giode]," Zonqua answered honestly. The man eyed the two of them with scrutiny.

"[North of the villages?]"

Zonqua nodded his head. "[Yes.]"

"[Now why would you two be out in the desert alone?]"

Zonqua took a deep breath as he licked his lips. 'Just the truth. Keep it simple.' He then started. "[I'm a crystal harvester. I was looking for more of them and found some trouble.]" The man then looked at the woman noticing her aggressive demeanor and her odd attire. Nuyani turned to the man, noticing that he was judging her. He stared at her eyes for a moment, then went back to Zonqua. A Thrum then passed through them, striking against her core and the contents of Zonqua's stuff. Nuyani gritted her teeth, feeling the urge to attack, but she was stopped when Zonqua moved to grab her hand.

"[What are you doing? Why is she moving?]" The man's tone grew harsh and loud.

"[She is not from here and doesn't know any customs.]"

"[Customs? Well then, what are your names, and why are you out here?]" The man rode closer to one side as another warrior moved to the other in the corner of Nuyani's eyes. She felt ready to burst, ready to fight all of them. As if Zonqua understood what she was feeling, he gripped her hand harder to keep her at bay.

"[I am Zonqua. This is Nuyani. We just came from the north and ran out of supplies. We were looking for crystals and ran into some trouble.]"

"[You came all the way from the north and passed the villages as well. It would take some skill to get through the city and villages.]" The man then looked over them once more. "[A war mount. Your spear seems of good quality. Tell me where the girl came from.]"

"[I don't know. She saved me from a swarm of worms when I was trying to find more crystals.]"

Zonqua then twitched and released Nuyani's hand as a rising pain and burning radiated in his neck. Nuyani could feel the thrum ringing from him, and she looked bewildered. She turned her attention to the man, ready to release a spell, only for Zonqua to grab her hand once more. Even as his body convulsed with waves of pain, he was trying to keep her still. The man then grunted as his neck muscles flexed. The pain radiating through him tightened the grip. Nuyani did not pull away but tried to match it with her magic, which strengthened her as she looked for the source. When Zonqua started to lean forward, the leader waved a hand.

The outside thrum then ended. Nuyani followed the receding echo toward the source and found the other man who sent the probing wave of edria wielding a strange ring with markings on the flat top but no gem. Nuyani then placed her free hand on his neck, releasing a thrum in an attempt to soothe the pain. Zonqua breathed heavily as he placed a hand on hers, not removing it but in thanks.

By his shine, is this not a reason to attack? Nuyani thought only to find her distorted waves of edria to lessen the pain proved that something was there. She could feel the bumps and paths of scarred skin on his neck. Nuyani looked in surprise as she felt a faint thrum lying within the wound like an edragaurio. "Why is that there?" she whispered. Nuyani thought of his constant shifting and fixing his collar. She did not expect there to be some mark that could inflict such pain. It mattered little as Nuyani fought to quell the anger rising within.

"[I am telling you the truth…]" Zonqua breathed heavily as he tried to ignore the fading pain.

"[Oh, I am certain of it.]" The leader's eyes narrowed at the two. "[I just want to know what a branded traitor is doing out here.]" The man moved closer to Zonqua, making sure his presence was felt more than seen, before moving to pull Zonqua's collar back. His eyes lit with a small fury. "[You're not even from this kingdom, are you?]"

"[I am, and I have reason.]"

"[What would I want with a traitor to the throne?]"

"[Passage and service!]" Zonqua's rush nearly set the owl lizards to fight as both mounts jolt, stopping short of their lunges. "[I was a court mage and can fight with any of the swarms. She's no different and can handle plenty on her own. Let some of your men rest on the way to Turu. We will earn our stay.]"

The man nodded his head. He then turned to the others. "[Search the bags and see if there's anything questionable. We'll see if you are worth what you claim.]" He then eyed Nuyani up and down with a judgmental glare. Nuyani narrowed her eyes at him but did not feel the same lustful pressure others had exuded. "[She saved you from a swarm? I'd like to see her do so. Release a sphere.]" As two of the guards moved to search the bags, Zonqua slowly lifted his hand and conjured a sphere of edria. With his strongest, he managed to create one as large as his head. The caster then looked to Nuyani and nodded his head. Nuyani blinked several times before following his example and creating a sphere just as strong as he did. She saw the strain on his brow as a vein bulged and new sweat started to rise. Zonqua stopped his conjuring and pointed up to the sky.

You want me to do more? Nuyani wondered. With another feed of energy, Nuyani's sphere grew enough to cover Lugna's head.

The warriors looked at the sphere suspended over her head as the blue glow was shown on all their faces. Nuyani then stopped the conjuring as she saw Zonqua smiling. *You were just hurt. He better have a plan*, she thought as she watched him speak with the warrior beside them.

"[Will that not be enough?]" Zonqua looked at him. The leader nodded his head a few times as he looked at Nuyani with the same intense glare but with a feeling of approval.

"[I think that proves you can handle the job, but let's see what you bring with you. The last thing we need is any contraband or stolen goods from an abandoned city.]."

Zonqua then looked to the ground beside them, where two of the warriors spread a sheet over the ground and began taking things out of the containers. They were not so rough with his equipment as they were just thorough. The bag of crystal shards was dumped into the center by one of the guards. Another guard opened a small chest, revealing several parchments that had been folded and put away. Next were the bags of dried meat, nuts, and bread Nuyani did not recognize.

There were two more fruits for Lugna to eat. The gourds were placed beside them, and the remaining bags had various tools, both for magical and manual labor, or tarps and sleeping rolls. There were extra papers and figurines of animals and the gods in pairs and singles of the god Do'alc. Seeing the figures, Nuyani wondered what they were for. Then, there were other gourds filled with liquid that Nuyani did not recognize, a few spare rags, stitching material, and armor for both chain mail and leather plates.

Nuyani blinked at the different metal items and found it strange that what she used to call ring stone from because of the sound of dropping a blade from the abandoned settlement, could be shaped so easily for different uses.

Once all the items were spread out and looked over, the lead guard then introduced himself, "[I am Idenka. I will allow you two to stay near the guard carriages, but you will adhere to two of my rules. Every time a swarm comes, you will be there. You will fight for us. Once the battle is over, you will not be with the people. Keep yourself separate. I don't need people learning there's a traitor amongst us, let alone a foreigner who came from a city. Be sure not to let the Te'marc learn of you. Am I clear?]"

"[Yes,]" Zonqua answered simply. His exhaustion seemed to have gone finally as he returned to coaxing Lugna. Nuyani did not notice but, the owl lizard was lowering her back in a crouch still. When the other mounts finally moved away, Lugna started to ease.

Nuyani could not blame Lugna but wondered if it was a male. She did not know what sex Lugna was, either. She let the question go as Zonqua dismounted from the saddle and started returning his things to the bags and boxes. Only two of the guards remained and watched from the side. Nuyani then leaped off Lugna and followed after Zonqua. As he placed several of the parchments in the small chests, each of a dark wood, and held a small thrum, she grabbed his arm and halted him. When he looked at her, Nuyani glared at him for a moment.

Before he could utter a single word, she pulled his collar to the side and pressed a hand to the wound. Her magic thrummed through the old wound, but she could feel the small bead of edria lying within just beneath the surface of the scar. Zonqua then looked annoyed and turned his attention to the ground before moving her hand from his neck to his brow. With a nod of his head, Zonqua wanted her to search his memories. *Fine then. Look. See what this mark comes from*, he thought as he stared at Nuyani with intensity.

Alright, Nuyani thought as she channeled a thrum to meet his mind. Both closed their eyes as the memories became vivid.

Nuyani's edria grew reverberated faster and faster until she could overlap the rhythm of Zonqua's own core. As his thoughts took shape, so did her mind. Before her was a large room with nearly a dozen or so people. From Zonqua's perspective, he was on his knees with both arms held in the grips of guards at either side. His head was pulled back by his dreadlocks, forcing him to face two people standing just on the other side of the room. It was a man and woman with regal bearings. The man was a tall, wide, and built man with long hair fixed into four thick locks bound by golden ties that reached his lower back. He had a wide nose and thick lips poking from the cloud of black making his sideburns and beard. Only a brass bead hung from the beard. His eyes burned with a rage that would give even Sutama's glare a challenge. He wore a dark brown sash across his chest with a gold disk stitched into the middle facing Zonqua. It had the mark of Do'alc and Do'alm engraved on the surface. Beneath the garment, he wore a dark brown robe with long sleeves reaching down to his ankles. Across his waist was another sash colored gold to contrast. His trousers were the same dark brown, but his sandals were different. The same dark brown leather is used for the souls, but fabric stitching passes through several loops on the edges of the souls.

At his waist was a nimcha with a metallic hilt instead of wood with a black scabbard bearing several symbols on the outside. Nuyani did not know or feel any pull of her mind like the others did. On each of his fingers were rings bearing black or white gems contrasting the gold they were embedded in. Even through the vision, she could feel a distant hum emitted from the jewelry.

Behind the man sitting on one of the ornate seats was a woman with a slender figure she seemed proud to show as her matching dress had a cut, allowing her long legs to show. Gold anklets and bracelets contrasted her brown skin, each baring gems of the same color as the man. She did not look much older than Nuyani, but even when she was sitting, it was obvious she was a tall woman. Her hair was in many locks with multiple golden rings in each one set apart at equal distances toward their ends. Around her waist was a red sash. As she sat looking away, she seemed to be nudging her breast as to draw attention to them in the open front of her dress. Nuyani noticed her demeanor was much different as she kept her legs crossed and leaned to the side, resting her head on her hand. Though she faced the side, and she wore a look of annoyance, she gave several glances toward Zonqua.

Zonqua was in a different state, however, as waves of pain and fear radiated through his body. A swollen knot on his head. Sore spots on his chest and torso. Sharp pains on his legs and shoulders. It was clear he was beaten. Before him, on the tiled floor of black and brass, lay a staff broken in half with bent golden threads running along the shaft, keeping two halves together though at an awkward angle.

The regal man then spoke with what sounded more like a roar than a voice. "[You will learn! I trusted you, and both of you failed me.]" The man looked at the woman, and she flinched as though he had moved to strike her. "[You'll get plenty of time to think, but you won't hold your status any longer, Zonqua. Brand him and move him to the prison. We'll make use of him still.]"

Two more men then moved into view as Zonqua's hair was yanked further to the side, exposing his neck. Unlike the guards around them, the men wore colors matching the man and woman near their ornate seats, along with long dark red shawls covering their torsos. Zonqua struggled, and his breath grew labored as he looked at a heated rod held by one of them. One man held what looked to be a salve ready in one hand, and the other then held the rod like a spear ready to thrust. The markings were those of the gods Do'alm and Do'alc. Before he could plead, pain radiated on the other side of his neck as the guard gripping his locks forced him forward. The guard holding the rod moved simultaneously and pressed the heated metal into his skin. Immediately, his thrum raced faster than it had ever done before tearing apart. A small shred of his edria drifted from the core and rose to the wound.

Nuyani shuttered as she wondered what the man had done to get his beating, but the woman was left unharmed, even daring to try and keep Zonqua's attention. The blinding pain met Nuyani's senses, making her wince as well. In the memory, he had been screaming in pain until the rod was pulled away, leaving him tired and limp. His senses were dull aside from the cooling touch of the other guard applying the salve. The thrum that separated from the rest of his tattered core was still attached to his senses but seemed warped as its rhythm had changed to meet both his base pattern and the foreign pattern created by the new brand. Before she could wonder what purpose there was to the hybrid pattern, the roaring man lifted his hand and released a thrum from one of his rings. The radiating echo met his new scar and reignited the sensation of burning and pain as if someone were digging their fingers into his very jugular.

The memory then changed, only to see the woman seated in the chair, bereft of clothing, and atop him. Her breasts swayed with every rise, along with her hair and pleasant pants. Nuyani ended the thrum and smacked the man on his brow. She backed away as heat rose in her cheeks. There was no glee in the man's demeanor. No sense of pride in being with that woman. Though it was him being with her at all that seemed to pull at something in Nuyani. It had barely been two days since she met him, yet the image was not one she wanted to see, not of her at least.

Nuyani tried to keep the heat from her face as she glowered and started putting away the items. Zonqua said nothing and continued to do the same. *Of course, that had to be the problem. Great lord, guide them; why would anyone break their union?* Nuyani thought.

As the two were escorted to the caravan, they were quieter than normal. Lugna became meek, looking about as if worried about meeting the other owl lizard. Nuyani herself took in more of the wonder of the separate culture and items that people had. The carriages seemed easier to use than the sleds that the hunters used in the drylands. The animals pulling them were also different; they were stout beasts with lazy gait about their stride. Each one had long snouts leading to wide noses but small mouths. Their large eyes appeared at the wide distance of their brows between facing forward and to the sides. Wide horns at the tops of their heads were completely horizontal and went to small points barely curving to the sky. Their legs looked strong, yet too thin for their bulk, but they were hooved. Their wide waists made Nuyani think the animals were more stomach than anything else and made her wonder how such animals survived in the deserts. The only thing that seemed familiar to Nuyani was the animals' bush-ended tails, which swayed back and forth with each lumbering stride.

They were complete opposites to the tall horns Nuyani saw in the drylands. Each creature seemed agile and swift. Their red and white fur made them stand out in the tall grass. Their thinner bodies allowed them to leap high into the air. Their thin bodies seemed more akin to wind. Even the pair of two knotted horns climbed vertically into the sky and not to the side.

Nuyani gawked at the other differences between her and the kelvertians. Though they wore dresses and tunics. Their clothing seemed thinner while covering more of their bodies. Those who were normal people wore lightly colored garments. Either a light khaki or blue contrasting heavily with the area around them, while those with specific occupations wore more or less clothing and in different colors. There were those who either traded or sold goods wearing clothing with more contrasting designs and darker colors, but these seemed to be the people who owned their own wagons or carts. Then there were the guards, who all seemed to wear the same clothing Zonqua was, making her wonder how he came to wear it.

Her thoughts turned to a different manner as Nuyani noticed the glaring expressions of disgust and anger. Nuyani narrowed her brow and looked confused to see such behavior, considering she had just gotten there. The people did not know her. Before, when people saw her, it was a look of fear and hatred because she was believed to be marked by demons. Now, when she saw such looks, they were brief and hidden, as they had been cast by other women in the village after they had been saved. She ignored their demeanor as they rode on.

Eventually the leading guards took them to the wagons and next to their carts and brought out some more armor. He gave Nuyani a helmet and a spear like theirs.

"[Tell your woman she needs a proper weapon. No point in tiring yourself out there]," the man said. He began to laugh wryly, "[Well, we'll see how well she does when the worms come.]" The man was of a thin size, matching Zonqua, but he looked noticeably younger by a few years.

"[And why are you so certain the nokragga will come by?]" Zonqua asked.

The guard gave the man a look. "[Maybe you've been looking for rocks too long. There are caravan trails that were attacked or disappeared overnight as they traveled. Even military trains are finding it hard to move about. Luckily, the worms aren't that strong aside from the large ones bringing their hoards with them.]"

"[What happened in the city?]" Zonqua asked as he handed Nuyani the spear. "[The cities are the greatest places for protection.]"

"[It wasn't enough.]" His voice nearly rose to a roar as he glared at Zonqua. "[The crystal didn't activate, and the nokragga started spilling in. Before there was even a chance to stop the swarms, the large one burst in and took out the tower.]"

Nuyani looked intently at their conversation. Zonqua seemed remorseful as his eyes went wider while the other man's face grew rigid, though both eyes had an intense burning of anger in them.

"[Do you know why the crystal didn't work?]" The guard looked up at Zonqua with a gaping mouth as if he were insulted but closed it with a vigorous snap.

"[I don't. Do'alc blast that. It's not enough for the trouble we must face with the war. Now we might have traitors if the rumors are anything to follow.]."

"[What are the rumors?]"

The guard looked at Zonqua as if offended by the question. "[The plague seekers. They think that we're to go to another storm god that makes the sandstorms. The worms are just the true forms we need to submit to.]" This time, Zonqua wore an expression as if offended.

Plague seekers? How could they get so deep into the guards to stop the towers? High born took care of those personally. Zonqua's thoughts raced at the information.

As the two were led to the side of the caravan they would patrol, Nuyani placed a hand on Lugna's head. The animal jumped and snapped around to see her, only to calm down and let her wide brown eyes dilate. She then walked normally as they settled on the southern outskirts of the caravan. Once there, Zonqua kept the camp light, knowing they would have to move once daybreak came. With their bedrolls on the ground, Zonqua then stood and held his spear in one hand, looking toward Nuyani to join him. Nuyani blinked several times until she remembered she was given a spear as well.

Time to practice then, Nuyani thought as she stood and retrieved the weapon from her own pack. It was not time for their shift yet as other roving guards passed by. Though they had at least four or five people with them. Nuyani's display seemed to have set them at a disadvantage. Nuyani took up the same stance and stood before Zonqua, mirroring his pose.

The man then nodded, turned to the side, and held the spear, pointing forward. Keeping both hands a comfortable distance apart to control the weapon, he held the bottom part low and the blade tip high. Nuyani did the same. She looked on as Zonqua stabbed in the air. The thrust of the spear was slow as he emphasized the turn of his wrist and the lean of his body. He looked at Nuyani, waiting. She squinted her eyes for a moment and then copied the move. When he gave a nod, he returned to the previous pose. Nuyani did the same. This time, the strike was real. Nuyani watched as his body went into a low sway to build momentum. His back arm flexed to bring up the back before springing forward to thrust the weapon outward. Even the rigid shaft of the weapon shook with the force of his thrust, if only by a few fractions of an inch.

When it ended, Nuyani did the same and thrust as if she saw a worm before her. Though it was a simple move, it felt good to use the spear. Next, Zonqua stepped forward with his back leg while raising the other end of his spear. Nuyani lowered her stance and looked at him, wondering why. Zonqua then took the same as before while he created a construct of a man's head and torso. The first stab went for his chest, but he dodged to the side and backward. The rise of the backend of the spear then caught the figure on the chin.

"We're fighting worms, though. Why are you showing me a person?" Nuyani asked.

As if interpreting her question, he returned to the first stance, and the construct changed to that of a worm's head. The worm leaned forward, ready to strike, only to catch on the blade. Nuyani looked between it and the spear and saw inches of steel buried in the shell. He then followed through with the rising back end and smacked the worm away. Aside from his spear, she could feel the second thrum from the ring conjuring the worm. The same principle but a different enemy. He then eased in his stance as the construct changed from a worm head to two small figures. One was of a man and the other of a worm. The worm came forward, and the man thrust the spear into its head. The head burst as a ball emerged in its place, and the body fell away. He then showed it again, but with the worm dodging the first strike altogether, then following with a magic channeled strike of the spear's other end, crushing the worm's head once more.

As night soon came, they practiced more swings, thrusts, and blocks. Nuyani threw herself onto the steps, trying to find a natural movement for the weapon. She attacked and blocked spheres of edria that flew around her. Often, Zonqua would have two or three flying about as the last one would sail underground and pop up to strike Nuyani's legs or back. She soon took to releasing a barrier covering all around her in mid-swing or channeling the energy through the spear to create a lengthened blade in a light construct of the same shape to meet the echo hidden within the ground. Zonqua then stopped and took a deep breath. To Nuyani's surprise, he was drenched in sweat more than she was. His hand started to shake, showing the strain of magic he maintained even with the rings.

"[That is all for today]," the man then looked to the sky. It was already dark, and soon, they would be on their first watch for the night. "[Let's move.]"

Zonqua then started to retrieve his bedroll, shaking his head as if they had never used them. Once they returned them to the saddle, Zonqua placed it on Lugna's back and started to fasten the strands. Nuyani did the same on the other side. Once she was done, she started to run her fingers lightly through scales and feathers.

"Nogowesa," Nuyani said with a smile. She liked the animals, seeing they were very independent. Asking for the names of so many animals, she learned the cattle were called kurru, and the worms were Nokragga. There were also smaller animals that seemed to be the easiest prey in the desert, called Buwamo. They were small brown-coated animals no taller than Nuyani's hip with long snouts like the kurru but no impressive bulk. The animals were used for their fur and some meat but seemed so weak that Nuyani was certain it was their domestication with people that kept them alive.

The different animals made Nuyani wonder which ones could be so large as to rival heavy horns. They were large, bulky creatures with two sets of tusks to fight with and long trunks extending their noses to the ground. They had wide fanning ears on the sides of their heads. Their legs were not hooved like the other herbivores but looked like tree stumps instead. Another opposite, Nuyani thought as they rode off. During the night and some of the day, they kept to the southern side, looking out into the night for any sign of threat. Zonqua was given a lantern that turned from blue to violet when in the presence of more prutosa. Nuyani did not like the signal so much, seeing how it was already changing closer to violet just from the environment they were in. The first night, they had yet to encounter any threats. Nuyani felt a bit disappointed, wanting to use her spear and making herself grimace at the stray thought.

A priestess wishing for battle. By his shine, Nuyani told herself as she looked at the wide opening. It was better to dwell on the dangers than it was for her to think of how Zonqua had received his scar. She never knew it was from an actual mark. The branding had done something to him, giving control or manipulating his body. The thought burned in Nuyani's mind as she never realized how much of a shackle that was. Her anger rose, and her breathing grew deeper to stifle the growing rage. What was done was done, and he got the worst of it. There was now the matter of learning how to use magic at all and to learn the language.

With relative ease, the first night was without incident. When morning came, the two were taken to one of the carriages for rest. Nuyani went to sleep first, while Zonqua went to take Lugna to a temporary stable where some of the other nogowesa slept. She quickly dosed off and was berated by dreams she had not had before. There were those of other leering men in the village who forgot the respect that she was supposed to have as wearing her priestess dress was not revealing but form-fitting. It was still more modest than her runner's wear, but she felt comfortable in the hardened leather. There was a purpose to the attire, which was meant for action while being a priestess felt like an ornament for others to cling to. After a decade alone, she was swallowed by a sea of fear, pain, and anger from others while playing a role she was never certain of. She was just the one who survived, not the one who deserved the praise. Though Lord Kelvert came to her and saved her, it did not make her feel any different about who she was. The woman in the cave who ran alone.

Once the two had rested, it became a repeat. Short meals then followed their shifts, which allowed them to practice more. All the while, Nuyani, and Zonqua tried to exchange some words and stories with their constructs. Allowing their edria to synchronize, Zonqua was able to use Nuyani's own energy to create larger and more elaborate constructs. He showed images of the desert map and the different lands, emphasizing not a battle against the worms but war. The concept seemed too strange for Nuyani to understand. Hundreds upon thousands of lives, innocent or not, caught in fights that could end their lives just for disputes. If not for the last sandstorm crippling most of the kingdoms, then the war would have continued even now.

Between the six kingdoms that scattered through Tuikon, they only broke apart three years ago and were once a single whole. The death of a single leader shattered the country while the worms were still manageable. Nuyani wondered how their people had gotten to the desert to begin with, as the maps showed only a far-off section south of the desert center. Though it had been centuries, Nuyani could not fathom the amount of travel they would need. Her disbelief grew as she saw her small section of the map compared to the desert, and the desert was so small compared to the rest of the land. Less than a tenth of the total land, Nuyani could not see her home when Zonqua shared his memories of other maps.

She let the thought go after seeing a girl peering at them from a set of rocks. Nuyani noticed her presence at first and smiled, only for her to shrink back and try to hide. *Guess the young remain curious,* she told herself as she created a small construct of a small field mouse glowing in the night. She sent it to follow the child, letting it run toward her with natural movements. The girl gasped at first, audibly catching Zonqua's attention. Nuyani pointed to the side, letting him know the child was there. A smile rose, and he let her continue to entertain their guest. The mouse then ran back into the open and went in circles. The girl then stepped out and watched as the construct stopped and looked at her.

The child was thin and wore a simple tan dress with traces of dust and dirt on the bottom of her dress. Nuyani looked at her, thinking she could only be a year or two older than her younger sister, Caluu. As the child leaned down, trying to catch the fake mouse, Nuyani commanded the construct to return in the same natural run. The girl's eyes followed and then widened when she realized that both Nuyani and Zonqua were looking at her. The child stiffened and lowered her chin as if she were doing something shameful.

Nuyani lifted her hand and created another construct of a small bird with a round body and short wings. The small construct flew about with as much life in it as the real thing and landed on the girl's shoulder. The child moved to pet it but stopped when she looked back at Nuyani. Instead of shrinking away or laughing, her expression grew serious as she looked at the two. Nuyani's lips went straight as she looked at the child, wondering what was bothering her. The child then ran forth as she opened one of her hands, showing several metal squares on a string.

"[Can you help us?]" the girl asked. Her eyes seemed desperate for an answer.

What are those? What are you asking me? Nuyani thought as she looked from the strange disks to Zonqua. His own expression became serious, even angry in comparison, though she did not feel it was as intense as he made it seem.

"[Where did you get those, child?]" he said in a light tone. Nuyani noticed that he was not trying to scare her but to get her to speak.

The girl seemed flustered as she jumped up and down. "[Please. Can you help us?]" Her eyes widened and grew wet as the gleam from the lamp brightened on the reflection of fledgling tears.

"[Where did you get those?]" Zonqua asked once more. His tone was becoming aggressive.

Then this is a serious matter, Nuyani said to herself. She looked at Zonqua with a curious glare.

The girl looked afraid as her breathing grew heavier, and she leaned backward. "[You are not in trouble. Just tell me where you got those. I can put them back. What do you need help with?]" Nuyani noticed the man's softer tone when the child looked back at him. The girl then clutched the string of disks in a tight grip as she seemed to calm down.

"[They won't help my father,]" the girl said. Zonqua blinked several times as if trying to parse the words. "[He got bit, and he's been sick since we left. A lot of people. They won't let us talk to him and want to wait for Turu.]" Her eyes started to tear even more than now as her face creased. "[They said they won't make it. I want to see him.]"

Nuyani looked between the two noticing that even Zonqua's expression was growing grim. He then created a construct of a man without any distinct features aside from a growing worm within his body. To show the passage of time, he recreated the sun and moons rotating until the worm was large enough equal the length of an arm or leg.

We've been out here a few days. There are people infected, and they haven't removed them yet. How had they slowed it down? Does that mean they can remove them? Nuyani questioned as she thought of the situation. There was someone still looking to save them, but how long would it take them to receive help? With so many things happening, Nuyani then wondered why the child had come to them. She looked at Zonqua and pointed at the girl, then to the small construct.

The man blinked. "[I don't know what you're asking]," Zonqua admitted.

"[Does she talk?]" the little girl asked.

"[She speaks a different language, child. Just give a moment and put those back, alright]," Zonqua said.

"[But we need help.]" The young girl's tone nearly turned into a high-pitched whine.

Zonqua blinked as his mouth shifted to the side, and he narrowed his eyes in a considerate manner. "[We will try, child but put those back. You may be causing others more trouble if they go missing. Do you understand?]" The child shrank away and nodded her head. "[Put them back?]"

At first, the child was reluctant to leave. She had approached, pleading to them for help. It was obvious she was not sure they would. Nuyani then gave the girl a smile, trying to ease her worries. Slowly, she turned and disappeared. The woman then turned to Zonqua with a look of confusion and worry. Nuyani then constructed the worms within the bodies of featureless figures. Zonqua then added his own construct of a figure and showed the figure using a sphere of edria to push through the body of the infected. Nuyani did not know what he meant and allowed him to influence her construct as the different rhythms then matched. The worm within moved toward the surface of the figurine it was in before soon rising out and trying to scurry back in. When the sphere pushed the creature out, the other figure then attacked with a spell orb killing.

Zonqua was not done with his example as he showed two more figures, one being normal and the other suspended a little higher and missing legs. *A spirit?* Nuyani wondered as she saw the halved figure shrink and enter the body of the other figure. The normal figure acted differently and started lashing out with random animal-like swipes. The curing figure then appeared, and, instead of using edria in a sphere, used the construct to break the core of the possessed figure and then used a cloud instead to push the spirit out before doing the same to the spirit as had happened to the worm.

They can be fixed the same way, Nuyani thought. Applying both magic and spirit was not something she was used to. Even with her time learning to control her own and the prayers of others, it was not something she liked to meddle with. The wishes and wills of others seemed too personal, too precious to others for her to use. Instead, she merely listened and took personal note of the thoughts and wishes of her people. Now, there may be a way for their prayers to help them.

Nuyani looked up and turned to Zonqua pointing out toward the camps. "We should help them," Nuyani said not caring whether he understood her goal or not.

The man looked at her flatly and narrowed his eyes as he created a construct of the two of them hiding from the other guards and a figure that seemed to be wearing the same type of elaborate clothing as the others in the memory he showed. It seemed that some or most men of importance wore longer tunics to their ankles and had plenty of jewelry as well. Nuyani narrowed her eyes. "Then I will hunt instead," Nuyani mumbled.

Zonqua blinked as he studied her demeanor. "[What are you planning? We can't be seen.]" He saw her jaw clench tight as she lay back. "[You're planning something. Just don't get caught.]" He struggled to keep himself from smiling. He then moved to retrieve something from his pouch, which drew Nuyani's attention. He then showed her the same squared metal disks. Each one was black but had a brass edge.

Nuyani leaned forward, wondering what they were for. Zonqua then pointed at his brow. Nuyani lifted her hand and was ready to connect their minds, only to pause for a moment as she looked at Zonqua. *You are too willing to do this*, she thought as she looked into his eyes. The man had already shown her both his adventures and misgivings, though it was not as if she were hiding anything. Placing a hand on his brow, the connection was made. He showed a merchant's kiosk in one of the cities with a short man wearing black robes and a brown headwrap. Dark green lacing etched into the sleeve rims. He wore a strange medallion with an ebony stone housed in the center of a brass disk.

Consistent, Nuyani thought.

At the kiosk were several different figurines, rings, bracelets, and small statues. Some bared gems while others remained simple pieces. Nuyani then saw Zonqua retrieve a string of the square disks, all sitting atop one another on a knot. Holding up the squared disk, he pinched the edges of the lowest one. Nuyani could feel the sensation of a thrum passing through his body and channeling into the disk. A second piece then fell away, sitting between his first finger and thumb. The pattern of the bras-colored edges was also thinner than the other, nearly half as far from the edge of the metal piece. Zonqua then moved the pieces to the tabletop, receiving a simple nod before the merchant handed him two figurines.

The vision then ended. Nuyani blinked as she looked at the ground. *That answers a question, but not the important one,* Nuyani thought. She turned to face Zonqua once more and created a construct of a worm, trying to emphasize the others. When the man looked at her, pondering what she was asking, she started waving toward the rest of the caravan.

You think I know where they are? Zonqua thought to himself. He merely shrugged his shoulders and created a construct of another person. This time, edria echoed from the small figure fading away the further they got from the beginning.

"Go look?" Nuyani said. "You do want to help." Nuyani started to smile. Without another word, Nuyani crouched low and started moving amongst the caravan. Keeping to the shadows of the carts or crawling beneath them. Nuyani released her thrum on occasion as she stayed out of sight. She especially found the task a lot easier wielding a ring to channel a second spell. As she searched for the sick, she also masked her presence.

The trick proved useful as two guards walked by on foot, both wearing rings. It was not odd for anyone to wear jewelry, but there were so many with items of duel nature that made Nuyani wonder what she could do with her own trinkets. Focusing on her task, Nuyani started to notice an increase in guards at the rear. With those at greater risk to turn, it made sense to keep them where they could be disposed of if needed. Nuyani grimaced at the thought but found another curious sign as heavy areas of edria sat suspended above the ground, covering most of the carriages' rear ends.

Slowly making her way beneath one of the carts, she brushed against the barrier and felt the presence of two people inside. Nuyani wondered why they were separated from only two of them but stopped wondering as she sensed the presence of two more guards.

The guards were speaking to one another in a low roar. To her luck, they were more preoccupied with their conversation than they were doing their job. Nuyani then placed her hand on the bottom of the carriage surface, passing through the barrier. She then sent her thrum out and studied two people who lay on parallel seats. Through the echo of edria, Nuyani could see their bodies and their conditions. One was a larger man with a heavy set with a straining swell of spirit seeming ready to burst from its own body. Within the confined torrents were separate swirls of prutosa. It was strange to Nuyani that she could feel the man's spirit so easily until she noticed the frayed core. She had shattered her core before and learned that it exposed your spirit to others. But to see one that was frayed made her question more of magic's nature. The other villager was in no better condition.

She studied their bodies and found the pressures starting to lessen. They did not seem like good signs to her. Nuyani instead focused her energy from searching to conjuring several finger-sized and finger-length darts to aim at the separate currents. She released the darts all at once, sending them into the currents to disrupt their flow. The entire pulls of prutosa halted at the disruptions. The spirit seemed to leak from the core. In a rush, Nuyani used her ring to create a barrier and formed it around the man's core.

By the great lord's will, don't die, Nuyani thought as she grunted and tried to hold the man's spirit together. She let out a few grunts, finding it difficult to continue switching and holding different spells. It took only a few moments for the soul within to start the flow once more. The threads of edria slowly started to mend. When his core was whole, it started to give a soft hum. Nuyani grinned. *Yes. This will work.* She turned her attention to the side where another set of eyes were on her. One of the guards looked at Nuyani with a curious stare. The other guard opened the door to the carriage.

The first guard waved for her to come out from beneath the carriage. The other remained inside. Nuyani did so slowly. She wore a stern glare as she came out from beneath it and stood. Nuyani fixed her eyes with edria, trying to get a clearer look at the guard's face. With silver lines making the outlines of his facial features, she recognized him as the first guard who gave her the spear.

"I've seen you," Nuyani said.

"[I don't know what you're saying, foreign girl, but this is not the place for you to be]," the man said. Nuyani raised a brow. His tone was both serious and friendly somehow, but she did not know why he would have such a conflicting demeanor. "[If you send a plague to the others…]"

"[I don't think she will]," a second man's voice said. This time, it was a thin, narrow-faced man with angular features on his face and a pointed nose. "[Whatever she is doing stopped the curse from taking him.]" He then looked at the torch in his hand. "[We may not need to burn any of them now.]"

Nuyani studied the man's demeanor as he lowered his shoulders and moved the torch further to his side. A shutter passed through her for a moment. The feeling that they were going to burn the carriage with the people in it passed through her mind.

The guard then looked at Nuyani through narrowed eyes as she tried to piece together his actions. There was enough light for them to see aside from the small space of shadow beneath them.

"[Look inside. The man is breathing easier now.]" The first guard looked between Nuyani and the other man before walking toward the entrance. The guard, still holding a torch, sighed as he nodded his head at her. "[You will prove useful if there's no trace of them.]"

Nuyani looked at him squarely. She was certain that the man knew she could not understand them. *Is he just trying to annoy me or scare me?* she thought.

The two then turned when the first guard returned with an excited and bewildered expression. His face, lit by the torch, showed disbelief as he looked at Nuyani. His voice was low as he looked at her, "[You were able to cure them. How?]" Nuyani gave a strained smirk as she looked at the man.

"[She doesn't know the language remember]," the second guard said.

The first guard wiped his face with both hands as he looked to the sky, keeping them cupped over his mouth as he sighed. He then turned his head to the other man breaking the fake seal as he asked, "[What do we do?]"

The other guard was calm as he looked at Nuyani for a moment with an inquisitive stare. The man then answered, "[Get her to do the same for the other villager. See if she can repeat it. Then we get the healer.]" He turned to look at the other man. "[By the winds of Do'alc, if she's broken the curse, then there won't be another life lost to the worms.]"

The other guard pointed a finger vigorously at the man as his expression turned to a glare. "[That works. Bless the goddess that should work.]" Nuyani looked at the man, thinking he was retaliating to an insult, only to see his wide eyes fixed on her. He tilted his head toward the carriage and started to walk. Nuyani looked confused for a moment but followed. She looked back at the other man, who merely nodded and looked about.

Stepping into the carriage, Nuyani felt the chill that often plagued an area filled with the raw energy of spirit. Though neither of the people there was dead or possessed, the energy still influenced others. Nuyani then looked at the other man on the opposite bench. Unlike the first cursed villager, the other was thin and much younger. He looked no older than fifteen despite his height. There was also a different pressure lying on the child. Despite several spinning currents within his core, the energy seemed to move slower compared to the other villagers. A Nuyani could feel a strange thrum radiating slowly from a medallion around the child's neck.

She moved forward and felt for the item. It had the design of a man with a nimcha in the center and what looked like wisps of clouds encircling him. *That must be Do'alm,* Nuyani thought. She looked in awe at the boy's face seeing the dark brown skin gain a tinge of gray. The cold emitted by him was suffocating. She then looked at the other man and saw life slowly returning to his face. Nuyani then felt a nudge on her shoulder.

When she looked back, the first guard was looking at her with great annoyance. "[What are you doing? Cure them,]" the man ordered. Nuyani nodded her head as she turned back to

the villager and started the thrum of her core. The vibrations
grew faster until the pattern became a blur. With a clear sight of
the villagers, Nuyani felt more confident in dispelling the
curse. She created several javelins once more for each of the
separate pools of prutosa. Releasing the projectiles, she broke
through his core and stopped the flow from continuing. The
boy winced in pain; his body lurched for a moment as if trying
to escape a switch. He then rested as the pools settled and
returned to the regular flow of prutosa surrounding his soul.

"There," Nuyani said, feeling nervous despite the
successful practice.

The guard then grabbed her arm and pulled Nuyani
away. She looked at him with anger and was ready to release
her nimcha only for the man to move her to the other side of
the carriage. Nuyani then sensed three more pressures
approaching from the other side. The first guard then looked
back around the corner before straightening himself out and
walking to meet the others.

As Nuyani waited, she heard their voices get louder
and even some rushing to the carriage. When she heard the
hard taps on the wood, Nuyani hid her presence. She waited as
the barrier fluxed and shifted. It washed over the area,
searching for any remaining signs of the curse. Creaks of wood
echoed, signaling that whoever entered was leaving. Nuyani
watched as his feet shifted, showing that the man was not going
to the others but stopping at the side. Rolling out and perching
atop a wheel on the opposite side, Nuyani hid. She did not
know why but felt that her presence might make their stay with
the others more difficult. Instead of waiting to be discovered or

at the whim of the other guards, Nuyani searched with a thrum toward the next carriage.

In a low crouch, she made her way to her destination and narrowed her eyes to obscure their glow. When she reached the carriage, she looked around to ensure that no one else would see her. Ever more cautious, she went beneath the carriage and felt for the limits of the barrier once more. *I'll have this curse gone. I'm a priestess. I must remove it. Lord Kelvert, guide me,* she thought as her thrum raced once more. A few moments later, she felt the imposing pressures and torrents. Moments later, they were gone and corrected. Nuyani felt a bit of fatigue as she left the carriage. Using magic to puncture through magic was a lot more difficult to do than striking worms. After a fifth carriage, Nuyani stopped and looked out into the quarantined area. There were dozens of carts still. She had only reached five.

I will have to come back. Nuyani thought as she turned and left.

In returning to Zonqua, Nuyani found him standing and waiting. When he heard her footsteps, he looked back and nodded his head. A smile crept over his face as he looked back toward the open desert. Nuyani blinked several times, forgetting that they were only stationary for the time being until they had to switch to a roaming patrol. *Are there worms coming now?* Nuyani wondered as she rushed to get her spear and looked outward.

Zonqua looked back at Nuyani with a confused expression as she stood beside him, keeping the same stance he had taught her. He then placed a gentle hand on her shoulder and released a coaxing thrum. Nuyani pushed back with her own and eased in her demeanor. She did look at him with a questioning glare. The man stifled a chuckle as he instead pointed to the side where a dim glow rose against a sand dune. Nuyani looked and could feel a low pulse of edria radiating from their direction. Exhausted as she was, Nuyani could not send her thrum so far, even with the aid of her ring and spear. Narrowing her eyes as she concentrated, the sight came into view. Four small wisps danced in a circle with a pale violet glow cast onto the sand. Nuyani wondered what they were and started to tiptoe toward them in careful steps.

Zonqua created a barrier around the two of them. Nuyani halted in her tracks as the same feeling or close to being lulled was interrupted. Despite the waves of edria being so soft, they were powerful yet subtle.

Zonqua then said, "[Must not be a usual for you, hunter. Focus with your eyes and look.]" Nuyani did not know what he was saying but, the caster made a pointing gesture to his eyes giving Nuyani a hint as to what he meant.

Eyes, she thought as she mouthed the word, trying to parse it from the sentence. Turning her head back toward the circle of wisps, Nuyani found the thrum radiating through the light. Dull as the glow was, it was still filled with a strong pull of edria with rippling waves of concentrated blue, much like the buzzing surface of her ethereal form. She then saw a few animal skeletons on the ground around the strange circle.

Looking at the wisps, they seemed to have thin forms amongst the glow. She was not certain, but Nuyani began to think of the same floating men that she first met the night before she ran into Zonqua.

"[Those are called fae or *tovreg*. Some are nice and all, but the wilder ones only think of anything or anyone else as food]," Zonqua said. Nuyani ignored the explanation, only lifting her spear while giving him a glare. "[No need to attack.]" The man still chuckled as he looked at the alluring dance. 'They can still be dangerous, but only if you don't know any better.

Nuyani returned to her seat, still looking at the circle warily. Zonqua then lifted his free hand and created the construct of the wagons. Her eyes then beamed with wonder as she stood and gestured for Zonqua to place his hand on her head. When the man did so, they released the thrums, letting the patterns course forth. When their magic came into contact, the waves meld together in one rhythm with little resistance. *That's getting easier,* Nuyani thought as she then closed her eyes and recalled her memory. This time, when meeting with a drained priestess, Zonqua was surprised to see that he could match her strength for the moment. His concerns went elsewhere when the visage in his mind showed Nuyani priming her core to strike at the separate swirling pools of prutosa from beneath the carriage.

It was a surprise to see how much control Nuyani bore over both forces. Her magic easily allowed her to shatter the cores only to risk the souls leaving, but she managed to keep the victims' spirits intact. Zonqua then looked back toward the rest of the caravan as lips grew tight and his brow furrowed. Nuyani looked at him, wondering if he was concerned about the actions she took or what the guards might do. He then sighed and went back to the saddle beside Lugna. He then removed a gourd from the side of the saddle and started drinking the alcohol before sitting. Nuyani moved to join him as he held out the gourd.

Ch. 5 Lack of Knowledge

The two then waited for their turn to start riding. Nuyani did not care much about it, considering she found herself traveling only in the same circle around the perimeter of the caravan, but that was the deal. Her thoughts trailed as the only real thing that seemed to interest her were the people and landscapes around them.

It was odd to see at first, but the desert was not just sand. Some areas of stone outcrops and small plateaus stuck out from the sands and had water springs sustaining a little life around them. The next day, they moved, and Nuyani gawked at a strange field of statues. A subtle yet heavy thrum resonated through the area, leaving sparse traces of prutosa.

With the sun on high, Zonqua leads Lugna forward along with a few other guards to scout the area. Nuyani released a thrum and searched the area, finding little spirit in the air or ground but plenty in the statues. Her eyes widened when she had a closer look. They were people like her or Zonqua but of the Kymac and Vorjecoudya. Several swarming crowds of the lizard people were on their way to attack a snake woman at the center. The kymacs were only about hip height but wielded axes and angular swords along with rectangular or rounded shields. Most had their armors stripped off, while some further in the masses still had pieces of rusted chains or plating clinging to the stone.

The vorjecoudya at the center had a blade going through her torso. Despite that grievous wound, her pose showed that she gave her last attack to petrify them, along with herself. Her body rose above the kymacs. Her arms were out, and her palms were facing outward. She was arched backward and facing the heavens. From the height of the saddle, Nuyani could see the woman's face filled with rage and anguish. She looked to be shouting, and unlike the other statues, this one had several cracks in her face that were noticeable from a distance. Most lingered around the eyes. Nuyani wondered if this was a similar action she had done to create the barrier to save the hunters.

She shuddered at the thought of releasing so much magic that it would harm her as well. Magic lingered still. Despite the battlefield being safer, Nuyani wanted to leave such a grave site. The thought of lingering amongst the dead for safety felt morbid. She could not complain when there were days when she thought of her home in exile as a tomb.

Her attention was pulled away when she heard Zonqua speaking to one of the other guards, who told them to move ahead along with four others. As they rode forward, Nuyani's eyes met two other guards who both nodded with a sense of respect. Nuyani blinked for a moment and gave her own awkward nod as well.

That's different, she thought to herself, wondering if it had something to do with her purifying the five carts. Her thoughts returned to their duty as if they were waiting, along with the suppressive presence of prutosa lingering only a few yards from the statues. The others watched the ground. It seemed to move. It was not compact dirt, but the amount of motion they saw clear signs that the worms were there. Nuyani then felt a strange surge of prutosa rising from beneath their feet. Nuyani erected a barrier, as the others did. Dirt burst into the air before several worms launched upward and went for the riders while others went for the nogowesas. Nuyani blocked the parasites that came for them. At the corner of her eye, she saw Lugna catch one of the emerging creatures and crush its head in her grasp.

Swarms of the worms continued to press their small group, forcing them back. Zonqua released several spheres of lightning to keep some at bay as the others got into a formation and created barriers to block the worms from getting through. As the worms gathered, the guards tried to push the worms back with their own offense. The swarm soon ended as only a few dozen of the creatures came toward them. When everything settled, one of the guards was sent off to the approaching caravan. Zonqua and the other guards used the time to clear many of the carcasses.

The smell of rot stung her nose and eyes. Nuyani fought the urge to close her eyes as the pain grew more familiar. She looked at the ground where the other nogowesa stepped, seeing the sand depressed like a sheet on a cushion. Her curiosity rose as she jumped down from the saddle. Landing on the ground, it felt wet and soft, as if merely damp. Zonqua looked down at her, wondering what she was doing. "Nuyani?" Zonqua questioned. She looked up at him as she crouched down and then dug her fingers with ease into the earth, taking out a fist full of dirt. The ground looked dry. The area seemed parched and hardened, something the worms would have a hard time passing through, yet it was not.

Zonqua kneeled and placed a hand on the sand. With his free hand, he reached out to Nuyani, waiting for her to connect with him. She paused for a moment, unsure what he

was doing. Feeling the faint echo of his thrum rising, she then
grabbed his hand and allowed their cores to synchronize. First,
Zonqua searched with a thrum radiating through the ground all
around them. The two could feel the presence of the devourer's
spirit saturating the area. No magic place and thicker than the
contents of the air. Zonqua tried to direct the senses to stretch
as far as he could. Covering at least two dozen paces before
them, he could feel the pressures of more worms hidden within
the earth. The parasites motioned closer to the surface, ready to
pounce.

[Too the sands. How are they doing this?] the caster
thought until he sped up the thrum. He started to notice the
prutosa was moving closer to him and Nuyani. *[What are they
using?]* His attention shifted once he felt a soul slowly
approaching him. Zonqua did not wait for any surprise as he
conjured a javelin with his hand and fired it through the dirt.
With his senses, the man could feel the concentrated pressure
rise and disperse. Zonqua then went to the saddle and retrieved
the shovel before he started to dig.

"Do you know what it is?" Nuyani said as she thought
of what it meant. He said nothing as his thoughts focused only
on the digging. Nuyani was curious but instead concentrated on
their surroundings. She could still feel the other worms close
by. The worms were smarter than their counterparts in the
drylands. As the thought of the safety of her home, Zonqua
finally unearthed what their senses felt.

Beneath the sand, the worms were using their insides
to soften the earth. All around the exposed crushed head of
another worm were soft boluses of dirt all around it. There
were smaller strands coming from the yellow pus moving like

threads, looking for more dirt to burrow in. Zonqua breathed heavily. Whatever control the false devourer possessed was expanding.

"[Wh-What do we do?]" the cadet asked.

"[Move back. I will burn this one and see how much we can get rid of them. We can't take the caravan over this]," the man said as he stood. The guard then looked to the others and waved for them to move further away. When Zonqua felt that they were far enough away, he then conjured fire. Nuyani felt the rhythm of the spell ring through her being and call to her mind. As his conjured flame fell to the earth, it burned shells and pus-like weeds. The flames trailed even within the sands as the ground shook and rumbled a few paces before them. Smoke bursts from small pours in the dirt.

"[Is that the last of it?]" another guard called.

Zonqua shook his head as he looked at the ground. Reaching once more as far as he could see, he then said, "[No. There is much more.]" They could feel the ground before them was free of prutosa, but the spirit seemed aware as the rest was sectioned off from the flames. The worms knew their demise was coming. In a low growl, Zonqua added, "[To the goddess, we need a solution.]"

As he said so, the prutosa started to reach out once more and parted around Zonqua and Nuyani in an attempt to surround them. Zonqua motioned for them to back away. When the presence began to recede, Zonqua motioned for one of the guards to approach. When the same cadet came forth, Zonqua then said, "[Go to your captain and tell him that there is a strange nest of worms on the path. I will need salt so we can purify it. Move.]" The guard nodded his head vigorously and cracked the reigns. Once, he tore off into the caravan. Zonqua then looked at Nuyani and showed her his intentions.

With short constructs, he showed a figure running in a circle with worms in the center. A circle was drawn into the surface then was surrounded by four smaller circles evenly spaced around it. With about six different figures, the circle gained more designs woven within it and around bearing more symbols that weighed on her memory. The more intricate design then brightened before becoming a single large light. Once the light faded, the worms were gone leaving only the figures.

"You're going to get rid of them. Could I learn this?" Nuyani questioned herself mostly. The solution she needed to seal the false devourer's powers was all the more tangible. The others waited, and more guards gathered with bags of salt in tow. Nuyani then grabbed a bag and was shown through mental pictures of where to run. Nuyani took off in a larger circle than the space controlled by the worms. With her speed, the worms were not able to catch her and went back into hiding despite their bodies creating bumps on the surface. Nuyani winced, feeling the soft patter of her feet against the tarnished dirt.

Once the circle was complete, she walked toward Zonqua, who had created his own circle and started to grab some of the contents. Nuyani stopped and stepped to the side as she watched him draw those same symbols in his space. He then yelled to the other guards to do the same and quickly formed the spell.

Nuyani looked with wide eyes as she tried to memorize the symbols. When he was done, he then controlled the thrum to synchronize with the other guards. Between the six of them, the energy vibrating through the area was numbing. Nuyani looked around to see if her arms and legs were still with her. Like the construct Zonqua showed, the salt began to glow blue and spread further toward the middle, making another path that encircled the softened earth. More symbols appeared in the path. When the light became blinding, it then formed a sphere cutting into the earth and sky. As Zonqua chanted to himself, Nuyani kept calm and focused on maintaining the thrum pace, as did the guards. She could feel the air rush around them, the souls buried beneath them, the links of will tethered to them going far beyond the horizon.

Once Zonqua finished his chant, the barrier rang forth, condensing the prutosa, and pushing it from the mortal realm. Nuyani had covered her eyes. When she looked out toward the circle, the grains of salt were all blue and glowing. The dirt itself had sunk low by a foot. Sticking up from the surface were dozens of worms petrified by the blow. Nuyani could feel the pressure of the area was finally gone. As the combined thrum of the six ended, Nuyani felt her legs give way. She dropped to her knees and fell forward, using her hands to catch herself. A wry laughter was rising as she found it strange she still had the strength to move them. She looked ahead as all the grains flew toward the center and dissipated.

Where are they going? Nuyani thought as she looked at the others. No different from her. They were all sitting on the ground as well. She then checked her core. It was a surprise to find that it was not as erratic as before but nearly dull. Her body did not meet with any pain, but just fatigue. Slowly, they all picked themselves up as more of the guards came by. Iranke first rode forth and ordered the other guards to keep a perimeter, barring the caravan from getting close. While it did keep them safe if there were any worms, he also wanted to keep Zonqua and Nuyani a secret from the high bloods.

"[Is it done?]" the man asked Zonqua.

He nodded his head as he tried to catch his breath. "[It is.]"

Iranke narrowed his eyes as he looked at the area. "[Tell me. How likely is it that there are more of these pits.]"

[Pits? That's a fitting name], Zonqua thought as he imagined them falling into the sand, caught off guard. "[If I were to guess along any path around cities and farms. This could be the very reason they are breaking into cities.]"

"[Do'alc gift us rain, then let's be vigilant. We are still days away. Can you teach that spell of yours?]" Zonqua gave another nod. "[Good. We will need that done and soon. Leave around the side and meet with one of the guards. Pass the lesson along and get to it.]"

Once the two had a breath and the other guards set the worms on fire, Nuyani and Zonqua rode around toward the back of the caravan. Nuyani found it surprising that the lesser pressure that normally weighed on her senses felt so light. The two waited for a moment as the caravan passed. Still, on watch, Zonqua looked out into the desert while Nuyani tried to recall as much detail as she could on the matter. The salt they had changed to magic before disappearing. The symbols all pressed on her mind, trying to surface as though they were memories. The strange pit had connections rippling from the far south. *Great lord, what secrets are out there? How can I use this knowledge to save them?* Nuyani thought as questions burned in her mind. She grunted and bared her teeth. Her core was unresponsive to her call. She could not conjure even a simple construct to ask questions.

With only the choice to wait, she focused on trying to relax.

As the day passed, Nuyani rested with Lugna while Zonqua went to the guards to show them what they had done. At the front of the caravan, he then held up a paper displaying the spell circle he used. With four circles to control the middle circle, it was balanced to control the flow of edria and prutosa. "[Use the symbol of Amovs. The goddess will take the power eagerly,]" he explained to two guard mages. Both were thin men near the same age as Zonqua but did not hold the same knowledge as the exiled caster. "[Keep at least two men in pairs for the spells or the recoil will kill one of you.]" The casters nodded with conviction and went to tell the others what they learned.

As Zonqua made his way through the caravan, his thoughts then went to what lessons he could show Nuyani. There were twelve days left before they would reach the city. He then went to some of the trading carts where merchants managed to take their goods from the chaos. He spoke to several merchants looking for more paper and charcoal to draw. To his dismay, the prices were greater than he had anticipated, finding that most were nearly three or four times the price he expected. Keeping his grumbling low, knowing that they were

all going through hard times, Zonqua removed a silver coin
from a pouch on his side and handed it to the merchant for the
items.

*[I wonder what she would think of a god who's name
for consuming was used to purify the land.]* the man thought as
he laughed, knowing the twist of words was meant for such a
negative goddess to prove useful. Still dwelling on giving her
lessons, he wondered what spells he should teach her to survive
at least. The offensive spells would be easy enough for her, but
that did not mean the same thing as breaking curses with more
than just something's will causing it or finding an item that
could harm her.

Once he returned to the outskirts of the caravan, he
found her shooting fire from one hand and ice from the other.
Both struck the same area. Nuyani stopped for a moment as her
hands started to tremble from the pain. It had barely been a few
hours, and she was still awake and trying to learn something
new.

[Good thing she's as eager to learn as she is to fight,]
the man thought as he walked to her side, gaining her attention.
He then held out the papers and charcoal piece. Nuyani paused
and took up the papers. She looked at the surface, finding it
blank, and looked at the pen. "[So, you can write.]" The man
said as he gestured, drawing on the paper. Nuyani blinked as
she looked at the papers and charcoal. Nuyani then placed the
papers on her knee and started drawing the symbol of sealing.
Nuyani inspected the mark, looking over the details and
wondering if it was correct. Zonqua looked over her shoulder.
He could see her placing the mark in a circle and randomly
placing other marks on the page. Random marks for different

gods were drawn onto the page out of order or out of place. *[What are you trying to do? Are you trying to recreate the spells.]*

Nuyani then looked at the mark of fire for one of the gods. "Sarcapno…" Nuyani said in a low voice as if trying to feel out the word. Zonqua looked at her with wide eyes.

"[You've managed to read out the symbol so soo…]" Nuyani stopped and looked up at the man with an inquisitive look. "[Bless the goddess, you're making this easier than expected.]" Nuyani blinked at the man, wondering what Zonqua was saying.

Soon after, the two started their patrol. For several days, they went through the same routines. During the day, they patrolled and scouted, while on the nights, they stood guard with only an overlapping third going from day to night, giving them time to rest. During these times, Nuyani would often sneak to the quarantined section, where Odba would wait for her and guide her to carriages with people still afflicted with the curse. It was not as though it did them a disservice, but Nuyani saw by the fearful look the other guards had that they did not want them cured or expected some issue.

Around the area, the security relaxed as the number of infected dwindled, some even managing to fight off the curse on their own. There was a man she saw on occasion who wore a long brown robe with intricate green designs on the cuffs and a few gold trinkets around his neck, fingers, or pinned to his clothing. He wore a black headwrap with a shawl covering his face. With a few inquisitive thrums, she could feel a stronger hum resonating from the man. He was a caster as well, but different in some way than Zonqua. His thin stature, with little help from his baggy clothing, told Nuyani he was no fighter like the others around him. Yet his authority was respected as he occasionally dressed down some of the guards around him.

By the great lord, why is he mad so often? Did something happen here? Nuyani questioned as she continued to help the cursed. After finishing another five or so carriages, she found her strength remained. It was beginning to become good practice for her as she worked. Keeping herself from overextending, she left after notifying Odba and made her way through the caravan. At times like this, she, too, wore a thin red shawl, hiding her eyes but allowing her to see clearly enough where she was going. Making her way through the caravan, Nuyani saw how different yet similar her people were to those in the desert. The clothing and colors seemed mostly to be the same, with greater mixes showing someone's status as more of a civilian while the less, or specific, colors one wore were a sign of one's position. Nuyani thought about the man who kept his face covered. His gold trinkets were not just simple pieces but were formed into either figures or symbols. With the figures often depicting a man or woman, Nuyani was certain that they were related to the deities in some manner. Her thoughts trailed to either one of the elders or herself, wondering if he was some form of religious figure.

Cutting her way through some of the crowds, Nuyani smiled as she felt some of the softer thrums radiating through the area. Though their edria was not as strong, Nuyani could feel their patterns and sometimes tried to replicate them. It was odd how casually the magic was used. Instead of any offensive use, their magic was often used to stop painful aches or soothe the pack animals. Sometimes, it was even used to coax children or elderly people to sleep. There were even those eating that seemed to concentrate their thrum into their mouths. Nuyani wondered if it were to help them eat or if the sensitivity somehow brought more pleasure to the taste. Another smile rose as Nuyani watched a boy and girl on the cusps of adulthood, controlling constructs of animals chasing one another in a circle, making a few children laugh. One of the children shrieked when a glowing field mouse climbed up their arm and over their shoulders before climbing down the other side. Nuyani felt a sense of joy seeing the people were willing to laugh despite their situation. The city was still six days away, yet they could enjoy what time they had.

She then felt a strange chill in the air, which made her shiver. The sensation immediately made her think of banshees. The memory of the violent specters made Nuyani stop. She tried to feel the direction in which the creatures were. A sudden scream then brought a shiver down Nuyani's spine. Powering through the sensation, she dashed off, leaving clouds of dust in her wake as she went through the area. On the same side of the caravan as their patrol, Nuyani's eyes widened when she saw a strange specter she had never encountered before. Green in hue, it was a transparent form of a man bereft of clothing with the head of a hound. Its ethereal teeth passed through the chest of a man, shaking as if cold. Nuyani could feel the radiating pressure of prutosa washing over the area. With every snap of its ghostly jaws, the core tore and released some of the spirit.

She then released a sphere of edria. The blue missile sailed forth and struck the creature in its head, making it lurch to the side. It snapped back, arching its back, showing a man's contracting back muscles. Its fangs were bared, and its arms spread out as if ready to grab with claws on each finger. Nuyani's attention merely focused on the pits of darkness that made its eyes, each with a simple iridescent glint at the center. Nuyani took a deep breath and let her thrum cover her entire body, blocking out the paralyzing sensation. Like a banshee, the animal-headed specter launched at her at a near-blinding speed. Nuyani matched the spirit, stepping to the side as its claws whistled through the air. Nuyani acted on instinct, creating a dagger of edria. She lunged forward and went for the specter's ribs.

The creature twisted and moved away from the blow before snapping at her with his teeth. Nuyani pulled her arm away before she could lose her hand. Like the real animal, it snarled and growled. The specter lunged for a punch. Nuyani released a full barrier covering her own body as she tried to gather her thoughts. The blow struck, sending a ripple through the construct's surface, and pushed her back by a few paces. Her heart gave a thud as the short contact revealed the violent torrent of spirit, making the creature's form. Denser than any specter she faced, it was almost as if it were solid.

She retaliated with another sphere of edria launched into the creature's chest. The specter lurched back as the projectile disappeared. Swinging at her again, Nuyani ducked as the emerald limbed sailed overhead. Nuyani tried to flick her wrist, only for the specter to reach back around and grab her. Her thrum then hammered away, filling her body with desperate strength as the specter snarled and pulled her forward. Sand collected in her sandals, raking the ground as her heart hammered away. Nuyani then remembered her ring and sent a thrum echoing to the gem. Sarcapno's name rang in her head, changing the pattern of the thrum and forming the energy into a new construct. A sphere of fire burst around her hand in a ring twice the size of her head. The specter's hand burst into green embers amongst the orange. Nuyani dived to the side as the apparition ignored the limb and swung at her with its other claws. A swish whistled in her ears.

Nuyani righted herself, kneeling on the ground to face the specter. Attempting to copy the creature, she molded her edria to form ghostly claws around her hands as well and went for a lunge. Sensing her intent, the specter moved to the side, dodging her slash. Nuyani continued to press with wild slashes but was evaded with ease. She noticed the creature's limb starting to reassemble. *No. You will not return,* Nuyani thought as she readied for another attack and fed the energy in her right transfer to her left. The edria changed and extended into a single piece, taking the form of a nimcha. She swung in a horizontal cleave, cutting into the specter's stomach. The damage was done but not crippling as it grabbed her right and pulled her to the side. Its maw widened and went for her throat. Nuyani made the blade dissipate, feeding the energy into another constructed barrier. The teeth slid against the surface of the shield, sending ripples along the way.

It growled and pulled Nuyani's arm lower, forcing her onto her back and slamming her head against the dirt. With her strength doubled, she fought the daze that would come with such a blow. The specter then raised its other hand, ready to strike. Before it could, a spear sailed forth and into the limb. Through the shoulder, Nuyani saw the gleaming red gem of the spear and grabbed the head before feeding her thrum into the weapon. She first released an empowered barrier expanding through the weapon to part the spirit. It released her and backed away as it was widened in a circle from the shoulder through half its torso. Its head nearly flattened and rounded.

"[Heganirri! Heganirri!]" someone shouted. Nuyani did not dare to look as the specter swiftly reassembled.

With a spear in her grasp, her range was far greater than before. Expanding the range of her thrum as she took a stance, Nuyani then released a second pulse, forming a sphere where the apparition stood. Aware of her actions, the creature leaped to the side. Thinking it was trying to escape, Nuyani thrust the spear forward, creating a javelin that extended to three times its length and skewered the apparition through its chest. A ripple passed through its form on contact. A howl echoed through the area, bringing a chill that washed over everyone but not Nuyani. She conjured another barrier around the specter, matching its height before condensing the construct further and further. The specter yelped and snapped like a desperate animal as its head was warped and pressed to the round surface.

Nuyani winced as she felt the concentrated prutosa was still too strong to contain for long, even with her ring and spear. Not wanting to risk the creature breaking free, Nuyani fed a thrum from her core to the ring, then to the spear. With another thrust applied with all her strength, the conjured javelin pierced through the sphere, indenting the construction only to shoot out from the other side in a needle of blinding light. A ghostly yelp faded in an instant as blue and green embers descended and faded away. Nuyani shook as she looked at the blank space. Darkness took over the area, making her adjust her sight. All her muscles were numb. Nuyani then looked to the side. Her hearing was gone for the moment, but the withering thrum caught her attention. Nuyani looked to the side and remembered what drew her here.

"[Nuyani. Wait!]" came a voice muffled and distorted.

She did not listen as she moved to the man's side and started placing a hand on his body. A larger man with a short black beard looked at her dazed as he shivered and coughed. His chest was lacerated with claws but was so cold and paled that the blood did not spill. His breathing was shallow and difficult. Nuyani did as she always had and fed her thrum into the man's body, looking for what problems lay beneath. Her vision was then dazed as she felt her strength begin to leave her. A pair of hands then grabbed her shoulders, though she did not feel them. Then, a thrum radiated into her as well, meeting her core and trying to create a connection. The sudden jolt of energy meeting her core awoke her, and she slowed her thrum, allowing the guards to synchronize with hers. Once in unison, she was able to increase the pattern once more and fed the energy to the wounded man.

By his shine, he can make it, Nuyani thought as she first healed the claw marks until they closed all the way, with a few parts showing signs of scarring. Next, she investigated his core and found areas that were torn. It was strange to Nuyani that a core could be torn or frayed instead of shattered. With such a wound, she felt a sense of doubt that there was something she could do to mend it. Digging deep, Nuyani first formed a barrier around the core to keep his spirit from leaving. She then tried to move the twisted and torn pieces back into place with subtle pulses widening to gradually move them back in place. Once they were all together and smoothed as best she could, Nuyani attempted to synchronize their cores. It proved difficult as the radiating pulse, which normally rose in unison, delayed at the sections that were torn.

Frustration gripped Nuyani as she wondered if she tried to think of something. His life could be lost if she did not act. Nuyani raced her core to the point that her thrum became a wall of energy. As the barrier containing his core reverberated, it began to force the man's core to change. His shaking grew more intense. Nuyani wondered if he was no longer feeling cold but pain. She continued to press until the torn ends of the core faded from her senses. Knowing she could not keep it up for long or risk other complications, Nuyani backed off and ended her connection with both. Sweat dripped from her brow as she looked at the wounded man. He had several white streaks going through his hair that did not fit his age, but his shaking was gone. He then looked at Nuyani with widened eyes. Nuyani smiled. The man then slumped even more in his position.

"[Goddess be praise, thank you,]" the man said. Nuyani was not certain what he was saying but felt that he was in thanks from his tone.

A grip on her shoulder reminded her that she was not alone. Nuyani looked at Odba only to find him looking toward the side. Several other guards were there along with a few civilians. Zonqua sat atop Lugna. They all stared. Nuyani felt her instincts telling her to run. They only ended when the other man who hid his face then appeared from the crowd. Zonqua quickly dismounted and started marching toward Nuyani as he looked at the other man. Zonqua did not stop until he stood between Nuyani and shawled man.

"[What is the matter, dear sage?]" Zonqua said in a tone Nuyani could tell was him playing coy.

"[Move. I will speak to the girl,]" the shawled man replied. His voice was strong. "[If she's the reason more people have walked out of quarantine, then I need to speak to her. Move.]"

"[I'm not a soldier, and she does not speak our tongue. Perhaps you should speak with me instead. I could give you a few answers,]" Zonqua stated.

"[This isn't the time for pride, caster. Move aside.]" Zonqua shook his head and widened his eyes. This brought an exasperated sigh from the shawled man. "[This is not helping you, exile.]"

"[No, but we are helping you. I am not asking you to speak through me and not to try anything we don't want,]" Zonqua stated. The shawled man eyed him for a moment.

"[We'll see how cooperative you are. Don't make any mistakes here. Follow me now,]" the shawled man then turned and walked away.

Zonqua looked at Nuyani and Odba. He nodded his head at the guard and waved for Nuyani to rise. When he saw she was having difficulty, Zonqua moved to help her stand along with the guard. Once she was on her feet, Nuyani then smiled and handed back the spear. Odba waited by the injured man as two more guards came by. Iranke waited at the front line of people and shook his head at the two.

"[I'm certain that this will bring great praise, but some trouble for you two as well,]" Iranke said. He looked solemnly at Nuyani.

"[Why do you say that?]" Zonqua asked.

The sage then said, "[Because whatever you can't prevent from now on will be a reason to hold you in contempt. Disobeying the quarantine and putting the caravan at risk. Follow.]"

With that said, Zonqua glared at the shawled man's back. Nuyani took notice and looked at him cautiously. *Great lord, guide me with your shine,* Nuyani thought as they went on.

The three soon left toward a carriage on the other side of the caravan with Lugna following. There were other guards standing beside the carriage. Both nodded at the three of them. When the man was close enough to the steps of his carriage, he sat down and released a thrum through the wood. Another barrier rose from the carriage containing all five of them and part of Lugna.

"[Now we must make proper arrangements,]" the shawled man said.

Zonqua glanced at Nuyani for a moment before he looked back at the other mage. "[How about a name? We never heard yours since we've arrived,]" Zonqua challenged.

The caster looked at Zonqua with a fixed glare, "[And you won't. I am a court mage all the same as you were. I don't answer to you, exile.]" Zonqua narrowed his eyes in an annoyed expression. The term did little to sting but buzzed around him like a gnat. "[Let's get to the point. Your efforts may have helped us, but I don't know who you are.]" His glare fell on Nuyani. "[I'd say good work and that you've been thorough thus far, but there's a reason the hall wants only priests and sages to take care of such matters. Some may be turned if they lack the spirit to sustain their bodies. That by itself requires more than enough reason to wait. Some may turn.]" The man then paused as he waited for a reply.

Zonqua lifted his hand and started creating a scenario with several figures. A small display of a woman trying to stop worms from growing but as some she treated leave, others did the same and turned.

"He blames me if others leave and still are cursed?" Nuyani thought aloud. "Then I will look for them." Nuyani then looked at the man resolutely and created her own construct with a simple figure radiating a barrier outward with other figures around it. One of the outside figures who are corrupted is revealed, and the center is moved toward them, and a javelin is used to stop the infection.

The man's eyes seemed blank, with his expression hidden. His hard stare told them that he was trying to decipher their method to converse. "[Interesting… How long has she been here? Have you taught her nothing of greetings or basic conversations?]"

Zonqua looked at the man as he answered, "[Only a few things such as greetings, but she has only been here maybe twenty days or so.]"

"[Tell me then. What brings her here? Why has she met with you?]" the man asked as he looked at Nuyani quizzically.

The caster looked at Nuyani for a moment. *[What can I tell him that won't get the temple involved? Can't bend the truth when her strengths have been seen.]* Turning back to the man, he stated the basic information, keeping the part of her connection to the crystals out as he recalled their travel. Even making sure to omit the nimcha she carried.

"[A lot for a few days. And to know that the storm even reaches outside of Tuikon. That shouldn't be a surprise, but it's enough to call someone to stop it. Some things you can hope for, but that is not a likely feat. Otherwise, the temple would've done so centuries ago.]" The man looked at Nuyani with narrowed eyes. He then released a thrum toward her, trying to see her strength. Nuyani hardened her stare, trying to keep her face devoid of emotion as she instead hid her core's thrum. The man narrowed his eyes at her before shaking his head. "[She's practiced enough in using the basics. I really don't see how she's going to seal Do'alm Kaddap. That's a tall order.]"

"[One we still seek to try,]" Zonqua said. Nuyani looked at Zonqua, noticing his tone grow stern.

The shawled man nodded his head. "[Then continue to work. I will not stop you, but I will ask that you double your efforts. You want to cure those people outside, but did you not think to check the ones that are left on their own? They are the main ones I'm concerned with.]"

"[If they are your biggest concern then why don't you check them before they leave?]" Zonqua glared at the man.

"[You see how easily she can hide her core? How many do you think could do that? How many children do you think could figure out such a thing? The desperate hide. Those too far gone, we kill or burn if it's too late.]"

Zonqua's brow furrowed. "[Then keep a watch…]"

"[There are literally thousands of people in this caravan with only enough supplies thanks to merchants we are compensating for. I don't just have the numbers of the cursed to watch but the injured, the sick, and other matters you don't have the rank to deal with. Or trust exile.]" The shawled man stood from the carriage steps and leaned back, puffing out his chest in pride. "[Take care of the cursed. Protect the caravan, and I will leave you be. When the time comes, flee to the city the day before, and may we never have to meet again.]"

Zonqua blinked. "[That's all?]"

"[Yes. The goddess blesses you; there are enough problems here. I just don't need you to be another. Just a warning, the spread of any curse or death to anyone on your side of the caravan and I will gladly apprehend you both and put you to good use.]" The man then shrugged. "[It's not like you haven't so far. People are getting better, livelier. You've found and given a solution to purging any pits along the way. And the heganirri…]" The man looked at Nuyani and nodded his head. He then turned and started down the path. "[May the clouds bare rain.]" The barrier then fell, and the other guards nodded to the two of them.

Zonqua nodded back and headed toward Lugna. Nuyani looked between the others and Zonqua.

"Anything we need to worry about?" Nuyani asked, trying to get some idea of their standing. The man had attempted to read her strength but seemed disappointed when he could not. The caster then turned to her before rising into the saddle and showed a construct of the two fighting the worms, curing the cursed, and finding any still cursed. He repeated her construct as well, showing what the man intended them to do. "He just needed clarity?" Nuyani wondered what the real reason for his approach was. Nuyani looked to the direction the man had left. She was not certain, but her mind told her not to trust the man.

Returning to the carriage, they found a sack sitting where they rested. The two looked at one another before Zonqua looked into the bag. Inside were a few pieces of fruit and bread, along with extra clothing for both a man and woman. Nuyani then saw a glint off the corner of one item. She reached inside and saw the same strand of metal coins. Nuyani was almost certain that they were the same ones the child had brought when she saw them.

She turned to Zonqua only to find his attention fixated on a paper. Fury rose in his eyes as he looked at the paper. *Another problem?* Nuyani thought to herself as she waited for the man to look her way. When he did, Zonqua sat on the bench of the carriage and faced Nuyani with a gloomy expression. He then raised his hand and created a construct of the paper in their hands as they moved to a city gate. The guards would greet them as if it were normal and then turn their weapons on them a moment later. Zonqua would be in jail, and Nuyani would be wearing thin attire in a lounge section of the city.

"What? What is that paper for?" Nuyani said, raising her voice.

Zonqua then looked at her eyes with his mouth agape. "[How do I explain this?]" he muttered. The caster then created a construct of Nuyani's memory. It was her brother running from the charge-horns. He kept the figures running in place in the air. He then pointed to the paper and then her brother. The man then pointed at her, himself, and the animals.

"A trap?" Nuyani said as she stepped back. Fatigue started to weigh on her. She did not understand the purpose of such a ruse. They were protecting the people. They were doing as promised. Why anyone would consider such deceit bewildered her. She held out her hand to look at the lettering and wondered what was needed for it. There was a soft, muffled thrum radiating from the piece. Nuyani then took the paper from Zonqua and placed her other hand on his shoulder. He looked at her in confusion for a moment but realized she was trying to link their cores once more. With her senses, he noticed the thrum as well and burned it immediately. Nuyani pulled her hand away from the sudden flame, letting the scorched parchment fall to the ground. Nuyani leered at the man, wondering why he would nearly burn her. Zonqua then pointed to his eye and ear before drawing a circle in the air overhead.

Someone is listening or watching? Nuyani thought. She then glowered at the man and conjured a figure near a hole in the ground with a blue flame sticking out of it. The figure then tossed the paper in. Zonqua lifted his hand conceding to her point. Nuyani groaned and moved to the other bench before closing the flap. Lying down on the bench she turned away from Zonqua thinking of the position they were in. Despite their help, there was still someone trying to stop them.

Zonqua rose and took Lugna's reins, and tied her to the horn of the carriage front. *[Good at magic but, too honest for politics. Her people must've kept things simple. Kelvertians. They don't know they're using her magic. I need to teach her somehow not to give that away. Any link drawn from her to the others, and they'll try to use her to control every kingdom.]* Further thought on the matter made his heart skip a beat as he thought of all the kings, highborns, and cults that would use her if they could. More for his comfort than Lugna's, he began to scratch the side of her head. The animal cooed in response.

The next few days had been eventful, to say the least. With the city only two days away, small parties of guards began to move ahead of the caravan, delivering messages and keeping the path clear. Nuyani and Zonqua remained with the caravan. However, as they attended to the cursed and defended the others, it became increasingly difficult for Nuyani to remain separate from the others as rumors of her skills grew. Some of the civilians, in appreciation, even conjured lights in orange like her eyes when she passed. Nuyani repeated the gesture but often kept the light far above and away from her actual sight. She found would-be suiters amongst them too eager to try and take Zonqua's place, though there were none.

Nuyani had enjoyed her time with them despite keeping separate. Her thoughts returned to some of the lessons she had learned. Heganirri were men who found their souls devoured by the same hounds. If the hounds ever died soon after, for whatever reason, too much spirit would linger and create the apparition. With a hunger for flesh and prutosa, the specter went for the living. It reminded Nuyani too much of the banshees. She shook her head and scowled at the ground, trying to rid herself of those thoughts. Months had passed since the entire village had moved. Nuyani found that the danger had never ceased. Hugging her arms, she wondered more about her people. She wondered if Caluu was all right, being related to her, and was considered a default priestess despite only knowing she had powers when everyone else could use theirs. Then there was Cuganwa and Sutama. Both were thrown into responsibilities that they weren't prepared for. The boy was too young to even be considered for any leadership but was seen as a priest while their father became an elder.

Nuyani sighed. The new positions and responsibilities felt suffocating. *I cursed my family with honors I don't think I can handle for long,* Nuyani thought. She then looked toward the south, where the false devourer was. *I just want to free you, mother. Free everyone. Let there be peace.*

Once Nuyani had returned to the carriage, Odba was there. The man was breathing heavily as Zonqua stood beside him. Both looked worried. Nuyani saw the two and walked faster. When Zonqua looked up, he then extended his arm. He was holding out Nuyani's sack. She took it up but looked at Zonqua quizzically.

"[Look at him,]" Zonqua said as he nodded his head toward the guard.

Nuyani looked at Odba, who was sweating even more than usual. Nuyani began to wonder if the man was sick. Without hesitation, she moved forward and grabbed the man's brow. Nuyani channeled edria into his head, letting it meet with the man's mind. The foreign force made the man hesitate, but he allowed the magic to synchronize. With an understanding of her skill, he showed her the last tribute from some of the people. Though there was another bag of food, it had another surprise. A large beetle half the size of her palm with the wings folded came out of the bag. It was large and brown, with several protruding horns at the front and a flexible abdomen with a stinger on the end. The beetle stung his hand, sending a sharp pain through his body. Nuyani could feel the blaring sensation of heat as though her own hand was struck.

She pulled her hands away and looked at Zonqua. Showing a construct of the same beetle, Zonqua shook his head. Nuyani looked at him with wide eyes as though demanding the man heal him. "[I have nothing!]" Zonqua bellowed. His eyes widened as he looked back at the man. "[I can't tell her but, you saved us. I hope she understands.]"

With his voice calm, Nuyani was certain that his sudden anger came from something. She tried to feel his emotions. Studying the rhythm of his core and the current of his spirit, she was certain that there was anguish and regret in his mind. Trying to decipher what it meant. *He's dying? Is it because of us?* Nuyani wondered as she looked at Zonqua in horror. He looked back through narrowed eyes. They were the target of the trap. Nuyani was certain. She fixed her spear in her hand and stood ready for a fight.

Zonqua grabbed her shoulders and stopped her. "[We leave,]" the man said. His sorrowful eyes still held a commanding strength. Nuyani scowled. She then turned back to Odba and pulled out as many herbs as she had. She pushed as many of the boluses into his mouth as she could and poured water into his mouth. Odba coughed but tried to eat as much as he could. Nuyani backed away when she found that she was nearly empty. She looked at the man with worry, only for Zonqua to place a hand on her shoulder.

Zonqua looked at the man, "[The goddess bless you, Odba.]"

"[Go,]" the man rasped as his eyes trailed not to either of them but the surrounding people. "[They are here. Somewhere. Leave.]"

The caster gave another nod and whistled. Nuyani bit her bottom lip, knowing something was wrong. The thrum of his core was growing weaker, but his spirit was still intact. Hopping onto the back of Lugna, the two rode forth ahead of the caravan. Several other guards saw them at the front. One of the men with a yellow sash told the others to keep to their patrols, letting the two pass.

Nuyani clung to Zonqua's back, feeling a sting in her eyes. She did not know why the man had died. She did not know why they had to run. All she understood was that there was someone trying to stop them. Lugna gave a dead sprint toward the city. They stayed on the outskirts of villages along the way as the wall of Giode came into view. Like Turu, the walls were made of large stones with crystal shards sitting in the mortar. The rounded towers on the outskirts of the wall had larger clusters of the shards on display. Pushing past the pain, Nuyani looked at the city, thinking of what they needed to do. There was someone chasing them. Yet, they needed to save them. As they neared the city, Zonqua pulled on his headwrap and revealed a second one for Nuyani. Lugna slowed down to a trot. They moved along the wall, waiting for a clear spot.

Zonqua linked his core with Nuyani, searching for the sparsest section of the wall. Feeling the thrum of those above, he sensed his opening and snapped the reins. Lugna stayed silent as she started scaling the wall in a single burst.

As quickly as they rose up, they were over the stone lip, went over the path and were down to the other side. Nuyani felt a strange sensation as the passed over. As though walking into a thread, the pressure snapped before she could understand where it was coming from. She could not feel the thrum but its presence. It still confused Nuyani how edria could go from a wave to an ethereal thread.

Too many mysteries, Nuyani thought as they stopped on a narrow path between several buildings.

Ch. 6 For The Record

Inside the city, Nuyani found it lively and cramped. Despite the countless buildings and alleyways, there were often plenty of people filling the spaces. Most of the areas were filled with markets, both large and small, ranging from fruits to trinkets. There were some people selling livestock. A feeling of disdain came to Nuyani when she saw that there were people who were part of that market, though she noticed they, too, wore brands on their necks. When they passed by a pole with the nearly broken people, Zonqua grabbed Nuyani's wrist firmly and walked with her and Lugna briskly through the crowd. Nuyani did not protest. She understood this was not a place she was familiar with.

The streets were filled with many of the same kinds of people that lingered in Zonqua's memories. There were large, wide men wearing trinkets who looked like they avoided work and were surrounded by bigger men with nimcha at their sides. There were thinly veiled women waiting at pillars or singing and dancing to entice people in the bazaars. Some of the women were veiled in much of the same manner but not so thin. The guards all wore light khaki instead of dark blue and green as others had but kept the signature sashes of blue or gold worn across their torsos. Their head garbs were simple wrappings instead of helmets.

Once they got to an area with a lighter crowd, Zonqua left and told her to wait by a pillar with Lugna. Nuyani sat on the edge of the pillar's base with the small room it afforded her as the nogowesa encircled her body around Nuyani and the pillar before lying her head down one part of her own back. Nuyani chuckled and scratched at the animal's feathers, realizing how long Lugna had been there. She needed something to take her mind off the guard they had left. Even with her efforts with poison suppressants, it did not guarantee that a sting would be lessened. Nuyani did not even know where the bug came from. She wondered if the beetle was native or not, considering the reaction of both men. Letting out a sigh, she sat back and looked at the ceiling of sheets covering the bazaar. Nuyani tried to focus on the colors as she waited for Zonqua to return. The shade beneath the ceiling did a lot to keep her cool.

From what she could tell, he was looking for a place where they could stay for at least the night, but that did not seem like the best idea with the approaching caravan coming in from the east. Nuyani then looked at some of the kiosks that bore different figurines, ornaments, or jewelry with stones embedded in them. As a man wearing black clothing spoke to someone who was wearing similar attire to the veiled man in the caravan, Nuyani noticed the shawled buyer placing down two of the shards on the kiosk's counter. The man in black then smiled and nodded his head as he knelt and retrieved a figurine of Do'alm; he stood ready to attack, or already doing so, as his arm was extended to the side and the blade was held out with the sharp end facing toward the rear. Nuyani sent a light thrum to the kiosk. To her surprise, almost every item had some trace of power within them. Even the items without gems connected to them.

Nuyani then looked at her own ring, studying the gem embedded in the band. The gem seemed so simple in its rhythm, as were the shards. She began to wonder, however, why any shard of Kelvert was considered only good enough to use for the wall or barrier and not the figures or other items. *They aren't a part of the same belief,* Nuyani thought, feeling it only explained a little of the question but felt flimsy at best. As she sent a thrum into the ring, she saw the simple pulse that rang under her influence. She then wondered what was so different from the shards of Kelvert. As Nuyani recalled the different pulses of people and animals she encountered, it never occurred to her how different they may be aside from the obvious spells. Even Kelvert's teachings on the matter were brief and basic. She wondered why Kelvert had left so much information out. She sighed, remembering that the (angel) was not tied to the same laws of reality as other deities were. Even more, it seemed that Kelvert did not possess the power. Nuyani did question that thought, seeing that the kingdoms were using the shards to protect themselves. *What exactly makes you weak if you have that kind of power?* Nuyani thought.

Amongst the kiosks, Zonqua found it difficult to move about as the crowd in the area remained thick. *[The refugees aren't even here yet,]* the man thought as he looked for a hostel. There had been plenty of inns and guest houses in the area, but so few would accommodate a nogowesa without a more expensive price. As he licked his lips and looked about, he wondered how bad the prices were for the other cities. Even for their short duration, just buying food had cost him three times more than he had expected. The constant thought did not sit well with him. As Zonqua moved about, he caught sight of two guards pulling a man through the crowds, forcing their way through. A thinned man with ragged clothing did not bother to fight as his swollen face told that there was forced compliance in his capture.

Zonqua fought the urge to fix his collar as onlookers followed the three to the bazaar's closest exit. The man then went down one of the alleyways with a few patrons and civilians conversing outside. Over the doorway of one building was a tarp hanging down that bared the image of cavalry fighters baring their blades in a silhouette of three overlapping. Looking at the building's base, it extended far beyond the marketing district. Zonqua bet his odds that this hostel would have a suitable stable, at least for the night. Entering through the doorway, he was assaulted with the smell of smoke thick in the air and sweet incense doing little to cover it. The inside contained a strange mist of vibrant colored veils obscuring the faces of other patrons in their rooms. Zonqua made his way to the front, wondering how annoyed Nuyani might feel while rooming in such a place. It was more likely to be quieter in the day than at night.

The only thing clear in the area was a counter with a thin-faced man with glowing green eyes behind it. A bustling kitchen in the back proved work was plenty as servants moved in and out of the entry. The man looked at Zonqua with an eager smile.

"[Isn't this interesting. How'd you get through?]" the man said with a loud voice. Zonqua's eyes widened as he looked about, wondering if anyone had heard the man's words. "[Guess court mages aren't always hiding things. I'm whispering and making them louder to you.]" Zonqua looked at the man with a glare. "[I'm waiting, exile. How'd you get in? Give me a reason before I have one to put you out.]"

Zonqua thought for a moment and stopped in his tracks. He released a thrum from his ring and felt the pulse of edria coursing through the area. There were two rhythms at play. One was soft in its pattern, augmenting the man's voice as the other felt subtle but stronger. A trap. Zonqua took a deep breath and looked at the man with a wary glare. Thinking the spell may do the same for him, Zonqua then answered, "[I climbed the wall. The guards did not seem to mind.]" A modified truth was all but enough to get the green-eyed man to laugh. Zonqua saw no point in covering too much. A highborn managing his own establishment was a good sign to him. It was possible he'd be eager to share a few things in the exchange.

The man seemed disappointed as he scowled. "[That…seems like a boring tale. But I think there is something else to it. Care to share?]" the man asked as he raised his hand in a greeting manner. Zonqua took it as a sign to approach and did so. Aside from the first thrum changing his voice, the second one remained at a stable hum. In approaching the counter, he found the man's expression seemed more annoyed than anything else.

[Not a warm greeting, but how does he know I'm an exile? Do I know him?] Zonqua thought as he considered his past. His training at the university gave him plenty of connections, but some students who were there for the temple were instructed to never show their faces wearing the usual attire but bereft of any symbols the closer you were to a first year. "[Just looking for a room and a space in the stables at least for a night.]"

"[But I still want to know what you are doing here. That mark. I have senses for it.]"

Zonqua fought the urge to brush the side of his neck, further proving his displacement, but then sent a thrum to the brand. A subtle echo of edria radiated to the spot interacting with the sensing thrum only enough to confirm it was there. "[I am here because Turu was taken over. There is no other place I could go without supplies. Worse, there will be a caravan of people coming along, so I just want to get a room before the rest are gone.]"

This brought a coy smile to the man's face. "[They were right about you.]"

"[They?]" Zonqua repeated.

The man nodded his head. "[A caster with a mark helped to protect us. Help him.]" Zonqua blinked. He remembered there were scouts who traveled ahead to secure the route to Giode. He did not think they would go this far. "[I sincerely apologize but, I will be helping you.]" Zonqua's brow furrowed as he backed away from the counter and looked at the man with a confused glare.

"[You will be?]"

"[The entire district has been informed of your arrival and, therefore, your capture. I suggest not using a hostel or inn. You stay in one, and the city guards will descend upon you.]"

Zonqua looked at the man with a mix of confusion and anger. He knew that the letter of passage was a trap, but he did not think that the guards of the same caravan they aided would willingly betray them. He bit back the anger that was beginning to seep into his tone. "[What do you know of the coming caravan?]"

"[All I was told was of Turu's fate and of a man to watch out for.]"

"[Why aren't you trying to take me in now?]" Zonqua eyed the man warily.

"[First off, you are alone, and I don't see a mount. Also, I think that if a man puts his life at risk for others, using their moment of weakness against them is a shame I could not bring myself to do.]" The man's tone was mocking as he placed a hand on his chest and made a serious expression in jest. The man chuckled but kept the serious expression. "[The room is paid for just like it is in any other hostel. But the court mage is just a bit too smart.]"

Taking the hint, Zonqua walked away from the counter and started toward the entrance. As he entered the market area, he wondered what he should do. Knowing that guards were aware of a branded man in their city did not leave many options. Worse, he knew trying to stay outside of the city would only bring attention to them. He waited by a nearby pillar as he stared at the ground. They needed a place to stay and one that would allow them some discretion.

[Baltik. He could be here,] Zonqua thought as his expression darkened. "[To the sands.]" he muttered. He knew his brother stayed in the city, but to find him, much less ask for him to take in two mouths, was not something he thought he could convince him to do. Especially not when it had been known of his loss of status. Zonqua released a low growl as he stood straight and went to one of the kiosks serving food instead of goods. Fresh fruit and skewers with diced meat were on full display. The aroma grew stronger and more enticing, making his mouth water. Giving four coins to the vendor, he

walked away with two slices of melon and two skewers for him and Nuyani.

He needed to decide soon for anything to work. Taking a bite from one of the pieces of meat, he tilted his head to fight his salivation. For a moment, he felt a sense of bliss. Chewing on the bite, he thought of what might happen if he did meet Baltik. What would make the man see his reason before shunning him? Either way, he needed to go to the scholars' lodge. His thoughts then returned to Nuyani. She could use a lesson book and scrolls for the languages and spells. Contemplating how much one of the gaurioxash bisrak edria would cost, Zonqua fished into his pockets, finding his coins were growing concerningly light and that they still needed more supplies. Even the crystals that he had collected were not trading as well as he had hoped.

[What work can an exile in hiding get from a city like this?] Zonqua thought as he grew closer to the market where Nuyani and Lugna waited.

When he reached the pillar where the two waited, Lugna took notice and twisted her long neck to meet his head in a way that was natural for a nogowesa as if turning an arm. Nuyani laughed at the thought of anyone else trying to do so would not be normal in that contorted manner. The man then held out the other skewer toward Nuyani. She paused for a moment before taking up the food. He gave a soft smile before looking around.

Something is wrong, Nuyani thought as she studied the tired expression on his face. His eyes were half open, and his lips were drawn back into a weak smile as though fighting the urge to make a scowl. *I'm not sure what's wrong, but we will fight it.* Nuyani took a bite of the food, lighting up her eyes. A chuckle from Zonqua made her laugh as well, but she knew it only masked the problem.

Zonqua then raised his hand and conjured a figure of Nuyani and her brother Cuganwa. Nuyani stopped chewing for a moment, wondering why he had shown her that. The figures then change, showing himself and then another man with similar features but a bit young. Nuyani then looked at Zonqua's face and found that he portrayed himself as a young man. Nuyani sat forward with interest as she looked at the figure. *You don't look so different. Maybe if you scowled less, you'd look the same,* Nuyani thought, but her attention returned to the other man. His robes were different from Zonqua's but had a studious air about them. With long, wide sleeves embroidered in elaborate designs, all she could tell was that it meant he either was another caster or some form of leader for the city.

Zonqua then finished his skewer before and handed the slices to Lugna. She cooed with pleasure as he scratched at her head. Nuyani then finished her own meal, and the three started off through the city. It was odd to Nuyani to see such a place. Though she had lived in the cavern with the village, it was far more congested in Giode. The people moved about as if taken by some great need, often bumping into one another or them. Their rush disturbed Nuyani as she scowled through the streets. She fought the urge to conjure a barrier and force the people to stand apart from them.

Like the market where she had waited, there were more sections in the city with kiosks and entertainment filling the area. Some of the smaller corridors had large men barring other civilians from entering, while more well-off rested and smoked hemp that wafted into the street. Her face creased as she felt the urge to sneeze.

Zonqua, on the other hand, strolled forth, pulling Lugna's reins along as they went through. Though she could feel him release a thrum to settle Lugna, she could see a rising tension in his demeanor whenever guards walked by. In keeping his head low, he seemed more like a worn traveler than a hidden convict. Curiosity nipped at her mind, making her want to look at the guards, but she knew better than to draw attention their way.

At the opening of the section stood two guards watching as the people passed through. It was not an elaborate post with only two brick walls, leaving enough room for a single cart or carriage to pass through. With so many people moving in and out of the way, the crowd's flow is slow enough for the guards to give a quick glance at everyone in passing. Zonqua tightened his grip on the reins. As they came up behind the other pedestrians, Zonqua kept his gaze forward. The guards looked at him and then Nuyani but did not take any action. Thinking they were in the clear, Nuyani felt her start once more, not realizing she was as nervous as Zonqua was.

They had entered through the side of a long horizontal corridor where most of the people went either left or right. Just ahead of them was another square with a sunbathed floor and loud drums playing. Nuyani looked ahead, wondering what was different about the area. Even small trembles of edria traveled her way as obvious signs that there were spells being used.

Once again, they passed by another set of guards and saw a nearly empty space that looked as if it could fit three of the other spaces in at once. What remained in the area were some stands sitting in corners with overhanging roofs covering the people and thin veils over the sides. Several people walked from the urns and back to the stands. The area faced a wide stage standing about hip height above the ground. There were a few other people there as well, sitting on a small single step that lined the entire square.

On the stage, two people fought. Nuyani gawked as she saw two an udrog and kymac wrestling one another on the stage. The udrog had no shirt, showing his dark brown complexion and low-hanging black beard. He wore a different style of pants. Nuyani was certain they were made from hide and not fur. It seemed like an uncomfortable choice, but she did the same thing for the first ten days in the desert. The kymac had red scales almost as vibrant as the cliffs and dark brown horns protruding from his head and part of his back. Under his chin, down his chest, and most of his stomach were khaki scales that had a softer, squared shape to them. His head was triangular with a pointed snout.

Nuyani continued to stare as she realized that in seeing their bodies through centuries old visions, she had thought both races were dead now. Yet before her the two took on a mock sparring match to entertain the people sitting in the stands. Zonqua then tapped her shoulder, returning her to her senses. He then guided Nuyani to the side so they could sit.

They live? Why did I think none of them did? Nuyani's brow then furrowed as she thought back to the statues and battles. *Why is this allowed? Weren't they enemies, even to us before? Why are they here now?* More questions reached her mind as she wondered about the safety of the people, both the entertainers and the people in the stands. Thinking that time had stopped the dispute from a few centuries ago, Nuyani eased her mind as she watched their battle. When the udrog fell to the ground, the two stopped. The crowd applauded the display. The performers waved to the crowd before descending the stage, letting the next performer rise. Nuyani was surprised to feel the same level of energy as herself. She saw the woman before her who wore little clothing like many of the women on the street but wore several trinkets of gold ornating her neck and arms. Nuyani was more focused on the woman's different features. Around her head, even replacing her eyes, were eight dark red stones. Each one seemed to radiate with their own pulse while acting in unison as well. Her skin was a bright violet.

Nuyani remembered seeing a similar woman from a spirit's vision. She was a part of the invaders but had blue skin. The woman wielded a wide blade too thick to be a nimcha. It had a golden disk-like guard and pummel with a rich brown handle and red leather. The woman started at the center, taking a tall stance and presenting her cleavage clearly to the onlookers. She kept the blade behind her back, letting its polished edge reflect the sunlight. She soon started with wide circles drawn by the blade tip. Trails of light lingered from the tip as the weapon cut through the air. Nuyani leaned forward as she tried to study the pattern of the thrum emitted by the woman. As the woman danced about, she started to sing. A sweet voice accompanying the display changed the trails of lights into separate figures. All were mist like being taking on the shape of men and women with their own weapons. Soon, the entire stage was filled with people fighting. Sword clashes and flashing lights in the mists brought others to the edge of their seats. The violet woman continued swinging her blade, extending the ribbons of light.

The entire area became brighter than the sun's rays, casting shadows from the stage edge. Her haunting song echoed through the area as some of the figures fell to the side. As the battle died down, the woman's voice did as well. She returned to the same beginning stance as her edria settled. Nuyani felt her skin prickle as she saw the woman gracefully saunter away from the stage. A few people walked along the stands with bags extended outward, waiting for offers from the onlookers. Zonqua wondered if that was why so few were around. With the supply of goods cut off from the cities and prices rising, few could afford to sit and watch a show.

Nuyani's mind was preoccupied with another matter. Her thoughts dwelled on the cloud illusions the performer displayed. Nuyani's brow furrowed as she thought of the rhythm resonating to her core. She had never used such spells, yet each new one still felt as though they had a presence or history with her. Instead of worrying about the familiarity, she tried to replicate the thrum as well. The strength was there, but not the right rhythm. With several patterns resonating through her mind, Nuyani could not separate them. Yet, they were so close. She let it go as another performer took the stage.

With squared shoulders and a tall figure, Nuyani was certain it was a man at the center. It was all that she could tell as he wore just as much clothing as the other caster in the caravan, along with a shroud covering his eyes. His clothing, however, was nearly all black aside from the embroidery of golden patterns on the sleeves. The Kymac and (dwarf) then returned, heaving a chest onto the stage with great care. The figure turned and regarded the chest as he lifted his hand to the side. A thrum then flashed outward so briefly that Nuyani was certain she would miss it if not for watching him. He formed a fist at his side as though holding something, only for the two green glowing lines to appear, one descending to the floor and the other rising to the sky. In their trail, a wooden shaft slowly revealed itself. The item seemed plane at first, but the thrum's strength doubled in its reveal. She studied his every move as the others left the chest on the floor.

With a quick tap of the bottom end against the floor, a thrum resonated through the area only to stop at the chest. The lid opened, revealing a large snake. Once its head rose, there was a series of gasps rising from the stands as they watched the serpent eye the man before it with anger. Yellow eyes fixed on him. Its mouth gaped open, revealing long fangs as its head coiled closer to its body, ready to strike. Nuyani felt only the fear rising from it as the snake's thrum vibrated sporadically. She noticed how larger the animal was, with a head twice the size of the man's and a body that was wider and far longer than even the parasites. Yet it was afraid of the man.

Nuyani looked at the creature, focusing on her sight and trying to see if there were any signs of abuse. Any reason why such a powerful creature was more afraid of him than he of it? The thought disappeared when the creature slithered out of the chest completely and headed toward the man. When it was close enough, the snake lunged at the man, only for his body to change into light. The snake twisted and reeled back in confusion as it realized it had caught nothing. Nuyani tried to release a thrum to study the spell. Unlike the woman with missing eyes, she could follow the few thrums that rang from the stage. It was similar to the other performer's spell but seemed distinct nonetheless.

The ball of light then disappeared just as the man reappeared three more times around the snake. It hissed and reared its head back once more, turning and twisting to see which one to select. It struck at another man only for light to appear and disorient it. One of the other figures then lifted their staff and tapped the snake's body as if trying to get its attention. On contact, fire danced around the animal's hide, covering the scales in an orange glimmer. Yet the snake merely turned to the contact point and tried to strike once more. The flames went unnoticed by the animal before dying out a moment or so later.

When the snake attacked the next figure, another tapped its hide with the staff, and lightning trailed along the scales; small fragments of static danced between the edges in an expanding ring from the contact point. Nuyani then noticed the animal's thrum. The same sporadic fear gripping the serpent was the same force displacing the magic used on it. Nuyani could tell the elements were at least real as the rhythms differed. The show continued with new false replicants of the man appearing, strolling along the area, and surrounding the snake. All in an effort to keep it in the center. The area flashed with whites, blues, and oranges, not just from elements but from other spells. Nuyani had no idea what they were. One of the conjured applications was a glowing green sap that poured over the snake and lingered for a moment.

The animal hissed once more and reeled back, letting the contents drip down its sides. The practice continued until the animal started to react to the sudden spells. Nuyani was aware that the animal had reached its limit. The defensive thrum began to weaken from the constant barrage. Even the snake went from a high coiling body to a low curling stance as if trying to turn into a ball. With the serpent trying to retreat from the battle, the caster then lifted his staff and created a ball of light before the animal's face. The snake shifted and hissed, trying to escape the blinding light. When there was no escape, the animal started to lash out once again. This time, the man used his staff to strike at the animal. Between the light and whacks of the staff, the snake was forced to back away toward the chest. When the snake was close enough to the chest, the caster created a barrier and lifted the large animal up and into the container. The serpent tried to fight only for another thrum to rise. The lulling rhythm caused the animal to ease in its efforts as he willed the chest to close once more.

Nuyani had a mix of feelings concerning the animal and the caster. While she wanted to focus on the spells cast to strike the animal, she did not care much about the fact that there was an animal being beaten and kept merely for entertainment. It did teach her a lesson, however. The abilities of different magicians. Some of the copies of the caster then moved to different corners of the chest and picked it up to move to the side. Nuyani's thrum could not decipher the secrets of the trick. There was no change in the thrum, yet light creating solid copies or beings was just too strange for her to believe. More of the performer aids walked around, approaching Nuyani and Zonqua with an outstretched bag. Zonqua then bowed his head and gave a silver piece to the man walking by.

He let out a low mumble, catching Nuyani's ear. She looked at him, then his pouch containing the coins. *How bad are things?* Nuyani wondered as Zonqua then nodded at her, and they left through another entryway. Nuyani stopped midstep as she felt a soft thrum resonate and linger around her core from her right. She looked to the side where the stage and stands were closer, only to find the violet woman smiling and walking away. The thrum then ended as she gave a small wave of her hand. Nuyani did the same hesitantly.

How is she able to see with those eyes? Nuyani wondered as she continued.

When they reached another district, the atmosphere was different from the other areas. The street was wider and far less congested compared to the rest of the city. Those traveling with an air of importance seemed to move with purpose and haste. The various buildings around the area were either planes with little decoration or unique shapes, while others had engraved murals of different warriors and people along with statues of the gods before the doorways.

Nuyani looked about as they traveled down the road. They made way for people in carriages to pass by or squads of soldiers to ride by on their steeds. Though the warriors had different colored clothing along with a few additional weapons on a person. Zonqua went back to Nuyani and held her hand. She was not certain why but could tell that there was something making him feel more uncomfortable out in the open. The group walked along until they reached a large building with a statue of Do'alc in front of it. His grip lessened, making Nuyani wonder what was wrong. They then moved to a pin where several other nogowesa waited, drinking from troughs of water that were open to the animals. It was a surprise to Nuyani how tame the animals were in such a small space only to find another lulling pulse used on them. Most were half asleep, lying as though they had just awoken and still did not possess the energy to rise. Nuyani smiled, seeing one of the animals chewing on the foot of another with soft bites. It had light khaki and brown feathers and was far smaller than the bigger counterpart next to it.

After settling Lugna in the pin, they made their way to the tall door of the building. Nuyani stopped for a moment as she felt something starting to pull at her core. When she took notice, feeling as if a thread were sitting on her, she released a thrum to sense its direction. Before she could trace the energy, the ethereal thread snapped, disappearing from her senses altogether. Zonqua looked back at Nuyani from the doorway, wondering if everything was all right. Nuyani looked at him for a moment only to smile and continue moving. *I don't know what that was, but we have to keep going,* Nuyani thought. She walked through the doorway, letting it close.

Their eyes took a moment to adjust to the dimmer setting, only to find that the inside resembled much like the inn and bars with their private booths and low curtains. Nuyani could feel the several thrums ringing through the area. Some were familiar to her dampening noise, while others were from spells she had not seen. Wisps of light floated around passersby, remaining bright enough to see but not enough to disturb others. Most of the people wore the same brown clothing with shawls hiding their faces and green embroidery on their arm sleeves. Nuyani looked about and channeled edria into her eyes until the outlines of the building became silver. She could see that the walls themselves contained spaces for rolls of papers or bound stacks as well as different items and figures that held subtle thrums within them.

Nuyani looked around seeing that those sitting at tables with their legs crossed on cushions were focused on the papers. She looked back at Zonqua. He found his attention was fixed on another person who was approaching them. It was another veiled figure but, their softer steps told Nuyani it was a woman.

"[Bless by the goddess. What brings you both here today?]" the woman said in a soft, cheerful voice.

"[May she bring rain. We seek a few items to study magic and language as well a space if there's one available.]" Zonqua said.

The woman nodded her head, and her eyes narrowed, eluding a smile beneath her veil. "[Yes. We have a few spaces available, and I can retrieve those items for you. Did you need the area to remain private?]"

"[Yes. That would be best,]" Zonqua said.

"[Alright. And your names are?]" the woman asked.

"[Nuyani and Zeppa,]" Zonqua answered.

Nuyani blinked several times, noticing the strange name he used, but managed not to look at him for her for too long.

"[Great. Then I will take you to a study and bring the items you asked for," the woman said before leading them down one of the corridors.

Nuyani noticed that there were other floors in the building as well, with open ledges to the front. More shelves came into view over the railings as a few floating lights or flames went by with their casters. When they went down the corridor, it did not take them long to reach a space. The scholar then stopped by the edge of a curtain and pulled it open for a moment before pulling it wide enough to allow the others to step inside. Rounding the corner, Nuyani saw the room was quite large, rivaling the common space of a family tent at home. At the center was a round table and several sitting cushions around the area. She sat down at the side of the table, allowing her back to stay close to the wall.

Zonqua also stepped into the space but turned to
address the woman. "[A moment. Is there a Baltik working at
this library?]" Zonqua asked.

"[Yes. How do you know of Baltik?]" the woman
asked.

"[Just an old friend from our days studying. If you tell
him Zeppa is here, he'll seek me out. Could you tell him I'm
here?]"

The woman blinked for a moment, studying Zonqua's
face. He only showed a pleasant and hopeful smile. The
woman gave a wider grin, evident only by the greater crease in
her narrowing eyes, and nodded her head. "[Yes. I can do that
for you. Just let me get your things first,]" the female scholar
said.

"[Bless by the goddess,]" Zonqua said.

The woman continued and let the curtain fall into
place. Nuyani looked around the room and felt the soft pulse of
edria radiate around the room. The room felt silent and endless,
though the space was still confined. Zonqua then dropped the
bag he was carrying onto the table. He sat next to Nuyani,
whose expression was serious. He smiled at her, seeing that she
understood that this was a place to learn. Nuyani then wore a
look of concern on her face as she remembered the sensation of
string snapping on her core. Twice in a day, there had to be a
sign, but for what reason, she could not tell. Thinking to at least
share the sensation through memory, she moved to reach for his
hand only for the curtain to open once more and for the scholar
woman to step through. In her arms were the papers bound on
one side with string laced through several holes and two statues
that held soft thrums within them. Nuyani looked at them both,

seeing one was a simple crystal ball fixed into black stone with shallow engravings on the surface that were hard to make out. The other was that of Do'alc, who stood in an odd posture. As if in midstep, one hand remained behind her, and the other extended over her head, with clouds forming around her. One foot was before the other in a normal stride but still bereft of clothing.

Nuyani wondered about the strange freedom of the goddess but the modesty that seemed to grip the people of the country. She left it alone as she watched the woman place them on the table along with several pieces of charcoal. Once she placed the utensils on the table, Nuyani caught the woman looking at her with a strange glare. With the veil on her face, she was not certain what it meant until she realized the woman was looking at her as if she had caught Nuyani attempting something. *Wait. What did you think I was doing?* Nuyani wondered as the woman's eyes turned away, and the same narrowing of the eyes showed that there was a hidden smile. 'By the great lord, does she think I was trying to take his hand?'

Nuyani sat straight and looked at the wall ahead, feeling flustered. Zonqua seemed not to notice as he instead took up the paper and charcoal piece. He started writing on the paper with several symbols from left to right. Nuyani looked at the symbols, wondering if they would bring a buzz or tremble to her core like the others. They did not.

"[Zonqua…]," the caster said as he went through the letters. Four symbols on the page made up his name.

"Zonqua," Nuyani repeated as she looked at the letters.

"[Yes. Now for your name,]" the man muttered. After a brief pause, he sounded out her name before writing it in a few more marks. The symbols were almost completely different, aside from the two. "Nuyani."

She then repeated, "Nu-ya-ni."

"Good. You at least see the syllables in your name. I'll explain mine later. For now, Do'alc will teach you more than I could," Zonqua said as he reached for the statue and placed it before Nuyani.

Nuyani looked at the figure, wondering more about what it could do. Zonqua then placed his hand on the base and fed a thrum into it. Symbols of edria lit with a dull blue light on the base as the cloud and eyes of Do'alc began to glow as well. Nuyani studied Zonqua's demeanor as his thrum pulsed with a steady beat, meeting the figure's. She then looked at the figurine and then placed her finger on it as well. Releasing a thrum into it, she felt her conscience being drawn from her body and into the thrum itself. Much like controlling her own projection, she was familiar with the disembodied sensation but still felt a little panicked at the figurine pulling her instead.

When Nuyani's conscience settled, she found herself in a world of blue with rolling sapphire clouds making up the entire area with bright glows piercing the edges. Nuyani felt a sense of ease as though her core was creating a lulling sensation that affected her instead of someone else. Zonqua stood in the cloudscape as well, with his attention focused not on her but on another construct that lacked the usual glow she had always seen with magic. The man looked back at her and smiled before waving for her to approach. Without saying a word, the construct created the same symbols that made up her name and his in a darker-tinted form as if someone had written them on the air itself. Nuyani walked slowly to Zonqua's side as she saw the display take place. More symbols rose from the cloud, taking their place in the air before the two. Nuyani gawked at them, wondering what else could be shown from this place.

Zonqua then looked at her, catching Nuyani's attention. Even without words, she felt his intentions and seemed to understand them.

"[Say hello,]" Zonqua instructed. Two construct further behind then rose from the cloud scape as indistinct people. One bowed their head as Zonqua's voice then echoed the greeting in a softer tone.

Nuyani stepped forward, seeming awed by the sudden display, and noticed some of the symbols appearing as the words reached her ears. *It's a lesson,* Nuyani thought. She started to compare the vision before her to the visions she saw when she was in the fallen settlement. With memory and energy stored in a single piece of knowledge, Nuyani wondered about the possibilities of the tool. A grin rose on her face. She did not know where to start. Zonqua then stood by her side and pointed at the letters floating before them. One by one, he named the letters as faint copies of them appeared and disappeared within moments. After reciting each letter, he started with simple phrases and terms, all illustrated by the figures before them. Zonqua showed bartering, directions, and the numbers they used, along with their names.

When he was done, he then turned to her and said, "Blessed by the goddess."

"Blessed by the goddess," Nuyani repeated, understanding more of the meaning of the words.

When he faded away, much like the letters, she could feel the thrum receding from the space around them. *Alright. I guess we will use the other later,* Nuyani thought. She felt the need to learn magic was more pressing, but it would not matter if she could not communicate with Zonqua to begin with. As she looked at the vacant space before her, Nuyani wondered more about the history of the land. With her thoughts focused on the goddess herself, different figures rose and fell, showing detailed images of various gods and beings who gave Nuyani the same tremble of energy as the symbols themselves had. When the two figures of Do'alm and Do'alc appeared together, it was after a fierce battle capturing another being. The being had a beetle's head and arms covered in small, thin spikes. The being looked like a man and was bound in tendrils of lightning. On his knees, the captured being was before another whose image remained obscured. The strange beetle-headed man was destroyed by his very binds in a flash of light before another arching flash traveled to Do'alm and Do'alc.

The gods seemed no different after the strike, but both turned toward Nuyani with strange eyes that looked like the starry sky. Nuyani recognized them before their feet, ships, and buildings rising no higher than their ankles started to appear. Only the bodies of monsters and strange beings rose higher but were slain, nonetheless. Both gods started to multiply as well. With two more copies of each, slight differences were shown. For both, one pair of the gods held weapons with the nimcha in hand, along with the strange three-sided dagger bared by Do'alc and a spear with same strange dagger as its spearhead. The next pair seemed more at ease wearing robes made of clouds. Only the strange dagger in both of their hands. The last pair seemed like a younger mortal form of them. The starscaped eyes were gone, with only voids of gray with silver light lining the brim.

What were they before they were gods? Nuyan thought. She thought of the lessons Kelvert gave and remembered that there were titans. Nuyani looked at the clouded floor as she hugged her arms. Before her were more gods, each with more power and proof to show it. She rubbed her arms for a moment before scowling. *The great lord is why I live,* Nuyani thought as she looked up and focused on letters. The plane replicated her thoughts to a degree. Considering what she needed for simple conversations, she decided to focus on the letters and greetings.

Zonqua stood, leaving Nuyani to her studies, as a sudden knock at the wall caught his attention. A man with a gleeful expression threw the curtains back and strolled in only to stop and a scowl to emerge. Like Zonqua, he had a thin build but a rounded face. He wore a long brown robe with trousers and a blue sash around his waist. His sleeves were embroidered in blue as well. His face was mostly trimmed aside from a thin mustache that covered his lip. With a glance, he took in Zonqua and Nuyani sitting at the table before turning around and walking away at a near trot.

"Baltik," Zonqua uttered in a harsh whisper as he followed. Passing through the curtain, he looked to the side, seeing his brother barreling through those strolling through the hall. "Dull witted…" Zonqua cursed for a moment before following at the same brisk pace, feeling absurd that he was chasing his brother through an academic building like they were ten. The lump in his throat grew as he wondered if he really held so much disdain for him after losing his position. It mattered little as he saw his brother slip through a set of double doors with a black rim over the wood. Zonqua was not as attuned to sensing magic as Nuyani was, but he could feel that there was something strange just from the entrance itself. His brother did not bother to yell or evade him, making the caster wonder why he had fled to the room.

With attention drawn to him, he moved to the door and opened it. The entrance was not barred. When he closed the door behind him, he could feel an enclosed silence surrounding him as darkness cloaked the room. Zonqua then conjured a light illuminating only some of the room. He looked around the space warily as the light only reached far enough to reveal a wide round table with cushions in front of him, along with a few items on it. The light only reached the end of the shelves closest to Zonqua but was not able to pierce the darkness any further.

What are you hiding, brother? Zonqua thought as he took slow steps further into the room. Once the door was fully closed, something warned him even as silence remained.

Leaning to the side, he felt the wind brush against his cheek as a large tomb swept by. Only the outline of blue from his conjured light revealed the assailant. Zonqua struck with a kick into the man's back leg. The assailant over-committed in his swing. The man toppled over with ease, falling to his knees and dropping the tomb. Before he could move away, he kicked him once more in his back and forced his arm to sit behind his back. The figure struggled, and Zonqua was certain he was even yelling as he put pressure on the arm, threatening to snap it. It did not help that the area still had a silencing spell remaining active. Zonqua then looked at the door, wondering who else might come to his assailant's aid if he could be heard. A thrum then rippled through the area. The grunts of pain then rose from the man on the floor.

"Mo'ede, why'd you attack him," came a man's voice from the side.

Zonqua looked toward the shelves, seeing his brother standing with a box in hand and looking confused. "I thought you were attacking me at first," Zonqua admitted.

"Me? I'm not so foolish," Baltik started. "You've got…"

"To the sands with you both. Get off me!" the man lamented from beneath Zonqua.

A sigh rose from Baltik as he looked at his brother, "Zonqua, by her blessing, let'm up," Baltik said.

With a smooth rise, the caster leaned away and transformed the light into a ball of edria ready to strike or defend. The man gasped and turned to the side of his good arm before turning over to rub his sore elbow and shoulder.

Like most religious acolytes, he wore the same academic robes but kept his face covered from prying eyes. Zonqua studied the man for a moment, noticing that he was thinner and shorter, making one think he was no older than a boy close to manhood. His opinion changed as the light revealed the aged lines of decades around his violet eyes. That could not be mistaken for anything else aside from age. Zonqua narrowed his eyes at the man as he wondered what he was carrying. Baltik then moved to the cloaked man's side and tried to help him up. The man called Mo'ede took it but could not help but glare at the man. Once all of them were standing, Baltik sighed and moved to the table as his compatriot retrieved the tome he was going to use as a bludgeon.

Zonqua narrowed his eyes at the bound book as he sat at the table, receiving annoyed glances from the smaller man. "Don't be angry with me. You attack first," Zonqua started. He then eyed the leatherwork of the covers, seeing strange symbols in straight lines pressed into the leather. "Where is that book from?"

"North," Baltik started.

"Hold on!" Mo'ede shot in.

"Far north," his brother continued. "In Elethyl about halfway."

Mo'ede leaned forward on the table as he glared at Baltik. "Do you trust so easily?" The heat in his tone told them both the man might even try to swing at Baltik if the conversation continued as it did.

"No," Baltik answered as he produced a figure Do'alc from his sleeve. Zonqua blinked for a moment. He looked at it and noticed the blue, glowing gem sitting in the middle of the statue's chest. With her arms and feet spread apart, the goddess stood on her own without a base. Small sparks of lightning danced in the air so fleeting and dim that it was hard to tell if they occurred. "I have my own questions. He'll be grateful to answer once we're done."

Zonqua hesitated for his next few words as Mo'ede looked back at him with almost a look of sympathy. Only a few expanding thrums radiating through the area that was silenced told Zonqua that the edragaurio was now synchronized with the space they stayed in. From the looks of the sparks, his brother was willing to imprison him here. "A lot of resources for someone who trades information," Zonqua commented.

"Caution keeps us alive. Something you might want to learn, brother," Baltik started. Zonqua narrowed his eyes, seeing the same disdainful look on his face as their father. Baltik blinked several times as if realizing what Zonqua was seeing and shifted his seating to leaning forward, propped up by his elbows. "I want answers, Zonqua. Are you a traitor?"

"No," Zonqua answered without hesitation. The few sparks surrounding the small figure started to lessen.

Baltik held an eager glare toward his brother as his breathing grew heavy. "What happened at the palace? Why are you branded?" his brother asked.

"The queen "invited" me to her chambers. Resist and be accused, or join and try to hide the truth," Zonqua said. The sparks did not show.

"What was she trying to get from you?" Mo'ede asked. The heat in his voice reduced to curiosity.

"Pleasure," Zonqua said with no joy in the words.

"Nonsense!" Mo'ede said with a chuckle. "The queen of Layoyem wouldn't put herself at risk for such a thing." Adultery after marriage was punishable by death.

"The king and queen had been separated for more than half a year. He needed to maintain the borders and negotiate with other kingdoms," Zonqua started. "There is not much to suspect that the lonely queen had her own consorts." The other men then glanced at one another before turning back to Zonqua. The shawled man then hefted the tome onto the table and rested his arm on it as though to keep it from flying away.

"That doesn't explain why the king would brand you a traitor," Mo'ede started.

"It means everything," Baltik said. "If he has to keep up appearances during a time war while everyone is watching, then it could be the only choice."

"That and King Yudo's past," Zonqua said. He was nearly switched out by a mistress at birth when his father had the throne. Learning that he would've had an entirely different life because of his father's choices, Yudo would never have done the same thing. Queen Marhekke, on the other hand, sees it as a royal hierarchy. I was there to serve both the court and them on personal needs."

Mo'ede narrowed his eyes for a moment with a look that seemed to tell Zonqua that he felt the man was blessed by Do'alc herself for bedding the queen. His look changed once he saw Zonqua scratch his neck. The mark afterward was not one he would wear just for a chance to do the same.

"Where did you go afterward?" Baltik asked. His tone sounding concerned.

"The city was attacked by a swarm. I escaped but got the help of some of the bandits," Zonqua answered. "They needed my help, and I needed a place to stay. I didn't do any raiding."

"To the sands with raids, what did you tell them?" Baltik said his tone grew stern. His eyes fixed like a beast on the game. "Did you give them anything that could harm us?"

"No," Zonqua said. The others stared at him. "They only wanted to steal goods from the others. Not join a war."

Mo'ede then spoke up. "What would a band of fools want with a mage?"

"I helped to ward off the worms and appraise magic goods," Zonqua said. "A few other things as well, but nothing so important to that threatened the kingdom."

Baltik looked down at the statue. The sparks no longer showed even as the gem glowed. "Why did you never come home or send word?"

"You can't be serious," Zonqua said. "Not only would they have found me if I came here beforehand, but they would've killed me and the rest of the family. It's a risk I didn't want to take even now."

Baltik took a deep sigh as he held his glare toward his brother. "So why are you here now?" Baltik grew tense as if he were preparing himself for a strike.

"I'm helping someone to stop the storms from returning and purging the worms," Zonqua said. The others were still for a moment.

Baltik was bewildered as he looked down at the figurine with no spark to find. Mo'ede broke his trance with a hearty laugh that would've drawn attention if not for the soundproofed space they occupied. The caster waited a moment for the others to collect themselves. Slowly, both scholars were looking at him as if he were a madman.

"What do you mean to purge the worms?" Baltik asked. "There isn't such a power lying around in any of the six kingdoms."

Zonqua shook his head as he replied. "There is, and we've been using it." The two remained silent for a moment until Zonqua removed one of the small shards that littered the world around them.

"No. There is no way," Baltik denied. "Y- You're serious, aren't you?" Zonqua looked at his brother with a blank expression. "How? Who is she?"

"Trade with me," Zonqua said plainly as he looked at his brother with the same calm demeanor.

"No. You are stuck in the corner with this one. I have no reason to help you," Baltik argued.

Zonqua kept his calm as he explained, "You wanted to know where I am and if I'm a traitor. I answered both questions and more without activating your lie seeker. Now look at me and tell me you have any grounds to act as some form of official." Baltik narrowed his eyes at his brother, seeing the man trying to catch his brother in a lie as well. When he remained silent, Zonqua continued, "Right now, I have a solution to Tuikon's problem. I need to know more, though, and for a price."

"A price?" Mo'ede questioned. "We trade. There is no buying."

"Not for coin but room and board until I can plan further. There are movements that could catch us off guard if we don't act fast," Zonqua said, breaking his cool as he looked at both men. "Let us stay with you, and I will explain what she is capable of."

"Who is she? Spark my curiosity, and we might start," Baltik said, lifting his chin and narrowing his eyes, making a smug expression.

Zonqua gave an annoyed glare as he told the man, "She is connected to the shards, and that's all you will know if you cannot agree." Zonqua remained silent as he looked at his brother. The only true leverage he had was with the man's interest in protecting the kingdom. He was still surprised his brother even bothered to return and not call the guards, though he was not certain guards were not waiting for him outside of the library.

"Fine. Tell me how you found Tuikon's answer," Baltik agreed. Both hands were now folded on the table, and a flicker of the small figurine meant that he had half meant it. Zonqua looked at the man warily. If the edragaurio had activated based on his intentions, Baltik would've received a powerful shock.

"Then we agree?" Zonqua ensured. "No guards or twists?"

"You will be welcomed into my home as a guest so long as you prove that this is not some joke or desperate action," Baltik said in a stern voice.

Zonqua leaned closer to the table and explained what he knew of Nuyani. Her abilities with magic and the reaction of the shards were proof enough that she could connect them. Even more so, his sole goal in the desert was to seal the Do'alc Kaddap for good. Both men looked astonished by the accounts, only for Baltik to have grown stern as he leaned his head to the side and pressed a finger to his temple. There was something he knew. Zonqua was certain as the guards that left would not have missed passing some bit of information along.

When the caster was done, they sat in silence for a moment, aside from Baltik's fingers tapping against the table surface.

"A *jornoxarra* (elemental)," Mo'ede thought with a sound of awe to his tone as he looked toward the darkened ceiling.

"You certain she has control over the stones?" Baltik asked.

"More like an influence. From what I've gathered from her visions, her deity gave her enough strength and knowledge to at least do that. But, it's not a named god by the accounts of the high pantheon, so it seems like mere raw magic for her," Zonqua said in a faster tone.

"And what do you plan to do with her?" Baltik asked. The figurine before them confirmed every word that the caster believed to be true.

"What do people know of her, or who might be after us? We have already heard that the rumors about her skills might draw the attention of the cults. I'd rather steer clear of any of them for now," Zonqua said.

"The cults are a larger problem than you may imagine," Baltik said. "You did well to avoid even my ears, but that does not matter when it comes to them. There are agents in each of the kingdoms. If they knew this, you wouldn't have made it to us as you've managed."

"No. This is worse than anything," Mo'ede whined. The others looked at him with knowing leers, but that did not stop his tirade. "Not only are you saying there's a person capable of controlling the stones, but her very presence throws everything into a chance of chaos. The cults will subjugate this Nuyani for power and destroy the kingdoms. For any one kingdom, she'd be the greatest asset to the war. Her very presence here means that things may grow worse than the storms and worms."

"They are already getting worse," Zonqua said as he looked at the smaller man, nearly out of breath. "Their pus or innards are softening the ground, allowing them to tunnel through. It's only a matter of time before they get here as well. There were already nests of the creatures along the path here.

Baltik sat forward and laced his hands together. "You mean there's another reason why the cities are falling?" Baltik thought aloud. Zonqua was certain the man was speaking of the rumors of the cults taking down the towers before the attacks took place.

"I believe so," Zonqua stated. "Not much else I could tell you, though I saw it with my own two eyes and purged the first pit."

"Do'alc's blessing. This is not the greatest news to receive, but this explains so much more." Mo'ede commented.

"Like what?" Zonqua questioned.

"No. That part you will not need to know," Baltik cut in as he raised a hand, signaling to block the other man's speech. "What you need to do is keep your own mouth shut tighter than the nogowesa's jaws. There are too many things that could go wrong with this. But what I can tell you is that there isn't a word of your location yet. Dead or living. All we can say is that you are forgotten for the moment while there are other matters that need to be addressed. How are you going to get the materials needed to begin with? Unless you plan on scouring the fallen cities for the crystals amongst the worms even, you are not in any position to use the crystals or a place to store them."

"That is why we are here. We need a start," Zonqua said.

"Who is this girl?" Baltik said, narrowing his eyes at his brother once more.

"I told you everything I know or understand," Zonqua said.

"To you," Baltik clarified. Mo'ede leaned forward with an eager gleam in his eyes.

"Just the person we need," Zonqua said plainly.

"Is this one married?" Baltik asked. Mo'ede's head reeled back as his brow climbed higher.

"I'm not looking to court her, and I don't think she is either at the rate that she's trying to get to the center," Zonqua explained. "Her first few days, she was making a straight line for the center of the desert."

"Well, fortunate for you," Mo'ede said with little attempt to hide his glee.

Zonqua narrowed his eyes at the man. The thought of putting him back in the armlock came to mind, but he instead directed his attention to the book that the man still guarded. "You said that tome is from the north. Why's it here?" Zonqua asked.

Mo'ede slid the book back as though removing it from sight would deflect the question.

"To the sands, just tell him," Baltik said. "This isn't much worse."

There was still a moment of hesitation in the man as he looked at Baltik before he turned to Zonqua and said, "We intercepted this book from Iocunaon." The caster blinked recognizing the name from a powerful family in Daibot.

"What do they have to do with this?" Zonqua asked. From what he remembered, their power came from the merchants and trade routes in goods for wood, both grown and imported into the desert.

"They have been making some interesting deals with magic items recently," Mo'ede said. "Strange items that would be considered dangerous in the wrong hands and mostly illegal."

Zonqua's brow furrowed for a moment as he then looked at the tome sitting on the table. He knew a lot of forbidden information could be brought in and cause harm to the kingdom if not vetted thoroughly. "What's in this?" Zonqua asked as he leaned forward, staring at the recently rebound leather, trying to pick out the text for any clue. It was clear the original cover was replaced but still bared text in another language carved into the surface.

"Soul and magic manipulation," Mo'ede stated. Zonqua blinked and looked at Mo'ede with an annoyed expression. "More importantly, soul-stealing, trapping, manipulation, magic forging." Zonqua blinked again as the last two words stuck in his mind.

"Magic forging?" the caster repeated.

"This book is called 'The Way of Demons' from what we've gathered," Baltik added.

"These are rituals and techniques for mortals to take and steal souls, using them to make magic," Mo'ede said.

The scholar then turned the book to Zonqua and opened it to one of the pages marked with a small wooden dowel near the spine. It showed clean pages with neatly penned marks in the foreign language on the right page and an illustration of several people on the other. There were four people garbed in foreign robes in vibrant greens and blues, with three of them extending their hands out toward the fourth, standing in the middle with a pained expression. At the center of each person was a circle with streaks surrounding them, depicting a shine. Yet the streaks that pointed toward the man in the middle and, following their outstretched hands, repeated until they pushed the other man's body, obscuring the lines within them and pushing the core further up toward the fourth man's head while the lines toward the top started rising like smoke.

Zonqua turned the page to another illustration showing a man kneeling as another standing before him drew his hand back. The same lines Zonqua assumed represented spirit were drawn in a current directing the energy from the kneeling man's body to the other. The lines of spirit were clustered around the circle within the standing man while the very core within the kneeling was almost out of his body. The same painful expression remained on his face. What Zonqua started to notice were the other wave-like lines that surrounded the core, only opening to the channels of spirit. *Magic and spirit then,* Zonqua thought.

"We believe Iocunaon is in league with the mad king," Mo'ede said.

Zonqua looked at the man with a sense of disbelief. Why would any powerful family on the other side of Tuikon want to join in the war directly or even ally themselves with a tyrant?

"This may not be a surprise, but his goods always supplied the armies with wood for their spears and staves,"

Baltik added. "If not for his influence and supplies, no one would have bothered with this."

"Why do you suspect him?" Zonqua asked as he looked at the man.

Mo'ede chimed in, "During wartime, his orders have gotten more diverse, but the biggest issue is his side comments to the royal family and the other families of power. He gave sound advice to a few of the other families to start keeping their goods in multiple cities in case of the worms when we got the first word but not before calling many of the others fools for doing so, to begin with."

"That does not sound so different from what a highborn would do," Zonqua said.

"Not until the comments get so specific that you see him questioning the other businesses that align with many of the fallen cities," Mo'ede said. "The problem, however, is that the cities he's mentioned aren't the only ones."

"Blessed by the goddess, a running mouth isn't going to get anyone incriminated with just scathing remarks," Zonqua said.

"Until they start matching days before the attacks," Baltik said. Zonqua looked at his brother. "There have only been four cities he's mentioned out of twenty or so that fell between Daibot and Layoyem, but a fifth is still more than expected, especially when Iocunaon has been sending messages out toward the other kingdoms."

"What kind of messages?" Zonqua asked as he turned the page and revealed another illustration of a pained expression from a man captured within a crystal. A strange hole or opening at one end of the container. The same lines of spirit poured from it and into the pained man as his core started to fall from him. Zonqua noticed his arms and legs were different. The outlines were drawn in the same wave-like patterns that he assumed were magic.

"All of them were coded to a degree for other goods like food and furniture, but the numbers do not add up to their inventory," Baltik said.

Zonqua looked at his brother with a look of worry. "You've had your eye on him for a while then," Zonqua said.

"That said," Baltik started. "This only means that there is more that you may face."

"I know," Zonqua said as he closed the book. "Follow me, and I will show you."

Before either of the brothers stood, Mo'ede took the book and raced back into the dark for a moment before returning as the two reached the door.

Fast when he wants to be, Zonqua thought as they exited the room. There were not many people still around but, the few who still lingered in the area looked at the men with wary eyes remembering that two of them rushed into the room.

Zonqua took a deep breath resisting the urge to brush his collar with so many eyes trained on them. The three then strolled down the hall until they returned to the space where Nuyani resided. Upon opening the curtain, they found Nuyani writing on a piece of paper amongst dozens with different letters covering each page.

She looked up and to the curtains with a look of surprise. She then greeted, "[Blessed by the goddess.]" Nuyani gave a smile despite the stares of both men.

"[Blessed by the goddess]," Zonqua returned before stepping to the side to give the others a clearer view of both parties. "[Nuyani, this is Baltik and Mo'ede.]" He followed with a wave of his hands to both men.

"Nuyani," she said while placing a hand on her chest. Baltik nodded his head as he gave a tired sigh.

Mo'ede focused more on her eyes. Nuyani started to focus on his as well. She showed more awe as she noticed the violet eyes he had. Though they did not possess a glow like hers, they were still far different than anyone Nuyani had seen yet. She then smiled and gestured to her eyes. The man nodded.

"[This is the elemental?]" the man said as he strolled around the table along the other side and sat down. Zonqua watched him warily, but he felt calm, sensing that Nuyani was keeping her guard up as usual with the steady thrum radiating through the room.

When did I get so sensitive to Edria? the man thought for a moment before sitting down as well on the opposite side of Nuyani and his brother across from her.

"[Why here?]" Nuyani asked after a quick glance at her notes. It was clear that she was taking some of the lessons for simple speech. Nuyani then pointed at the two men.

Mo'ede then answered in a cheerful tone, "[We are here to learn of your skills. We might be able to help.]"

Nuyani blinked for a moment before looking down at the papers. "[Help?]" she whispered, trying to find the word. "[Help.]" She then looked up at the man with wide eyes.

"[Yes. She doesn't have that great a grasp on speech yet. What were you two doing all this time?]" Mo'ede questioned.

"[I have a theory,]" Baltik added, giving Zonqua an annoyed, accusative glare.

"[Don't. We were busy trying to find a place to stay. There are a few things she understands, but that does not mean that she can just go off trying to speak, especially not with other concerns,]" Zonqua said.

"[The cults?]" Mo'ede asked.

"[Exactly]," Zonqua said.

"[We'll see]," Baltik went on. "[Just remember Walgo was also just someone you passed by.]"

Zonqua waved his hand, signaling for his brother to drop the subject as he scowled. Mo'ede and Nuyani glanced between the brothers, but the silence that followed was broken by the scholar's eagerness to know Nuyani. The shawled man then presented two more black stone items, each with a subtle thrum. One was nearly a flat stand with eight levels rising like steps toward the middle. The steps were small and went around in a ring, making the small stand seem more like a disk. The other stone piece was another figurine of Do'alm with his sword raised high and dagger in hand. Nuyani glanced at the shawled man and noticed that this was the first figurine of the man god she had seen, and it was bereft of clothing. If Do'alc held knowledge, what would the god's purpose be?

The man then placed a hand on the base like stone and fed a thrum into it. From the lowest rung up to the fifth, blue symbols glowed on the surface. The faster his thrum went, the further it climbed. Nuyani watched as she studied the thrum. *You need this stone to show you strength, or mine?* Nuyani wondered as the man stopped. He started breathing heavily but then gestured to the stone for her to try the same. Nuyani then glanced at the man with narrowed eyes and then back at Zonqua. The man nodded his head, seeing her hesitation. *You brought more people to test me?* Nuyani thought. Seeing that he was not worried about the test, Nuyani placed a finger on the stone and released a thrum into it.

The rungs started to rise, going up to the fourth level, with different symbols showing. Nuyani looked at the glyphs, trying to see if she recognized any of them from magic or the language. To her surprise she recognized some of them or at least their shapes. What came as a surprise to the others was the fifth rung's symbols, from the bottom to top, had a dim glow. Nuyani had looked at the others wondering what she had done to bring their astonishment.

"Jornoxarra," Mo'ede started. Nuyani's eyes narrowed further as she drew her hand back. The man's enthusiasm was more than she felt comfort with as her thrum continued to race. Zonqua placed a hand on her shoulder. She gave him a warning look which only brought a smile. Mo'ede's expression changed as he looked at Zonqua. "[Is something wrong?]"

"[Your joy is a little much for her. Take no offense, but she has not seen the best of the country since she arrived]," Zonqua explained.

"[Oh]," Mo'ede said with a saddened tone to his voice. "[Well, I meant no harm.]"

Nuyani looked back, noting the softened tone and softer hum of his core. *He's not planning something,* Nuyani concluded as she looked at the other figure. *Zonqua is here, but I still feel that he is too trusting. He only mentioned his brother.*

Zonqua then leaned forward and tapped a finger on Nuyani's ring, getting her attention. He then tapped on the small platform. She looked between him and the ring before piecing it together, and he wanted her to use it as well.

Mo'ede looked dumbfounded, looking between the ring and Nuyani. "[How far could she go with aid?]" the man asked.

"[Wait and see]," Zonqua said. He then gestured to the stone.

As they waited in anticipation, Nuyani then did so feeling some unease at displaying her abilities for a show.

When she fed a thrum into the ring and then the platform, the levels alit rising to the fifth but that was all.

The look of awe grew in the strangers' eyes. Nuyani stopped as she gestured to them both. Zonqua then created a construct of a man only a few inches tall creating a ball of edria. The sphere was as wide as his torso. The caster then pointed to Nuyani before creating her smaller counterpart and showing a sphere large enough to cover her, a few carriages, and people within its space.

"Does this mean you found a way to get the crystals?" Nuyani asked. Zonqua looked at her, wondering what she was asking. *I get that I'm stronger.* She sighed and then looked at the constructs. She gestured with a wave of her hand. "[Why?]"

"[Oh, that's what you're asking]," Zonqua said as he then placed one of his bags on the table. He then took out several small crystals and placed them around the constructs. He then changed the constructs from people to the same platform and cliffside, just small enough to fit within the perimeter of shards. He then created a figure of a woman behind one of the shards before taking a line of magic from one shard to another. The bright line of magic stayed while it was anchored to the other shard. He then repeated the display with another before showing the full line of six connected. The barrier then formed from the closed line over the area before a brighter glow started to show beneath the layer, and the barrier created bulged but did not give.

Mo'ede nodded his head at the display. Zonqua then noticed why Nuyani felt a little uncomfortable around him. The man seemed to have an excitement burning within him. He did not know what it meant, but he already had to trust his brother and they him.

"[Alright, so we see the plan, but can she do it?]" Baltik asked. Zonqua and Nuyani looked at him. "[Can she control the stones as you've said?]"

"[Yes]," Zonqua answered annoyed.

"[Show me]," the man said. "[Bring those together and use it.]" Baltik was now glaring at Nuyani, but she saw how he spread his hand out over the table and then drew his fingers together.

Nuyani looked back at Zonqua. The caster picked up one of the shards and fed a thrum into it before taking another and pressing them together. She raised her head, realizing what he was telling her to fuse the shards together once more. Nuyani then took up two of the shards and fed a thrum into both. She felt no resistance as both started to brighten and take on ethereal glows instead of their hardened forms. Baltik and Mo'ede gawked at the sight, watching intently as she pushed the two together. With a single, brighter bead of light, Nuyani released her thrum when she felt the two pulses synchronized as one and stopped feeding the piece apart of her thrum.

When the hum died out, a larger rounded form of the shards then emerged. Nuyani herself looked at the shard with curiosity wondering why the piece became solid once more. She then tapped the piece on the table thinking its solid state should still be postponed until she noticed the others looking at her. Zonqua smirked while the others were dumbfounded.

Nuyani sat straight as heat rose in her face and she put the crystal down.

Mo'ede then clapped his hands together and laughed before he said, "[This will change everything. This could stop the worms completely.]" The man laughed as he leaned forward, placing his elbows on the table and gripping the top of his head. Before a word could be said to the man, tears stained his shawl as he looked down at the table surface. Small pools of drops collected beneath them. Baltik reached out to the man and placed a hand on his shoulder.

What has he gone through? Nuyani wondered as her discomfort dimmed slightly but. *Everyone has a past.* Nuyani tried to remember as her thoughts went back to the citizens who lost their homes in Turu.

Nuyani did not think but raised her hand and pointed toward Mo'ede's head. The man blinked as he looked at Nuyani, wondering what she was trying to do.

"[She wants to see your memories]," Zonqua said.

"[See my... But only sages and priests...]" Mo'ede ended his protest when he looked at the caster and saw him shaking his head. He then looked back at Nuyani as he whispered, "[Elementals.]"

"Nuyani," she corrected as she pressed her fingers on his brow softly. With the waves of edria passing from her core to his mind, she met the barrier within him before he eased his thoughts and allowed her to synchronize with his magic. The memory was not short as Nuyani saw the different visages of the man's past. There were others sworn to secrecy and tortured just in training as ways to keep their minds sharp. Worse was the training needed as Nuyani saw the man in one image suspended in a cave with worms beneath him and the occasional bar pressed to his arms and legs. Dim lights showed several people in similar attire and shawled, but the colors were different, along with several trinkets. A single man larger than the others stood at the tallest ledge with brown and black as his robing and gold embroidery on the sleeves. Around his head sat a strange circlet of gold depicted as one of the worms.

Thick curtains of shadow were only pierced by the dim glows of spells orbs suspended over their heads. The man looked down in the pit, seeing the larger worms picking apart fresh bodies. Nuyani even felt uneasy seeing both the corpses being made a meal and the bruised legs of a man who seemed to be starving as well. The man winced as a hot rectangular plate flew forth, glowing a bright orange. It landed flat and stayed in place on his chest. It did not matter what little strength lay in his beaten body. Pain forced his piercing scream and desperate dance as he dangled in the air, looking for some release from his anguish.

Nuyani gripped the cushion with her other hand as she watched. The people were now talking as the plate suddenly went cold, as if it were submerged in water and the heat was never there. The plate flew back, taking skin. Mo'ede whimpered as he looked on. A sudden rush of edria filled his body, keeping him awake, keeping the pain low for a moment and the fatigue at bay. He saw the others looking at him, and words were spoken in a commanding voice, but Nuyani knew not from who. Before the speech could be finished. Arrows shot from the shadows, followed by javelins of edria, catching the people off guard. Several men in long black cloaks emerged from the dark with nimchas and spears in hand. The group of black robed people lost several of their members before they could act.

The large figure with a circlet on his head did not react as Nuyani felt the sudden end of someone's thrum. The tall figure and two others disappeared in clouds of dust as Mo'ede plummeted. Several of the black-cloaked figures reached out toward them with their own magic and pulled Mo'ede and a few others toward the ledge. More screams were heard as those who did not flee either met the blade or were thrown into the pit. A man with a black head wrap and a short wild beard like a bush then stood over him. He started speaking to Mo'ede; his vision doubled as the edria keeping him awake had already ended.

Nuyani pulled her hand back and curled her fingers into a fist as she looked into his eyes. She nodded her head. *Everyone has a past or a reason. By the great lord, there's always a reminder,* she told herself. Nuyani then looked at the man's eyes, seeing that he had strength behind them. The torture he went through both for training and then in actual life made her question what sort of position the man was in. She fought the urge to try and console him or connect to heal whatever grievous wounds remained. The man seemed to have his own strength still.

"By his shine, you have endured," Nuyani said. Mo'ede could only guess at Nuyani's words, but he nodded his head, and his eyes narrowed in a way as if smiling under his shawl.

Baltik then broke in, "[If she's at ease now, then we can start planning. The only problem for now are supplies]."

"[A problem?]" Zonqua asked.

"[Of course]," Baltik said. "[I trade in information. Not goods. What you will need for your plan will take months and resources beyond what I can give.]"

"[You work with the courts. What can't you get or give?]" Zonqua asked.

Baltik looked at the brother with an annoyed expression on his face. The man then explained, "[Information on me. Not only am I going to reveal some intention on my part that can be exploited, but this can also be used to sneak others' interests into my affairs. Also, I may have a position, but that doesn't mean that I have access to everything. Maybe a court mage can, but that's not a privilege I have.]" Zonqua's jaw shut as he started to frown and sit back.

"[There's limits to everything,]" Zonqua said as he looked at the table where the larger crystal sat. "[Can you at least point us to the cities that have fallen?]"

"[What? Why would you want that?]" Baltik said. He then paused. "[You… want to use those crystals for your source?]"

Zonqua answered, "[Correct. If we use something that no one else would suspect of being taken by you personally, then you are safe, and we are safe.]"

"[No]," Mo'ede chimed in. Zonqua looked at the man. "[The city is already sending platoons to try and retrieve the crystals if they can. That and having spies watch over the fallen grounds for looters or other kingdoms to take supplies. More so, there is a friend of yours who has been rumored to appear around some of the fallen villages.]" Zonqua straightened his back and took a deep breath.

"[Does that mean she is taking the crystals, though?]" Zonqua asked in a more abrasive tone. Nuyani raised a brow as she studied his face. Zonqua looked more insulted than anything, but the others did not seem to be poking fun at him.

Picking up the words "[she]," Nuyani wondered if they were talking about an old lover of his. She fought a smile seeing the man start to fidget but stopped shortly. Nuyani then looked at the others as they spoke.

"[From what we know, she's been taking as many valuables as possible but not too focused on the crystals]," Mo'ede said.

"[The best advice I have for you is to harvest them as you have been]," Baltik said. "[The cities are doubling their guards with what forces they can, but that only makes the wild safer than being in a village. I wouldn't go to any cities unless you have no other choice.]"

"[To the sands...]" Zonqua cursed but blinked for a moment as Baltik laughed. Mo'ede and Nuyani looked at one another for a moment, not seeing what was so amusing.

"[Then let's plan these things out first]," Baltik said. "[You need a place to lie low and get the stones so you can store the crystals. You will need to learn the spells and plan for any setbacks. More so, you will need a way to hide their power because if you collect too much magic, they will call the worms and others to that place as well.]"

"[That's another thing I needed to ask you. Do you know of any maps with the abandoned or cleared caverns by the cities?]" Zonqua asked.

Baltik looked at his brother with a bit of surprise before he said, "[I can get you a map of cleared cities, but that does not mean they will be abandoned. If there isn't a cultist or a worm in there, you'll be dealing with animals instead.]"

"[To be fair, that would be preferred]," Zonqua said as he looked back at Nuyani.

Baltik narrowed his eyes at his brother and at her. "[What did Nuyani do before she came here, brother? How did you meet with her?]"

"[That I've told you. She saved us from a swarm of the nokragga before one of the larger worms emerged from the ground]," Zonqua said.

"[Yes, but what was she doing before she came here?]" Baltik asked.

"[She's some figurehead for her village]," Zonqua said. "[Seems more religious than anything.]+9+"

Baltik slammed his hand on the table, making the others jump before pointing at his brother. "I knew it," the man said. "Another queen. Another leader. If we want to quail a war, let's send you to the other queen and see if we can stop their forces with infighting."

Zonqua, this time, looked at his brother with annoyance as he started to laugh.

Once the conversations were over, Mo'ede returned to the back room after leaving the Do'alm figurine for Nuyani. She could feel a thrum from it, but she did not know what it was for. After gathering their supplies and the papers, Nuyani and the brothers left the library. It only took a few steps, but Nuyani felt the same small thread pressing against her core. Before she could pause, the ethereal thread broke while she was midstride. Nuyani paused and looked about. Zonqua then looked at Nuyani with a curious eye. Baltik took notice as well.

When the man placed a hand on her shoulder to get her attention, Nuyani then held out her hand and conjured a string of light that started to snap in the middle. Zonqua's eyes were serious as he looked at her.

"[Brother, are there trappers in the city?]" Zonqua asked.

"[Yes. So many refugees come this way, on criminals…]" Baltik stopped. "[Come with me now. There will be few eyes or ears near my home.]"

"[Are you certain?]" Zonqua's eyes shifted about in a cautious manner.

There was something to them? Nuyani thought, wanting to kick herself for not thinking of the display sooner.

The three then moved to the pin and retrieved Lugna before walking off toward another district.

Ch. 7 High Born and Classes

Baltik took the lead. There was little trouble or scrutiny from the guards as they passed through the long halls of the city. Nuyani noticed that many of the guards even seemed to avert their eyes as if he was a walking taboo for the group. She glanced at the man and then at Zonqua, who seemed to notice as well.

"[Not too many want to look at you, brother]," Zonqua commented as a pair of guards approached him. They noticed him, then moved to one side and turned their backs to the wall. The act so blatant that it made Baltik stand out.

"[Some positions come with consequences]," Baltik answered. "[Sometimes the price for information can cost lives if the wrong people find out. Innocent or not.]" Zonqua turned his head slightly to look at his brother's expression. Pain radiated from his glare as he looked ahead.

As they walked along, the group then reached a district with more homes than official buildings. Only a few large carriages were to be seen as most of the people passing by either wore an assortment of regal clothing and trinkets or wore tan-brown tunics and trousers often tattered and with a blue sash around their waist or none at all. Most of those wearing the tan attire had worn clothing with tears or holes in them while their expressions remained solemn. Nuyani could feel the soft hum of edria radiating from their attire. A sense of binding rose on them. Nuyani's grip on her spear tightened as she felt the urge to burst out. Her own core pulsed rapidly as though she were ready to fight.

Zonqua and Nuyani both stopped when they heard the commotion of two men across the road. One was beating the other with a stick, the one wielding a stick wearing a rich robe of light blue and white while the other wore a tan tunic without a sash. The anxiety had to go somewhere, and Nuyani took up her spear in both hands and moved to face them. Before she could fully turn their way, Zonqua's hand shot back and grabbed her arm. The sudden move made Nuyani move reflexively, nearly shoving the shaft of her spear into his wrist, but she stopped when she saw the man's expression. He looked as angry as she was but said nothing. Zonqua shook his head and released her when he saw that she was not continuing. The wails of pain from the other man rang in their ears. Nuyani's face creased as she looked at the ground.

'I'm a priestess. I must help him. Can I help him? Why are they alright with this?' Nuyani thought. Knowing there was a difference between her people and those in the desert, she only grew frustrated as the constant noise echoed in her mind. The woman then moved to the opposite side of the group, furthest away from the cries. Baltik continued walking at a faster pace but did not seem bothered by the situation. *Great lord, I'm ignoring this. I'm placing my judgment on this man. Is this right? Please guide me with your light,* Nuyani thought. She gripped her spear, trying to soothe herself for her decision. As they walked along, she thought of the fact that the spear was in her hands. There was food in her stomach. The men around her were willing to aid in the same plan. As much as the situation was different, and so many traps around her, Nuyani was still better off than many she had seen. Another question started to rise in her mind. What would they do with her once the false devourer was sealed?

She found her grip tightening and her face continuing to crease. "By his shine," Nuyani whispered.

The group then reached Baltik's home. Like many of the others, it seemed to have a high wall of brick with scarce placements of shards in the wall's mortar. Only the roof could be seen, and the home was separated by small alleyways between homes. Nuyani never thought much about the spacing but tried to compare it to the tents of her old village. The three then entered through an opening in the wall where a large man sat in place on the opposite side. He looked only a few years older than Zonqua. Similar to the guards, he wore armor and was armed with a nimcha, but his tunic was maroon, and his trousers were dark brown. Even his footwear was that of sandals and not the same sturdy boots that Nuyani had seen the guards wear. Overhead was a tall, thin tree growing out of a pot that shaded him.

"[Blessed by the goddess, sir. You have guests?]" the man greeted as he retrieved a rectangular metal piece and a small rod before striking the two together.

It let out a soft chime that seemed to travel through the entire front courtyard.

Even as it lingered in their ears, slowly fading, Baltik then said, "[Yes, Mirrega. We have two for a few days before we can rearrange a few things. Just let me speak to Gelvo before he leaves for the night.]"

"[As you wish, sir]," the man said as his eyes then peered at Nuyani. Nuyani took notice and he gave a soft smile.

One she meant but did not deter her from squeezing the spear tighter.

Nuyani was unsure about the city as most seemed too eager to leer at her. The longer she stayed in the city, the more confused she felt about it. In the village, there were guards, but they also did labor, and there was rarely a hand that could not do almost anything to help the village. For there to be positions and seating for almost everyone to do one thing and the entire city surviving almost baffled Nuyani. Her mood shifted, however, when Nuyani saw a small girl looking only seven or eight years of age, then stepped out of the main home wearing the same tan clothing as those subjugated. The child seemed thin but healthy, and her hair was covered by a headwrap. The girl then walked forward and lowered her head when she stopped in front of Mirrega.

The man leaned down and spoke to the girl in a soft tone, "[Tell Gelvo that Baltik is here and wants to speak to him before he leaves. Then prepare a room and bath]," Mirrega said.

"[Perhaps two rooms]," Baltik said as he looked back at his brother.

"[Enough. But you are correct]," Zonqua said as he kept himself from smirking. The personal guard also seemed to smirk as he glanced at Nuyani as he stood. Her grip tightened further as her expression remained stern.

"[Don't bother, Mirrega. She's here for official reasons]," Baltik said as he strolled toward the home after the girl. Mirrega straightened and turned his head in the other direction, and a smile rose on his face.

Nuyani blinked, noticing his change in demeanor as Zonqua walked ahead. Once they crossed the courtyard, another woman older than them appeared at the home entrance and took up Lugna's reins. She then guided the steed around the side. Nuyani barely noticed the clicks and caws of other animals from the side, which was a sign that there was a stable somewhere else. In entering the home, Nuyani was surprised to see so many rooms on one level. The area did not seem so large, but each room had different items in it and for separate purposes. One or two had cushions in them with small stools and tables, along with large mattresses for bedding. There were several people in another room that had people cooking in it with fire pits sitting in urns and letting the heat rise to cook either meats or vegetables. Nuyani was surprised to feel the heat rising from the area alone, nearly making her brow sweat. They passed by another room with a low table and several stacks of papers, books, and scrolls all around. In another room almost identical to the other, a man then sat at the table and was writing on a piece of paper as the young girl spoke to him. He wore attire just like Mo'ede.

The three then passed on, and Nuyani started to see the man had more influence than he let on. Reminded of the village elders, Nuyani wondered what questions she could ask him. Once the two were shown to their rooms, the girl then returned to Baltik's side, waiting for further instructions. Nuyani studied their interaction. The girl did not seem afraid of her dwelling, and even the clothing she wore was in good condition compared to most of what she saw. 'By his shine, village hands were supposed to be volunteers at most for their position if the help was needed, but this did not hold the same sense of pride in it.

Nuyani's thoughts dwelled on the setting as they toured the home. Shown both their bed chambers and where they could eat, it was not long before Nuyani was taken to the washroom. The young girl who guided her looked with large eyes at Nuyani, staring either at her eyes or at the spear in her hand. The girl seemed in awe that Nuyani was a fighter.

Why is she wearing them then, Nuyani wondered. With curiosity on her mind, Nuyani approached her and pinched the tunic. The girl's expression changed to a look of fear. Nuyani then tried to parse her mind, seeing only brief glimpses into her memory of the girl climbing the wall to steal some figs from several urns in the back. Hunger drove her, and she was without a home. When someone went to check, one of the urns fell over, spilling the fruit all over the ground. The child was caught and taken to Baltik. The rant and rage on his face seemed too dramatic for someone who forced her to wear the robes. What Nuyani was surprised to learn was that the robes were brought in from another place as the child was forced to wait in the man's custody. He spent some time and even had food brought to her having a conversation. When one of the other house hands returned, they brought not just the robes but a scroll as well.

The girl looked reluctant to write on the paper, but she did. Once the writing was done, the paper started to glow. A portion of her magic was cut from her core, leaving a painful ripping sensation to echo through her body. The girl winced as the same page turned into green strands that floated toward her hands and landed on the sleeves. The visage was unnerving as the string became animated like worms. They radiated with magic as they dug into the clothing sleeves and laced into the intricate circles and waving lines making up the design.

A little thief spared a harsher punishment, Nuyani thought, recalling the actions of her village. Theft at almost any age was seen as a severe crime that often led to severed limbs or, worse, death. The girl blinked, wondering what had happened, but left to clear her head. Nuyani smiled and waved to the girl. Nuyani looked at the room and saw how different many of the spaces were. A low trench with a few holes for drains in the corners of the walls was built into the ground. Small slits at the same corners of the walls replaced the windows. The orange-colored rays peering through the slits showed that night was soon to come. Nuyani undressed and took up a rag to wash. Once she was done, Nuyani returned to her room and started looking at her notes. On one of her stools sat the three figures with Do'alm, Do'alc, and the crystal ball. Nuyani looked at her notes, trying to remember the phrases and terms that she was shown.

Looking over some of her notes, she started to piece together some of them, but the conversations taking place only seemed to lose her. With Zonqua's attempts to explain what they were saying, she had an idea of what they were doing. Baltik was the one who could get them the information they needed and perhaps more resources. Whatever position they were in, the three men, however, seemed to have different skills that would help. She stared at the ceiling, letting her mind wander for a moment before looking everything over. The room was a simple square space but seemed almost as large as her old hut within the cavern.

The room was illuminated with another magic ball of light, creating an orange glow instead of the usual blue. It was suspended from an edragaurio made of iron and was the figure of the goddess with an outstretched hand. Nuyani wondered why there was such a fixation on the goddess, only to remember even some of the villager's clothing wore the mark of Kelvert, representing his shine. It did not help that the deity may have been their standard for beauty. She let the thought go as she looked at the rest of the room. The windows were small and squared, seeming only wide enough to pass her fist through. She lay on a large cushion with half a dozen more sitting on it with various vibrant colors. The stools were made of dark wood with polish, which brought a shine to them. Nuyani then looked at the second stool, where a wooden tray sat with a pitcher, and a set of cups sat with wine in it.

This feels too soft, Nuyani thought for a moment, seeing so much comfort. A few layers of fur and a leather bottom to keep out water and pests were enough to let her sleep. Yet the soft cushion beneath her seemed to let her sink in, threatening to never let her go. Staying vigilant to study, Nuyani sat up and kept her feet planted at the edge as she brought her attention to the crystal ball instead. Though she could not speak either language, she could at least try to form a grasp of the symbols for spells.

Picking up the crystal ball, Nuyani radiated a thrum into the sphere. The center of the crystal shined with a blue glow as her mind transferred to the small item. She found herself inside the crystal ball as though she had been shrunk and trapped inside, though she could still feel the weight in her hand. Clearing her mind, Nuyani then thought on reflex to the number of gods and those above. A great sigil then rose with the symbols of each god contained in a circle. There were eight sections splitting the gods apart. Nuyani blinked for a moment, remembering their numbers as she felt her body tremble. It felt as if she just discovered new body parts as the tremble continued.

How many are there? she questioned, only to see them divided by the sections. Finding sixty-four different symbols, Nuyani pondered the numbers as she looked at them.

When she studied the eight symbols at the center, the tremor was strongest, while at the edge, with four symbols in each section, gave the weakest sensation. *There are stronger and weaker gods,* Nuyani thought as she looked from one to another. Using what few words she knew, Nuyani repeated the name Sarcapno, and the symbol of the fire god flared. Nuyani stepped forward, noticing the symbol strengthened with the thoughts. Recalling the flame in her head, then brought another set of symbols lining up in a row beneath the circle. They were made up of the gods' symbols, but together, Nuyani had a feeling she could recall the word.

As her mind turned with information rising, she then said, "*Tosgam* (fire)." Three more of the symbols in the circle flared. Nuyani looked at them, seeing that she had called not one god over flame but four. "Why?" Nuyani wanted to ask but stopped as she looked at the symbols. New information rose from the depths of her being.

Their names grew clearer as she recited them as well. "Aczuriv. Thurygo. Elemus. Sarcapno." Each of the deities held the flame but with different meanings. *Alright, more gods have the same powers, or different but...* She stopped for a moment, wondering how she could get more information. Thinking of the element gave her some idea, but using the god's name gave her the symbol. Nuyani sighed as she wondered what to ask or think so she could see which gods were in control of sealing. More so, she started to think of how the seal broke to begin with. With the thoughts of the cultists, she wondered if they could break the seal if she placed one. Finding herself in a constant loop, Nuyani breathed deeply, trying to clear her thoughts. Her attention was taken away for a moment when she saw her own body mimicking the gesture.

"I will just see what god does what and start from there."

After some contemplation, Nuyani found herself discovering a dozen names and seeing that Do'alm and Do'alc were indeed not in the pantheon. Strangely enough, their names did make the symbol of Sarcapno shimmer only a little. Nuyani blinked, surprised to find that the same god had controlled it as well. Following the same steps, Nuyani quickly found different relations of the gods to one another as wind *yojowa*, only to find air, *heidul,* with the god Heonsha. Though the word "wind" appeared, she was surprised to find that it was not associated with any god in the pantheon, only air was.

Nuyani continued to study the words and spells, exiting the crystal on occasion to test the spells. She held out her hand to one of the cups on the tray and recited "*yojowa*." Her thrum raced but merely created a cool breeze in the room surrounding Nuyani, jostling some of her papers. She stopped when she saw that the breeze was not strong enough to push anything around even as she fed more strength into the thrum. She felt a small portion of her spirit leave her core.

Holding up her hand once more, she thought of calling Sarcapno's name but remembered the deity's powers covered more than just the wind. She could cause a fire to land on the cushions, which would make things difficult for her and their host. Nuyani then wondered about Do'alc's abilities to summon various elements. Cautious of her actions, Nuyani faced the stone wall and created a sphere of edria. The ball of magic pulsed steadily above her palm. Nuyani concentrated on the goddess's name. As she focused on the thrum, letting it race faster, she could feel the ties to the elements falling into her grasp. Yet, compared to Sarcapno's name, the control was difficult to collect. She continued her attempt to call upon the forces until the thrum of her core nearly raced to its strongest before the wind stirred. The rhythm at play had now been met, but not without issue.

What was first an encircling gale became an enclosed tornado, causing the papers and cushions to circle about. Nuyani yelped as the larger cushion she sat on started to rise on one side with her and folded inward. The tray on the stool performed a chaotic dance as it tipped over, only to repeatedly collide with the wall and fall to the floor with the picture and cups teetering to fall, but never spilling a drop. Nuyani released her thrum just as mist and sparks of lightning began to appear in the air. The room settled only a moment later, and Nuyani looked around at the mess of papers all over the floor, the figurines lying on their sides, and the stool.

"By the great lord. Why did that happen?" Nuyani first wondered. "Is that why they still use other spells?" Her mind raced with questions, only to be replaced with thoughts of the encroaching pain taking over her body. The same tensing anguish took over her muscles and forced her to lie down as her hands clenched and opened with enough strength to shake her body. Nuyani breathed heavily, waiting for the pain to pass. It eventually eased, and she sat upright. She gave a small chuckle as she looked at the papers on the ground. *I won't be trying that again. Not without Zonqua to explain it,* Nuyani thought.

Her attention then went to the door as Zonqua and Mirrega both appeared through the entrance. The two stopped and looked at the scattered papers and cushions, and then Nuyani. She gave a small grin and created a construct of herself performing a spell and the room spinning in the breeze. Omitting the cramping pain that came with too much excessive use of magic. The others laughed seeing the mess and Mirrega even pointed to the tray with the pitcher and cups sitting on it but somewhat haphazardly.

"[Must a strong spell to surprise you]," Zonqua said.

"[If that's all that happened, I'll return to the front]," Mirrega said before giving a side glance at Nuyani. A sense of heat rose in her face as she realized she was not as covered as before. Wearing a simple tunic and skirt amongst the clothing she was gifted with seemed more exposing as she saw the skirt rising nearly up to her hip. Quickly fixing her clothing, she then stood and started picking up the papers.

"[You're a bit too strong, I see, for using some spells]," Zonqua commented. Nuyani glanced at him, not understanding what he said, but she wondered if this was his way of trying to get her to learn the language faster. With that thought in mind, she tried to parse out the words.

Zonqua then started picking up the papers as well. She then stole another glance at Zonqua. Even in their travels, he had rarely been without two layers of clothing, mostly wearing his armor over his long tunic. Wearing a simple green tunic with short sleeves tucked into his trousers, he revealed his thin frame, though he was still as toned as some of the hunters from her village. The simple dreads that dangled from his head seemed as cared for as most of the men did their beards with few frays out of place. Nuyani found herself pausing for too long and continued to pick up the papers. Before long, the room was cleared up, and the stool was reset, with the edragaurio sitting back in place.

Zonqua took up the third stool and returned the wooden tray to the last. He then looked at Nuyani with a smile as he then asked, "[So what happened?]"

"You want to see if I understand you? I will try," Nuyani said as she gave him a wary eye and reached for one of the papers and the charcoal piece that now skewered the cushion. Nuyani then drew the symbols of Do'alm and Do'alc, then created a ball of edria in her opposite hand as she pointed to them. "[This strong]," Nuyani said with difficulty. She then turned back to the paper and started drawing the symbol of Sarcapno. As she worked, Zonqua started finding his eyes trailing up and down her leg, sitting over the cushion side while the other remained folded and propping her up. Her simple tunic did little to hide the curves of her body. He then blinked and brought his attention back to her drawing as she pointed to the deity's symbol. "[This easy.]" Recreating a second ball of edria, the entire sphere transformed into fire glowing on her face, then freezing winds, then lighting. "[Why?]"

[Stronger? She meant harder or difficult], Zonqua thought.

Zonqua looked up to the ceiling, looking for the proper word to say. He then looked back at her with an idea. "[Prayer.]" Nuyani blinked as he stared at her, wondering if she understood. With silence starting to take place, he then showed a construct of her performing her prayer in the morning. "[For you, it's Kelvert. For me, it's Do'alm and Do'alc.]" The construct then changed to a small blue version of himself wielding his spear before the symbol of the goddess appeared behind him, and lightning streaked from the tip of his weapon.

Your prayer to the god grants their gift? Nuyani thought. *But what's the difference? Why are there gods with the same powers?* Nuyani then looked from the construct to the man's face. "[Why…two? Why… twice?]"

"[Twice?]" Zonqua looked at her for a moment, trying to understand what she was asking. "[You mean the gods?]" Nuyani blinked for a moment, showing she was contemplating the words before she nodded her head. The man thought for a moment. "[You mean gods for the same spells?]" Nuyani scowled as she looked to the side, trying to see if she could follow his speech. Still silent after a moment, Zonqua then illustrated his assumption with both symbols of Do'alc and Sarcapno before creating lightning in between them. Nuyani looked at the construct and nodded her head once more.

"[Oh. For weaknesses.]" Zonqua said as he changed the construct to the same circle of glyphs that Nuyani saw in the crystal ball. She did not understand the word but wondered what he meant. The only difference in his display was new circles separating the glyphs even further. On the outer rim, groups of three contained the symbols that gave the weakest thrum. The next inner section was in fours, with symbols growing noticeably stronger, and the final section, with those standing alone toward the center, was held the strongest. Zonqua then pointed to the opposite sides, showing the symbols that countered one another. As he pointed to Sarcapno, he showed the opposite symbols in the furthest section. The same strength in pulse radiated from Nuyani's core, looking between either side.

"[Now create fire]," Zonqua said as he converted one of the constructs into a simple ball of edria. Nuyani followed his lead, not certain what he wanted until he repeated Sarcapno's name. He dispersed his own construct before flames or cold could be conjured.

Nuyani repeated his words and focused on the fire aspect, trying to keep it as a flame, but it continued to change from one form to another. Despite its fleeting form, Nuyani was still able to maintain it with ease.

Zonqua then recreated his construct and the glyphs before uttering the name of Lorkep, a god of poisons, toxins, plagues, and diseases. Nuyani was not certain why at first, but the name made her stomach turn as she looked at the sphere of edria twist into a sphere of vapor and mist. The color changed to a dark blue glowing with some traces of light blue on the edge. Nuyani noticed Zonqua started to sweat, and his face somehow grew drastically tired as bags started to form under his eyes. With his free hand, he waved to her to extend her hand outward as he did so. Turning his hand to face her,

Nuyani was reluctant, concerned that he was growing sick. Only his continued gesture for her to do the same convinced her to follow along. Nuyani did, and as the spheres collided, the thrums clashed and recoiled back to their cores. Neither continued. She gawked at Zonqua, surprised that the magic would merely end. She was even more surprised that the man's complexion returned to a healthy state.

"[Now for another pair]," Zonqua said as he gestured for her to create another conjuring. Once Nuyani did and repeated the storm god's name, Zonqua then fed magic into his ring, doubling the strength of his thrum. Uttering a new name, he called "Amovs." With the name of the goddess of binding and torture, Nuyani felt a restrictive nature echoing toward her from the spell. As though she knew it was meant as a trap and worse. Zonqua's body seemed stiff and devious at the same time. Repeating the connection of the spheres, on contact, Nuyani's spell not only dispersed but changed to a stronger thrum. The recoil of the spell converted to a strange binding that made Nuyani feel stiff. A ghostly sickness weakened her muscles as she felt her mutinied core being the only thing keeping her physical form together. Her mental thoughts of doubt and fear grew heavier, even to the point of bringing tears to her eyes. Nuyani fought the sudden whiplash of emotions, changing her next thrum from the storm god to her pure will. With all her might, she broke through the influence and forced the recoil of Zonqua's spell back on himself. Or so she was hoping as anger flared. The man had stopped his own conjuring the moment she had fallen.

"How? [Why?]" Nuyani asked.

Zonqua then showed a pair of figures lacking in features, with one being a woman placing her hand on the head of another kneeling before her with what looked to be ropes binding her arms and legs. The symbol of the goddess was placed on the standing figure's face. Nuyani looked at him for a moment, glaring at him. Zonqua waited for her to speak or say something. He could not tell if she was angry or had a lot of questions. Her focus was on the thrum and ring. She wondered why he had to use the ring. Nuyani then leaned forward and tapped the ring.

"[Why do I use this?]" He then took it off and pointed to the glyphs once more. He ran his fingers along the ridge with the weakest thrums of the gods. He then placed the ring in his hand. "[With a ring, I can do these.]" He ran his finger along the inner circle.

"That's why the strengths of magic are so important. [Why?]" Nuyani looked at him, wondering what had stopped him from using the others. Zonqua merely chopped at his neck, simulating a blade cutting him down. "Y-you die?" Nuyani then returned her thoughts to Kelvert. She remembered that too much magic would release your soul from your body or do too much damage. With the spells and gods being finite in their requirements, she thought that most spells were safer.

Zonqua then pointed at Nuyani. "[You are jornoxarra.]" He then pointed to the inner ring. Zonqua then reached out toward Nuyani and grabbed her hand. She looked between his hand and eyes wondering what he was doing. She felt the heat growing once more but stopped as she saw him grabbing her ring and taking it off. He then looked at her and told her to call a new name. "Seyoata."

Nuyani repeated the name as she conjured a sphere of edria. The pulse rushed faster than ever as the magic conjured different emotions in Nuyani, along with various colors and starlike lights within the sphere. Nuyani looked in wonder as her sight grew stronger. The same sensation she felt when sending edria to strengthen her eyes as silver light seemed to replace the glow of the magic torch, and many of the shadows that lingered were now brighter. Nuyani then felt a strange elation coming over her as her thoughts flashed from running into the desert and seeing new sights that they hid and to wondering what a partner would be as she looked at Zonqua. She blinked at the thought as a strange compulsion started to rise. Taking control of herself, she stopped the thrum before the fantasy continued.

By his shine. Nuyani glowered as she looked to the side and placed both hands on her lap. *Too many men at home and I'm looking to finish this travel with his help. Stop it.* Nuyani then turned back to him as she saw him and looked at him, puzzled. She smiled at him, only making his brow rise and blink.

[I don't understand this woman.] Zonqua then smiled as his mind wondered about the possibilities if he told her the titan of lust instead. He let the thought go as Nuyani scratched through her hair.

Another question? Nuyani looked to the side as she tried to gather the right words to speak. When she turned back, she raised her hand and created a construct of two deities, one of Do'alc and the other of the goddess Amovs. Zonqua then looked at the constructs suspended in the air and watched as

Nuyani mimicked the encounter of the spells with her hands instead. Zonqua nodded his head and first pointed to Amovs before forming a fist with the same hand and acting as if he were going to attack the construct of Do'alc. Nuyani blinked, wondering if such a gesture would prove blasphemous, but remembered that they were all a part of a greater scale than Nuyani had any part in. Zonqua then handed back the ring before creating his own constructs of Amovs and Do'alc. He then created two more figures with extending staves in each other's direction. The spell with Amovs influence beat out Do'alc's, but the tie changed in a second illustration as the figure using the storm god's influence now sported a ring along with his staff. The second clash had the two matchings, but Nuyani knew that second rings or items could allow the thrum to grow stronger. Just to match the higher god, more power was needed.

Nuyani committed the lesson to memory but, then, looked at Zonqua, seeing that the man was now sweating. Letting a coursing thrum echo over him, she could feel the pulse of his core growing a little unstable.

"[You well?]" Nuyani's expression changed to worry as she looked him in the eyes.

The man shrugged. "[Tired. Perhaps tomorrow, then. More lessons.]" Nuyani nodded her head. "[May the goddess bless you.]"

"[May the goddess bless you]," Nuyani said hoping it did not come off obviously that she was copying him and not saying something foolish.

The man then rose from his seat with a faint smile and walked out of the room. After he left the room and passed the entrance curtains, Nuyani placed her items on the stools and turned to sleep on the cushion. Though she felt some fatigue as well, her mind was racing with the possibilities of spells. With more references to different spells and their relations between the gods, Nuyani's brow furrowed as she thought of the lessons. Instead of the elements canceling each other out, it was the relations between gods on the glyph that determined it all. When she thought back to all the gods she had yet to study, her mind started to race. She imagined the different symbols and circles needed to create the seal. She wondered which spells would be needed to guard the outside as much as the inside. She wondered about the writing that was needed.

Taking a deep breath, she tried to let the thoughts go. Part of her started to think of Zonqua taking her ring and the use of Seyoata's influence. Her curiosity grew, but she did not know her thoughts would dwell on the body, not with so many other matters coming into play. With another deep breath, she tried to quell her racing heart. Sleep soon took over, and Nuyani started to dream more about her home and what the others were doing. She saw her brother shouting at the others as he pointed into the distance. Caluu was holding something at bay, but her magic radiated stronger than ever. Worry and guilt grew in Nuyani as she wondered how good of a priestess she was; if she was about to spend more time in the desert than she had with her own people. The guilt grew that she found herself forming her life away from the others. Enjoying more from it than from those she knew. She rubbed her fingers together as she thought of the lives that were lost and those still in danger. A part of her wished she had never known there was more to the world, yet she was happy that there was.

Ch. 8 Shaken Foundations

Several days later, Nuyani was waiting in one of the larger plazas as the rush of the crowds marched on. With so many people filling through the streets during midday, it was the best time for her and Zonqua to move about the city. It also helped that both took on completely different attire while having false names registered in the city. Aside from her spear and glowing eyes, there was little to recognize her as she wore a longer brown robe that draped over her body. She still wore the leather wrappings and armguard Zonqua gave her, but she kept the rest of her runner's wear bound within her satchel. With the robe reaching ankle length, it covered her loose trousers and tunic. What some seemed to notice was the lack of embroidery on her sleeves. Between the headwrap, veil, spear, and her leather sandals meant more for battle, Nuyani learned that she looked more like a hired hand for security.

Only a few seemed to want much to do with her since then, as a sense of disdain was felt by those in her presence. The few who seemed to notice her demeanor or strength was not so tarnished were the performers and merchants who measured most who walked by for good customers or not. She often went back to the same area where the performers stayed and tried to catch glimpses of their acts and mimic some of the spells that echoed from them. Even as she gave the coin to the performers, they smiled back at her for visiting the show along with the wave of edria the violet woman sent her way trying to identify her. Nuyani considered sending her own wave back at her but decided not to, knowing that the customs were different for everyone.

When the show was over, she started down one of the lone halls devoid of people, trying to keep to herself. Zonqua informed her to walk in a rush; otherwise, she would meet the eyes of those who wanted to see more than just the robe. Confidence in her fighting abilities never waned, but Nuyani knew that when two blade jaws fought, it was often the third that would win. Keeping a decent pace, she tried to remember the few simple phrases she remembered for the people around her. For her, the practice was a daily exercise, such as walking around the city and buying food. Nuyani liked the idea as she met merchant after merchant, trying to find the items Zonqua asked for. With some luck, she made it through but found that her lack of knowledge could grow costly as she noticed many trying to take advantage of her ignorance. She quickly grew accustomed to counting when she was only given enough silver and gold coins to purchase some rope, phylactery, and pieces of iron.

It was a surprise to Nuyani to see a blade smith at work for the first time. As the fire heated, metal then struck to take form from another piece of metal, making her jaw drop. She watched the sparks fly. She did wonder what all the pieces were for but thought it was possible that each of them was for different lessons. A part of the lesson that she learned was that the hidden names of the gods also lay in everything, sometimes alone and others in groups. With that said, she tried to read the thrum of her spear, wondering where the wood had come from. With a mixture of hidden rhythms also obscured by the gem housed in the metal, Nuyani could hardly make out the names. Making her way to a fruit vendor, she tried to send a thrum through the wood of the kiosk as the man went to retrieve two melons. She found a nasty surprise, with a shock to her hand, reacting to her magic and forcing her to yelp.

Catching the vendor's attention, he gave her a look, and Nuyani struggled to explain that she was studying magic. The man barely understood but was content with another silver piece for the trouble. Walking away with the food and at least a little pride in settling a matter on her own, Nuyani walked away with some joy, knowing she was getting better. She did count the pieces afterward and started to feel that her spending might get out of hand.

Walking the alleyways, Nuyani wanted to go to the library once more but was told by the others, at least not to go without them, explaining that trackers and trappers were special kinds of guards that went to different cities or countries to take people in. Worse than ever, Nuyani had broken two lines, already alerting at least one or two men that there was a target. It only became a learning experience for Nuyani as she took alternative routes into smaller neighborhoods that took in some of the refugees. With more people to feed, it pained Nuyani that there were so many who could not find work, and she found herself wanting to speak with them but knew that she had to keep anonymity. Clutching the medallions around her neck, she often forced herself to look ahead when a familiar face came by.

Nuyani wanted to smile, at least when she saw the same girl who called her for help wearing scholar's clothing instead of casual attire. Accompanied by her parents and the same shawled man as before, Nuyani surprised her with a small hummingbird construct to hover around her. The child laughed, and the parents saw the construct before it faded away. Feeling a little relieved, she made her way down one of the more crowded roads too wide for the same canopy ceiling to give shade. Before she walked too far into the open, Nuyani felt a familiar thrum brush toward her. Recognizing Zonqua's presence, she turned to see the man wearing a pained smile. His neck twitched, and his brow furrowed on occasion.

To keep his cover, he wore a red robe with a leather collar and shoulders that rose in the back to cover the neck from attacks. He wore simple brown boots and had a solid color blue for his sash, tunic, and trousers. On his head was another dark blue head wrap covering his dreads while his helmet remained in his bag. With a closer study, Nuyani could feel the sporadic pulses of his edria. They were weaker than normal as Zonqua staggered toward her. Nuyani quickly moved toward him as he propped himself up with his own spear. Nuyani held out her hands to help steady him, but Zonqua pulled her through another entrance into a small market alleyway. Though there were no guards at the front, the area did seem to contain a cluster of kiosks.

With the first time seeing the area, Nuyani could tell it was a more private and expensive venue with the kiosks accompanied by gilded merchants and serious-looking guards in different uniforms. The items they sold were either completely made of gold or other metals and had gems fixed in place or embroidered with various designs containing stories of their own. *No place for a light pouch,* Nuyani thought as they moved along.

Along the walls, however, were spaces with small tables and cushions, and the smell of smoke filled the air and stung her throat. The two found one that was empty, and Zonqua dropped to the floor and clutched his neck. The pain grew worse as his fingers curled, threatening as if he would claw into his neck. Nuyani knelt beside him, letting her spear drop to the side as she cupped her hands over his. Sending a thrum through his body whether he could agree or not, Nuyani felt the same strings wrapping around his core and the placement of the mark. What seemed subtle at first now felt like a rope pulsing like a drum beat and taut against his magic. The resonating thrum stifled not only his magic but echoed the curse in his neck.

Nuyani felt a sense of rage boil within her as her thrum went from a thin wave to a rushing beat. With her mind clear, she focused on the ethereal cord and tried to break it. Her magic did nothing, even as she reinforced it with her ring. The snare's thrum seemed far too powerful to be a person, or only one. Seeing she lacked the strength, Nuyani did the next thing she could and instead used her ring to form a construct to block the foreign thrum from activating the curse. Immediately, Zonqua seemed more relaxed as he breathed heavily and sweat ran down his face. He looked at Nuyani for a moment and nodded his head as he tried to collect himself.

"[We must move.]" His voice was rasped and tired as he struggled to stand. The two looked back toward the entrance seeing a pair of personal guards looking at them accusingly but neither removing their blades. "[Sorry, we will leave.]" Zonqua said as he pulled Nuyani closer to him. Both seemed to smile and walked on.

Nuyani wanted to beat both men until they apologized if their smirks meant what she thought they believed. She instead turned her attention to the edria hindering his core. *By his shine, how do we remove that?* Nuyani wondered as the two made their way to the other side of the market area. Through the next entrance were normal city guards. They eyed the two with suspicion but did not move to stop them as they turned their attention to those trying to enter. With her mind preoccupied with maintaining the barrier around the curse, she noticed the stronger thrums radiating from the cord. As they went into the crowd and tried to make their way toward another entrance, Zonqua stopped when they saw that there were two more guards approaching the entrance. From the dozens of paces, he could see one of the new guards talking to the others as his partner started surveying the crowd and stopped at him.

The two could not go back as the flow of the crowd had carts, animals, and travelers entering from the southern gate. A quick glance showed one of the personal guards also escorting two city guards to the entrance they left and pointing them out.

"[To sands...]" Nuyani bemoaned as she tried to look for another exit.

With another thrum racing toward them, Nuyani instinctively created a barrier. The blue dome knocked over a pushcart beside them, sending an older man tumbling to the side as his belongings were thrown about. Nuyani winced and held her spear defensively as the barrier rippled. She looked up at a man standing on the wall above the road. Unlike any guard she had seen, the man wore leather armor dyed blue over his white tunic and trousers. He had a straight blade equal in length to any nimcha but was sharp on both sides. Leaping from the top of the wall to the street, others screamed at the action. Nuyani did not move as she felt she was still blocking something from striking them. When she looked at the rippling surface, what seemed to be a golden claw or fang continued to press into the ethereal wall.

The man strolled closer to her and narrowed his eyes. He had a salt and peppered beard reaching down to mid-chest and a physique that seemed on par with any of the other guards yet with a fiercer demeanor. On his right arm was a gold gauntlet with spider-like engraving on the surface and gems in the place of its eight eyes. There were small divets with the same fang-like pieces sitting in them. Except two were missing out of eight. Nuyani glared at the man, seeing he was not a normal person. Even more so, she found it strange that such magic was concentrated only on the item and not echoing as so many others had before.

"[Do'alc's glory, may we find a way]," Zonqua said as he looked to the opposite end of the area and saw more guards filling the road. They let the people pass by and created space.

A booming voice then called from the man, "[Traitor, why did you come to the city? Finding you is annoying.]" The man spoke with an eased posture unthreatened by Nuyani's presence.

Nuyani's anger started to rise, but she instead turned her attention to the needle. With a clearer focus, she could feel the same reinforced rhythm concentrated in the weapon as she felt from the cord holding Zonqua. Realizing this, Nuyani then turned to Zonqua and grabbed the man's hand, bearing his ring. Surprise rose on his face, only to fade when he realized what she was planning. With both synchronizing their thrums and feeding the energy into his ring, their strength doubled. This got the trapper's attention, and he swung his arm around as if throwing a net. Nuyani could feel the ethereal coils wrapping around her barrier, but her combined strength with Zonqua's broke them with an erect barrier, snapping all the lines in place. A series of groans and yells sounded as the surrounding guards buckled in their stances. The trapper himself looked almost unfazed. He narrowed his gaze and took a glance at his bracer. All but two of the legs were gone now, and four of the gem eyes were cracked.

Nuyani felt the urge to smile but stopped, remembering that letting her guard down would only make her vulnerable. With the guards hindered, the two started toward the far-off entrance. The guards there were still standing, showing they had not added their power to the binding. Before either could get far, Nuyani felt the flow of edria heading her way and turned in time to block an arch of edria that flew toward her. She gawked at the man wielding his ida. In its scabbard, she did not feel its magic but quickly collected herself, seeing that the man was well prepared. Before either could get far, the man swung the blade horizontally as another wave of edria flew forth. Nuyani created a smaller barrier around her spear tip and stabbed at the arching wave, dissipating it with ease. The trapper then raised his hand with the spider guard and released the last two legs along with another wave of edria. Zonqua, this time, erected a barrier between them and the man, letting the projectiles collide with the reinforced wall. The man did not wait for them to counter as he raced forth and fed magic into his gauntlet.

Adding some energy to the ida, he swung at the barrier but stopped short, forming a sphere of edria at the tip of his weapon. With only a wall between them, his construct flew behind their defense as the blade tip scratched the surface of the opposite side. Nuyani turned into a blur as she ducked the sudden attack. Behind her veil, her eyes glowed with fury. Nuyani then extended her hand to the side and created another sphere of edria at the barrier's end. Copying the same tactic, she let the sphere sail toward him. The man seemed to know her next move as he jumped back before the sphere expanded into another wall-sweeping area. Zonqua changed their defense into a javelin and fired it at the man just as he landed. The projectile collided with the flat of the ida knocking him off balance. The caster then grabbed Nuyani's arm, and the two ran for the exit.

The other guards fired simple spheres of edria but, their forces were no match for Nuyani and Zonqua's combined reserve. With simple walls to push them aside, the two first made their way through the entrance, only blocking the guards from following. As the two made their way down the plaza, Nuyani felt a different pressure covering them. The ground started to shake. They saw pedestrians struggling to keep themselves right. Before a single word could be said, the ground opened with a hole dozens of paces wide, sending people screaming as they were swallowed into the depths.

"No!" Nuyani yelled as she watched another kiosk fall in and worms rise from within. Without a single thought, she started jabbing at the first parasite, shattering its head and sending chunks flying back toward the void.

Yet, with one fallen, three more rose. The two began immediately battling the worms as the other guards struggled to right themselves. Still synchronized, Nuyani erected a barrier nearly three dozen paces all around, sending worms flying in all directions, and a few magical items started to activate on contact. Nuyani then called for cold and pointed at the hole, freezing the shifting earth mixed with debris, worms, and pus in a blanket of ice. Zonqua looked at her with surprise, but he only saw worry as she looked from him to the guards.

A sense of fear rose in the man. "N…" he tried to yell but saw that Nuyani would not sacrifice them. People from outside began to flee the markets as more worms rose over the walls and started attacking the people. With some experience in the attacks, even civilians fought the worms with what magic or items they had. Nuyani saw one of the gilded heavy pedestrians firing a few spells himself while others escorted him through the crowd. Despite her distaste, she could respect the effort as most worms were not in his path. Zonqua joined Nuyani on the other side and fired several spheres of edria and lightning into the invading hoard. Several guards scrambled to right themselves before they met the end of pincers. Nuyani then created a barrier sweeping around the area to knock away the worms. Wide blue arcs of edria flew forth, severing the heads of parasites as a few had their bodies pierced by the small golden fangs of the spider guard.

With some effort to keep the spilling hoard at bay, the others were able to get on their feet and fight back. Zonqua then grabbed Nuyani's arm and pointed for the exit. "[The people! The tower! Go!]" Zonqua said, keeping the words simple.

Nuyani paused, wondering what he meant, but recognized the word "people." With a nod of her head, she ran off. Passed the gates and into another alleyway, Nuyani found herself amongst the injured and wounded as worms climbed the walls and descended on them. First, creating a barrier for a temporary roof, followed by an attack on the worms themselves. Edria, filling her spear, stabbed, slashed, and struck each parasite she could reach. With a second breath, the worms fell backward. Nuyani allowed the people to flee. When most exited into buildings or out of the hall, she then converted her barrier to flame after shouting, "Tosgam! (Fire)!" The barrier roof roared into the sky, sending any worms standing on it upward before descending as charred carcasses. She then moved toward the next hall and market, trying to clear as many of them as possible.

Zonqua growled as he found himself striking down a group of parasites. With Nuyani so far away, the connection broke, and his magic returned to the same state. Zonqua looked toward the tower and found it did not have the same shine as anyone would expect from the erected barriers. Before he could take a step, the idea rose before him, meeting his neck. The caster met the eyes of the trapper. Despite the same wild stare, his look seemed understanding and measured. He then lowered the weapon and let Zonqua leave as he moved to fight with the others. The caster ran off after giving a weighing look at the man.

Passing through the entrance and bounding over stone debris, Zonqua tried to make his way toward the tower. With the worms making it this deep into the city, the larger crystal was their only defense from the swarms. Worse, the quakes passing through the area meant another large worm was seeking to reach the tower and keep it from activating altogether.

If there's any place she'd go, it would be there, right?
Zonqua questioned. He was not sure, and it angered him. The
only thing he knew was Nuyani's fervent will to fight. Unable
to find a clear path, Zonqua climbed some of the debris and
onto the wide walls. He rarely ventured on them but knew that
most were pathways for other guards to move and transfer units
across the town without hindrance or if any party of bandits
tried to hold a market hostage. The only thing the man met
were more worms taking up pathways and proving to embed
themselves further in the city. Zonqua thought of his brother,
hoping he had found safety.

As Nuyani went from bazaar to plaza, she cleared
away as many of the creatures as she could. With luck, she
found her way to the performer's plaza, catching them and the
few guards around during battle. Like the trapper, the
edricoudya (magic person) Nuyani learned was the woman of
violet skin who sent waves of edria sailing from her blade and
carving through the worms. The udrog (dwarf) and kymac took
to fighting with battle axes. The kymac did the same but
fought, clinging to the wall's surface by his feet alone. He
stayed suspended above an entrance as several people exited
the area from another. The last man sent offensive spells
toward the creatures. He used his illusions to bait many of the
parasites away from the actual crowds. Nuyani found herself
feeling exhausted as she looked around the area, trying to see
what she could do.

She remembered the tower housed the largest gem and
was meant to erect the barrier. Remembering the word, Nuyani
spat at her lack of memory before looking for a way to reach
the tower. Seeing that so many worms were rising from the
walls, she wondered if there was a path or tunnel inside them.

Taking a deep breath, she raced toward the wall and sent javelins through many of the worms in place. Killing at least a dozen or so, it freed the others to move to safety. She then climbed what debris she could and reached the hidden path. Worry struck Nuyani as she found the dead bodies of three guards with the marks of blades left on their bodies. Unlike the corpses of those who had fallen, missing small pieces from the worms devouring them, these men were murdered. Remembering her goal, Nuyani ran along the path, trying to find the quickest way through the area.

The path was not even, as some sections were low enough for ground level or deeper. Others were nearly flush with the walls' height, making any cover impossible. While she ran along, the number of paths available became disorienting. On occasion, she ran into more worms and more bodies. A morbid thought told Nuyani that she was on the right path. Rising out of the wall once more to meet an entrance coinciding with a building wall, Nuyani saw the wooden door fly open before a blinding light forced her to close her eyes. Reflexively, she raised a barrier blocking an unseen attack as she felt an opposing thrum collide with her barrier. When Nuyani tried to step forward, the ground had become slippery, and she fell over the side of the guard rail only raised to hip height. Nuyani yelped as she flipped over and landed on an outstretched tarp. Then, it ripped, sending her to the floor, dazed.

Across the side, Zonqua saw the sudden flash and ran along the path toward it. He did not know what to expect, but he was almost certain it was Nuyani. When Zonqua reached the area, he looked around. A section of the floor was covered in a sheet of ice, and he looked down the side of the wall. There,

Zonqua found Nuyani lying on her side with worms almost set upon her. Releasing javelins from his spear, he skewered the worms through their heads before descending onto a tarp pole and using the ripped tarp to lower himself to the ground. Zonqua then collected Nuyani in his arms, sitting her up as he sent waves of edria from his core to hers, trying to wake her. Nuyani's eyes snapped open as she looked at the man and then the area around them, and a loud clicking sounded in her ears. The ground fell in as more worms burst from the hole in the street. Nuyani then looked at the wall and saw the shards that lay within. Taking up the chance, she gathered her spear and held Zonqua's hand. Their minds and magic synchronized instantly as a flash of her memory with the larger crystal shard met his mind.

Concentrating with all their might, the thrum raced faster than ever before. Nuyani took up the crystal she had fused in the library and funneled the edria from it into the wall. With the intent to erect a barrier, the others did the same, causing small barriers to erect from each shard and cascade across the walls and buildings of Giode. Worms across the city shattered on contact with the walls while others on the ground halved in force, with people still fighting the hoards. The cascade moved along the buildings like a beacon, rising around them until they collected into large domes covering the structures before reaching the top of the tower and doing the same. The barrier erected ran through the entire city and beyond the few farmlands and villages on the outskirts.

With the area drenched in a blue glow, the worms all turned to shattered shells and pus. Nuyani felt as though she were being split a thousand times over. Her body was numb, and her vision was dazed. This was not the same as her core merely breaking or shattering as it did before. With what dull thrum she could manage, the pulses felt like they set on direct courses encircling her soul. From what she could tell, her ethereal drum was now frayed into threads, and her spirit was leaking. The coolness of her body slowly took over as Zonqua caught her. Both his and her ring were shattered, but that did little to protect Nuyani, who had a more direct connection to the shards.

"[Nuyani! Stay awake! You just gave the city a chance!]" Zonqua bellowed as he looked at her. The man then looked around and found the crystal Nuyani had used, which was now a fist-sized sphere of light. Thinking quickly as the thrum remained active, Zonqua lay Nuyani on the ground and used his magic to keep the pulse strong. With a different rhythm, it was still a hard task to perform. The radiating thrums made him aware of her spirit seeping from her body. Zonqua did not have his spare items with him and instead tried to use the spear, though he was certain it would backfire. He fed magic into the crystal from his weapon, letting the thrum repel and expand at once. When he gained control over the thrum, Zonqua expanded the edria into a barrier and lowered it within her body. Controlling the intent, her soul and damaged core passed through with ease. He then receded the barrier to fit Nuyani's core, sealing both her edria and spirit. Before releasing his hold on the magic, he waited until her core was strong enough to hold.

On contact, the core began to transfer pulses to the foreign barrier, taking control of it. Within a few moments, the threads started to fuse into the construct and take hold of it. The cold that ran through her body lessened, and she found her conscience returning gradually. When Nuyani awoke, she turned her head and saw Zonqua looking at her with a smile on his face.

"[You saved the city for now]," Zonqua said. Nuyani blinked as she felt the small tremors of his memory seep through the construct. With a desperate move, he had saved her. Embracing each other, they took a moment to relax before the familiar clicking returned. The wave of blue had gone. Whatever remained of the worms was returning. Zonqua then brought Nuyani closer to him and pulled out a small green replica of Lugna tied around his neck. Feeding the edragaurio, the thrums resonating from it did not echo out but faded.

With little control over her magic, Nuyani could do little to move. The feeling of sharp pain resonated through her, making any motion she made excruciating. It did not help when Zonqua picked her up in his arms and ran with her toward one of the halls with both of their spears in the other hand. Behind them, more worms spilled from the hole as they ran toward the empty streets. Luckily, few had returned to the area. Yet those that lingered were only the guards trying to clear the areas. A few large units ran along the walls to reach the tower. The ground shook again, reminding everyone that the worst was yet to come.

As Zonqua ran into another plaza with more of the worms coming into view, he felt relieved as the sound of furious cawing rose from overhead. Lugna descended from over the wall, slashing into two of the creatures before lowering her body before Zonqua. The saddle was already set with supplies; he wondered if Baltik had thought ahead. Climbing onto the mount, he took up the reins and placed the spears in the saddle sheath before they tore off over the walls.

Now heading for the city edge, Zonqua and Nuyani could see the towering creature once more making its way toward the city. Evidence of the initial repulsion showed the worm was unearthed with large dirt hills reaching toward the sky. With the worm advancing, the outer wall had been broken down. Nuyani watched as she saw distant fire spells upon the worm, from flame to lightning. Even cold did nothing to slow the creature. Every action from the city guards was brushed away like water drops. It was clear that there was an effect on the creature from the erect barriers.

The pungent smell of rot filled the air. Yellow streaks clashed with the creature's brown shell. Zonqua said nothing, keeping his eyes to the south.

I will stop you, Nuyani thought as she glared at the worm. Feeling more of her strength returning, the two managed to get to the outer wall and down the side before sprinting off into the desert, heading south. They cleared hut after hut, along with the few spots of grass in the area. Many homes were now sinking into the earth as animals roamed freely. Spots of turned-up soil showed signs that the worms had also surfaced and attacked the single homes. Even as the city began to grow smaller behind them, Nuyani could feel the pulse of the shards growing. Her own core seemed to react more to them than she knew. Her heart pounded as she wondered what would happen if the barrier reached them.

As the worm continued to advance into the city, another blue glow erupted from the tower, bringing a silhouette to the stone and parasite. The barrier raced through the area and collided with the colossal parasite before crushing its head into the rest of its body and sending the carcass rolling further into the desert. The magic continued to expand further, passing over its body and reducing it to a shell as the same fate met every other worm within the barrier's reach. Worry collected on Nuyani's face as she watched the ethereal construct close the distance between the city and them within a few breaths. Nuyani tried to reach her core and synchronize with Lugna to move faster, but it did not matter as her view was filled with the burning light as it passed over them. Her core reacted on its own, with a barrier erupting from it and engulfing them all. They were suspended in the air as Nuyani's body was wracked with pain, sending spasms throughout her being.

All that raced through her mind was her wish to escape. The area around them warped and darkened as blackness enveloped them before taking their view, before draining into the middle of the center and revealing sunlight once more. With the sudden strain on all their senses, they all fell unconscious in the desert. Yet there was a thrum sitting on her core. Unaware of their situation, Nuyani felt her body being lifted and placed somewhere as her arms grew tight behind her back.

Before her eyes could open, a voice said, "*Prameif.* (Sleep)." The thrum fell over Nuyani and Zonqua, keeping them unconscious.

Ch. 9 Mutual Benefit

The rocking was the first thing to stir Nuyani as she groaned from her body's dull pain still radiating through her. As she raised her hand to rub her head, Nuyani realized that she was swaying, and a soft breeze met the back of her arm. With the soft crunch of sand beneath turning wheels reaching her ears, Nuyani's eyes shot open. They saw the inner canopy of a wagon. Her head flung up from her seat, not knowing where she was or where her blade had gone.

A soft chuckle then met her ear as Nuyani found she was not alone. To her side was Zonqua lying unconscious with his head resting in the lap of a woman. She sat on the bench stroking the man's hair as his headwrap lay on the floor along with Nuyani's arm guards and bracelet. The woman exuded confidence in her smirk and her posture as she kept her legs crossed and her free arm resting against the wagon wall. The woman looked to be around Nuyani's age and had sharp black eyes, a thin nose that broadened at the base, and luscious lips. Her long dreads dangled to the side, spilling out of a blue head wrap. She wore simple wooden earrings with the symbols of Do'alm and Do'alc carved into opposite sides of their coin shape. She wore a strange red tunic beneath her leather breastplate with a plunging front showing breast stretching the fabric and reaching only to her mid-rift, protecting little of her. Along both of her bare arms were circlets of gold, silver, or iron with precious stones or magic gems embedded in the metal. She even sported several rings covering almost every finger. Around her neck sat an obsidian stone polished smooth, sitting in the center of a golden medallion hanging low enough to reach her cleavage.

Around her waist, she wore a leather belt instead of a sash engraved with repeating symbols of the god and goddess as pouches sat on the side. Covering her legs was a long green skirt with dark brown boots poking out of the bottom.

Nuyani narrowed her eyes at the woman, wondering why they were there. The woman continued to smile at her, showing she did not see her as a threat. Worse yet, Nuyani was certain she was not. With a weakened thrum barely rising above a mumble, Nuyani could feel the echoes of edria radiating from the strange woman. The priestess thought back to her old friend Lamoy, one of the few huntresses from the drylands and a leader of her own party.

The sense of danger flared in Nuyani's mind as she studied the woman's demeanor. With a well-toned physique showing that she was not shy from labor or battle, it felt as though she were in the presence of a blade jaw lying down but eyeing you all the same. The priestess reached out with little control of her edria and tried to create a construct around the bracelet. In an instant, the woman released her own thrum from a simple ring covering the entire wagon with an invisible barrier suppressing Nuyani's magic before another ring then commanded the air to lock around her. Nuyani's eyes opened wide for a moment before looking at the woman with a glare.

The strange woman lifted Zonqua's head and sat him down while sitting forward and grabbing the bracelet. She narrowed her eyes from the small crystal to Nuyani's as she looked her in the eyes. In the low-lit space, Nuyani could see the gleam of her burning eyes on the woman's face and metal pieces. Her captor then fed a thrum into the small bracelet, revealing the nimcha. The woman looked at the weapon as if it were a rare item, mostly focused on the rounded guard and pummel. She then looked at Nuyani with a widening smile before it became a chuckle. She released Nuyani from her hold as she inspected the weapon.

"[He never travels with simple company]," the woman said. "[What is your name?]" Her voice was playful and soft.

With all her confidence and effort not to become rude, the priestess replied, "[Nuyani. Who you?]" Her inflexion at the end sounded a little more childish to Nuyani than she had wished, but the language still eluded her somewhat.

The woman's eyes lit up as though she gained a new secret, and she looked at Nuyani with a mischievous grin. "[Blessed by the goddess, Nuyani. I am Walgo.]" Nuyani blinked and, for a moment, remembered the name from Baltik mentioning her and Zonqua looking to keep the subject vague. "[From that look, you've at least heard of me. Your speech tells me you aren't a native of Tuikon altogether. Where are you from?]"

Nuyani was silent as she tried to look for the words. She looked about and gripped the edge of the bench. Unsure how to answer, Nuyani was not certain they were safe and considered her options: fighting the woman instead of answering. With the pause taking too long, she answered, "[N-north.]"

The woman nodded her head as if regarding a child's wild stories. "[North of North? That's a far way away from here. Where would that be?]" Nuyani blinked and shifted in her seat as she tried deciphering the woman's words. "[Well, I guess your lessons aren't finished just yet.]" The woman then released a thrum into the hilt, returning it to a bracelet, and handed it back to her. She then looked to the front end of the wagon, where the rest of their items were. Nuyani looked at the woman and then at Zonqua. Catching her prying eyes, the woman wore a prideful smirk as she placed two fingers to her lips and then pressed them against Zonqua's as the man remained unconscious.

A pinching sensation rose in Nuyani as she shifted in her seat again. Her eyes darted from the front of the wagon to the woman's grin and back. A chuckle rose from Walgo. "[Not mine, girl. Just another story.]" The woman's demeanor changed as she looked down at the man with a smile, still holding good memories and pain. Nuyani's brow furrowed. She looked back at their luggage. Her face grew hot as she felt like she was watching another couple having a moment.

Before the situation became awkward, the canopy flaps opened, and a man wearing a red headwrap and shawl covering his face poked his head inside. "[We are reaching the entrance]," the man said, completely ignoring Nuyani and taking his head back out of the wagon.

[Entrance?] Nuyani questioned, trying to understand what they meant.

"[Good. We are here now]," Walgo said as she rose to move to the end of the wagon. Still needing to bend low to keep her head from touching the ceiling, she exited the wagon and dropped down, showing an auburn glow to the sky above the sands. With a quick glimpse, Nuyani saw several men all wearing mismatched armor and weapons as they kept their faces covered by shawls. The woman then opened the flap and waved for Nuyani to join her. Nuyani reattached the bracelet and donned her armguards before exiting the wagon again. When she hopped down from the wagon, she found the woman waiting beside her.

Looking around, Nuyani saw mostly men and guards in the caravan as they approached a lone plateau. Along the path, banners with a black symbol of what Nuyani thought to be an animal's head were hung from pillars that held up the stone. Distant lights of the fading day showed through the gaps of hundreds of pillars along the sides. Their path was well-worn and free of most sand as it dug further into the ground. Slowly, the lights died out, and the further they traveled into the depths, the darkness. The others in the caravan created wisps to follow the path and veered a little to the left. When Nuyani reached the turn, she wondered what led down the other path. Her weakened thrum only allowed a short distance to sense things.

She could feel a trace of a small thrum lining the dirt. Trying to extend her magic toward the dirt, she winced but managed as something glimmered in the blue light. *This is the safe way,* Nuyani thought only to question what may be on the other side if they had to mark their road.

When Nuyani looked forward, she found the other woman looking at her with a curious smile. She froze for a moment, wondering if Walgo would say anything, but the woman turned around instead. *I don't trust you,* Nuyani told herself as she looked at her. After some time, the group then reached a circular opening in a stone wall reaching the ground. With a gradual descent, Nuyani wondered how far below the surface they traveled. The air remained moist, and the smell of dew wafted into Nuyani's nose, making her realize how parched she was. When the group entered through the opening, Nuyani looked about, seeing different levels of naturally formed ramps making up the cavern as tents strewn on nails embedded into the stone took up most of the room. Some areas only had tarps to separate different sections. They descended one of the ramps to a lower level. Nuyani caught sight of another opening going deeper into the cavern with little light. Just from focusing on her eyesight, she saw trees in the distance. She watched as a pair of men emerged from the dark carrying what looked like a small charge horn but without the hump and only one pair of eyes.

Though the man carrying the creature was large, the animal on his back was at least twice as heavy. Her attention broke away from the hunters as she saw some of the young children running her way to greet the party. There was a peculiar air about it, making Nuyani think of her father's hunting party and how the village would greet those who returned. It was crowded with at least a few hundred just in the front alone. Walgo waved to the few smaller children while other adults greeted her with the usual phrases Nuyani understood. Some people glared at Nuyani as though she were a threat before speaking to Walgo in whispers. Giving a few commands, the traveling party slowly broke apart as lone riders on the nogowesa moved to the sides, and the kurru led wagons to other areas where the wagons could settle. Nuyani then looked at the low basin where some water started collecting.

"[How? The water?]" Nuyani questioned. The forest and lake below ground were the strangest things to Nuyani, seeing that most of the plants she knew relied on the sun. The water did not seem so odd as water reached any place it could, but what was odd to her was the lack of insects she would've expected to come from such a collection.

At the water's edge, however, there seemed to be people using another edragaurio. From what she could tell, it was around hip height and about as wide as her torso. As slow waves of edria emerged unseen, they were only revealed by the lines rippling across the water. *It's cleaning it,* Nuyani thought for a moment. It took a moment for her to see that many of the others were looking at her with weary glances before leaving. It did not take long for Walgo, Nuyani, and the two guards following them to reach another tent far larger than the others. When they reached the tent flaps, Walgo stopped for a moment and waited for one of the guards to hand her Nuyani bags.

"[My things,]" Nuyani said, but Walgo wore a coy look on her face and strolled into the tent. *Why does she want to speak to me alone? Where is Zonqua?* Nuyani thought as she went in. Once inside, Nuyani saw the room was set up more like a study in the library, aside from a few clothes sitting atop one of the large chests tucked into a corner. A bedroll sat on the opposite side of the tent. An edragaurio remained suspended overhead. It was another figure of the goddess outstretching her hand toward the sky as a small sphere of light shined from the palm. In the center was a round wooden table with several maps, books, scrolls, and writing utensils scattered across the surface. Nuyani wondered what the woman was planning and remembered she was considered a bandit.

By the great lord, if I weren't with Zonqua would she have killed me? Nuyani thought for a moment. *Or does she think I'm high born?* Remembering her eyes were a trait like some well-off families, Nuyani contemplated the meaning as Walgo sat down and placed the spear and bags beside the table.

The bandit leader had spoken to another woman beforehand who seemed to be working on one of the scrolls. She left the tent instead, not batting an eye at Nuyani. When the priestess turned back to the bandit, Walgo patted the table before her with a smile. Taking this as an invitation, Nuyani sat down on the cushion opposite of her.

"[I know you know little, but there can still be ways to speak]," Walgo said as she propped her head up with her elbows planted on the tabletop. Nuyani looked at her for a moment, trying to decipher the woman's reasoning.

She felt like prey waiting for charge horns to trap her on all sides. Her biggest problem was that she was already in the middle of it all.

The woman then pointed to the map and set her finger on Giode. "[This place]," Walgo started. "[How'd you escape?]" The bandit then reached over the side of the table and retrieved a figure of a worm the size of her thumb before placing it on the table next to the city she initially pointed out.

Nuyani mulled over her words as she noticed Walgo place the figure turned on its side instead of reeling up like a snake. The woman then continued to retrieve different pieces and place them in various locations on the map before her, but only for the northern section of Tuikon. Nuyani recognized Giode. What made her eyes widen were the dozens of cities and villages where Walgo continued to place worm pieces. Closer to the center of the desert, there were more cities, at least citing the worms, while several villages fell to them.

"[Escape? Escape? Leave?]" Nuyani said as she looked at the woman. The woman nodded as she started placing new pieces on the map. Each piece was of Nogowesa and their riders in pairs and facing one another. Knowing too little to explain the story as she saw it, Nuyani created her constructs and showed her and Zonqua surrounded by the town guard from her point of view. Walgo's face first went from excitement to fear, seeing Nuyani's sudden abilities as though she recognized the trapper they faced. She became more composed as the battle started. The snap of the ethereal threads, the dance of their weapons, and the sudden rise of the worms played before her. Soon, Nuyani went through the entire ordeal of crumbling stones, crawling parasites, and crowds of people all fighting for survival. As she went through her memories, Nuyani soon came upon the scene of the bodies found in the wall paths of the city, but no worms. Walgo narrowed her eyes, which seemed to indicate she thought it odd as well. It was confirmed as Nuyani was eventually blinded and knocked off the wall by someone at the entrance.

The memory then cut to her in Zonqua's arms as more swarms surrounded them. In a final effort, she connected with Zonqua, and together, they activated the barrier leading to the tower. With her memory growing hazed once more, she only saw Zonqua trying to fix her core before carrying her away from the area. Soon, they were riding Lugna and away from the city. Her memory then blacked out as the last thing she saw was the sweeping wave of edria rushing toward them. Nuyani ended the memory. The woman stared at Nuyani with a look of astonishment. Nuyani felt heat rising in her face as she wondered why the woman was staring at her for so long.

When Walgo took a deep breath, the woman looked at the table at the one city that did not fall among the others. "[Do'alc bless us all, you... You control the crystals]," Walgo said as she looked at Nuyani. "[Zonqua does not keep normal company.]" The flaps to the tent then opened, and the woman who had left earlier returned with a gourd and two cups. Nuyani felt a soft thrum rising from the gourd and looked at the woman, wondering what was in the drink. The woman still paid her no mind as she placed the cups on the little table surfaces that remained exposed before pouring cyder into both, then corked the gourd and placed it on the table. When the tent flaps closed, the woman created a barrier around them that hummed with a similar thrum to the shawled man at the caravan.

"[I want you to commit this to memory then, Nuyani. I think you will be the best thing to happen to this country in the past decade. If you control the shards as you've shown me, then Zonqua will have a lot of 'help' on my part]," Walgo said. Nuyani blinked, not understanding a single word the woman said. She did get the feeling that there was a declaration made which she was not sure was good or bad. The bandit leader continued to look Nuyani over before she pointed to the map. "[North, right?]"

Nuyani stared at her with a blank expression. She was not certain what this woman wanted from her. It was odd to her that Walgo was asking so many questions of her. She asked questions before Zonqua could answer or interpret what she was saying. Sensing her distrust, Walgo smiled, trying to persuade her for the better. "[Why be cautious now? You've told me enough already.]"

"[Where is Zonqua?]" Nuyani asked. She kept her eyes locked and unyielding to the woman. Though, she was certain her weakened state could do nothing to keep Walgo from beating her. The bandit leader's smile deepened as she raised her chin and placed both hands on the table before sweeping them outward, knocking away some of the small figurines and marking the placement of units and nests. Nuyani watched as the wooden pieces fell to the floor. The woman held a glare despite her smile. The thrum raced through Walgo at a pace matching much of Nuyani's, but only a thin wave radiated from the woman's core and passed over her. The bandit leader was trying to get a read on her. Nuyani dampened her core, trying to hide her strength, though she was certain Walgo already knew. Seeing a competition would not benefit her situation, Nuyani refrained from letting her anger get the better of her. "[Where is Zonqua?]" Her voice grew more confident as she looked at the bandit leader.

Walgo sighed and looked at the drinks, which were still waiting to be emptied. Her smile remained, but Nuyani did not bother to follow her gaze. With only an afternoon, she was already certain the bandit leader was only asking questions or leading her on to get more information than would be safe. Nuyani did not know what she would have that would jeopardize her life until she remembered Zonqua's warning.

Her ember eyes widened as she recalled his construct, showing that some chose to sell people as well. With her abilities, the very cities could be in danger or saved. Nuyani was now taking deep and measured breaths.

"[Take a drink]," Walgo said as she picked up one of the cups and downed it in a single gulp. Nuyani looked hesitantly at the cup only to feel the thrum of the woman grow faster and stronger, though not to any abnormal degree.

Is she being forward? Nuyani wondered, feeling some frustration. The woman then looked at Nuyani with a smirk and narrowed eyes. Walgo reached for the second cup and downed it as well before setting both on the table and refilling them. Grabbing her cup once more, she held it up to her lips before narrowing her eyes in an exasperated gaze toward Nuyani. After the brief pause, the bottom of the cup rose, and she had her third. Nuyani could feel nothing change in her from the initial drink nor when she sent a thrum through the cups and gourd housing the liquor. Her mouth twisted as she realized she was already giving in to the woman's taunts. As she reached for the drink and took a sip.

As if the cool liquid was turning into soothing energy, it rushed down her through with a brisk touch before settling in her stomach and warming her body. With the subtle thrum, it even began to strengthen her core. Nuyani held out her empty cup, looking for another helping. The woman smiled with a victorious grin on her face as she poured another. Nuyani felt hesitant for a moment but realized that she was letting her thrum radiate like a fire's light.

Shaking her head, Nuyani cleared her thoughts, ignoring the faint burn at the back of her throat. The priestess glared at the bandit, determined to get her answer. "[Where is Zonqua?]" Nuyani then stood. Walgo then looked to the side, shook her head, and stood as well.

"[He's healing, Nuyan]i," Walgo said as if it were obvious. "[He was hurt. Not you, though.]"

Nuyani froze, recognizing the word hurt as she looked at the woman. "[How?]" Walgo looked at her gilded hand as if scrutinizing the jewelry before opening her palm and creating a construct of what she saw. It was her, Zonqua, and Lugna sprawled in the sands near a small village still in view of Giode. Smoke climbed from the far-off city, but it still stood. A faint tremble rose in Nuyani, and she fought the sensation from making her handshake. She kept her gaze from meeting Walgo's eyes. She did not want to give a hint of weakness, not to her. Sending a soothing thrum through her own body, Nuyani managed to beat back a tremble. Flashes of pincers and worms tearing into civilians made her stomach twist. She started to wish she had taken a second drink.

Her eyes went back to the construct, which showed Zonqua had landed on a stone with some blood trickling into the sand around his head. Upturned dirt surrounded all of them as their belongings were scattered further ahead. They did not just appear but were thrown from her teleportation. Nuyani tried to search her own memories, mostly to stop looking at the city. A small question rose, making her wonder if she would ever see one that did not fall apart. When nothing came to her, it only left questions.

"[Now then]," Walgo said as she ended the thrum and walked around the table until she came to Nuyani's spear. With a swift thrum coming not from her hand but from near her lower leg, the spear was wrapped in edria and levitated to the woman's hand. She then smiled and sauntered toward the entrance as Nuyani watched her for a moment before she hurried to catch her. When the priestess exited the tent, she tried to find Walgo only for a figure cloaked in black with gold embroidery on the edges of his shawl and sleeves to reach toward her with a sphere of edria large enough to encase her. Nuyani's eyes widened at the sudden ambush and the fact that the thrum was stronger than normal. With a wave of his hand, he raked the air with his hand toward his back as the sphere flew forth and into a cleared space that had seamster and seamstresses, cleaners, and workers only a moment ago. Nuyani wondered what was happening for a moment until she was tossed to the dirt. Anger grew in her as she looked around. There were two more figures standing on opposite ends of the rounded stage.

Guards stood at the edge of the cleared space as the three figures worked together to keep Nuyani bound. The rapid thrum was evident enough that they were linked. Even more so, she was certain that the cloaked figures also had edrategria in their midst. With her spear missing and the ring she held shattered, Nuyani fed a thrum into her hidden bracelet as small white lights shimmered over the ground's surface.

Trying to summon the nimcha, a softer thrum was released as sent to her arm. It did nothing to harm her. Instead, the thrum was severed, and Nuyani lost control of the nimcha. The lights no longer showed, and when she turned to face the assailant, one was already sending a sphere of edria toward her.

Nuyani coated her own hand with magic and swung at the projectile. Countering the spell, it was sent back to the caster only to phase into his body. Nuyani could feel the thrum lessen as the next two started lifting strange knives before conjuring their own spheres. Nuyani twisted around, dodging the second sphere approaching her left while facing the third, creating her own sphere of edria, and firing it back at the last figure blasting through his construct. The man reeled back for a moment, standing his ground, until the sphere of edria collided with his stomach, sitting him on his rear end. Nuyani remembered Zonqua mentioning her strength and wondered if she did too much damage as she had cracked a brick wall before.

Her worries proved unfound as the man breathed heavily and maneuvered to stand. The priestess did not wait as the last standing figure was preparing to attack. The echoes of his thrum were weaker than before but still seemed strong enough to do harm. Turning to face his attack, Nuyani stopped and leaped backward, seeing that there was a fourth person trying to attack her with her spear. Terror colored Nuyani's face as she saw Walgo pass by with the tip of her blade piercing the air. Nuyani dodged backward once more as a follow-up to the weapon's backend streaked across her view. With a second chance, Nuyani then sent a thrum into the bracelet once more and summoned the nimcha. The blade sprung forth as if thrown from its small confines.

As Walgo turned the spear for a second thrust, Nuyani gripped the blade and swung it in a rising arch, knocking away the bandit's second attack. This did not deter Walgo as she merely pressed the shaft into Nuyani's side and pushed her. She was not alone in her attack as one of the remaining figures fired more spheres.

Why are they only attacking with spheres? Nuyani wondered as she used her better speed to evade both attacks and slipped through Walgo's left arm.

The woman whirled around and pointed the spear tip at Nuyani while taking a low stance. The thrum of the other three then reconnected and strengthened its radiance. The others started cheering for Walgo and the cloaked figures, with a few cheering for Nuyani. Bright born was cheered repeatedly, but Nuyani had yet to know they meant her. As the others prepared themselves for another attack, Nuyani sent an arching wave from her blade toward Walgo instead. The blue arch twisted and wrapped around the woman a few feet away from the bandit before fading altogether. Nuyani did not feel or see a single thrum emit from her to block the attack. The entire time she was with the bandit leader, it never seemed as though she was completely forward about her strength. Nuyani was now narrowing her eyes at Walgo with exasperation.

Instead, she turned her next attack toward another of the cloaked fighters, who seemed to be hiding from the fight. She pointed her blade at the man and created a javelin instead of an arch. The ethereal force sailed faster than any other spell but passed through the man as if he were not there. Feeling a faint thrum coursing through the area, she was certain he wasn't. Nuyani remembered then that the performers at the lone plaza used the same tricks. Her mind wondered how many people knew such tricks as she resorted to the same. First on her list were illusions. Copying the rhythm as she remembered, there were four of Nuyani. Even Walgo seemed surprised, though it was not effective in stalling her as Nuyani sliced at her, trying to force her back. The woman dodged backward with a reinforced leap.

The group did not bother to blind fire at the copies; instead, they chose to send a full thrum radiating through the area to dispel the illusion. Nuyani did not falter as she lunged for one of the men. With a stronger thrum directed at him, she created a wall before him as she pushed forth. The wall of edria swept him away and falling to the side. No noise was made, making Nuyani wonder if the other side had a long descent.

Nuyani darted to the edge only to find shadows, then turned to the others, who only wore wry smiles on their faces as they looked at her. "Do you not care?" she asked the others. Answered with a simple flash of light nearly blinding her, Nuyani created a barrier around her body, trying to collect herself. She increased the thrum, hardened her concentration, and waited for the effect to wear off. Nuyani gripped the nimcha as tightly as she could and looked through a narrowed eye trying to see the others. To no surprise, they continued to attack her, riddling her defense with simple spells. Nuyani concentrated on the barrier, lessening the ripples of each impact. With a deep breath, her barrier then burst outward, covering the space and dissipating the blinding spells and their collected thrum. Her will only focused on keeping the others from using their spells, which made the woman laugh as she took up another stance, readying herself for a fight.

The priestess lunged toward the woman, trying to use her unusual speed to carry her through the battle. The others did the same, surprising her. Nuyani lunged at Walgo, seeing the spear as the most difficult weapon to face. The bandit leader lunged forward and stabbed, aiming for her chest.

Nuyani dodged to the side while striking at the spearhead to deflect it in the opposite direction. Despite her natural speed allowing her to move fast enough to parry arrows, Walgo was keeping pace with Nuyani's slashes. Worse, she was exchanging attacks and pushing her away. The priestess's confidence waned as Walgo even began to knock the blade away.

The heavy blows and swift strikes of the spear were difficult for her to block. Often, Nuyani was forced to step back, and it only got worse as the last two figures joined. It took a moment, but Nuyani could feel that the others were still able to enhance their strengths even within the space of her thrum's radius. One of the figures tried to stab at Nuyani with the blade, only for her to parry the blow at the last moment and respond with a kick to his chest. The man fell backward with a loud grunt. Nuyani recovered quickly as the spearhead flew past her ear and cut into the shawl. If not for her edria filling the space, Nuyani was certain she wouldn't have known to dodge. She then twisted and rolled toward the fallen figure, snatching his strange dagger. With a closer look, the weapon looked like an animal horn with several horizontal striations running down the blade. It was slightly curved in shape, reminding her of her own ivory knife, but the hard steel made it look functional. Nuyani's attention, however, remained on her last two assailants. Even with the added support of the blade in hand, Nuyani felt it only gave enough power to stabilize her thrum, which was growing difficult to maintain as the battle went on. As Nuyani continued to swipe and dodge a flurry of attacks from the others, she found herself remaining on the defense.

The figure wielding his blade only came in on occasion, either trying to bait her attention or steal attacks to make openings for Walgo. Nuyani backed away as far as she could. With a brief pause, she considered her options. The nimcha was not meant for casting. At least, that was how it felt to Nuyani, but she tried to send a weakened sphere of edria toward the cloaked figure. With his own blade, he stabbed at her magic instead of defending. Pain radiated through Nuyani as the missile broke and the recoil struck Nuyani's core. Not relying on the weapon as a conduit, Nuyani was able to maintain the larger thrum, keeping the battle somewhat even. Walgo then lunged for another attack only to force Nuyani into the grip of the cloaked figure from which she stole the blade.

As he wrapped his arms around her, Nuyani tried to release another thrum but channeled through the ridged blade. She felt something familiar in the attack, something akin to Zonqua's curse. As her thrum passed through the blade, the hidden spell activated. Nuyani's own magic expanded into a sphere around her body. The cloaked man pulled away as she was enveloped. Nuyani could feel the thrum converted into a pattern she had not used before. Clouds formed within the sphere, soon followed by lightning. She looked about only to find the haze obscuring her view. Before she could understand what had occurred, Nuyani felt several shocks dance across her body. She screamed at the touch. Her mind went blank for a moment until the familiar pulse of the nimcha helped her to focus. Nuyani struggled as her body convulsed from the shocks, each one starting to make her black out. Most of her magic was being converted to the blade and its trap.

From outside of the spear, Nuyani's dome had dissipated, and the others gathered themselves. Even the fourth member of their side had returned. One of the figures stepped forward with his blade. "No. Wait till she learns," Walgo said. The man looked back at her then to Nuyani before lowering his hand and stepping back.

With her thoughts blinded by pain, Nuyani tried to focus on one thrum wavering in the blade. Gritting her teeth, her shriek ended, and she sent the pulse from her blade to the knife. Disrupting the flow of edria, she was able to cease control of her power and dispersed magic. Nuyani looked at the others with pain on her face as she tried to remain standing. The cloaked figures looked surprised as the Walgo merely started to chuckle. Nuyani found it difficult to release the strange blade as her fingers were fastened around the hilt. The others started to move forward, closing in on her. Nuyani lifted the nimcha with the tip pointed at Walgo. The woman smirked and shook her head. The bandit leader then thrust the spear with magic, reinforcing her movements. She became a blur as the spearhead raced past the blade and her head. Nuyani could not move. She could not think. The fight was over.

One of the children came by with a gourd, baring a soft thrum. To Nuyani's surprise, the others started to help her move. The figure she kicked laughed as he fought to loosen her fingers. Nuyani looked at her hand, seeing it did not do as she wished. She let out a sigh.

"[Are you done hazing her?]" Zonqua's voice called as he walked up the slope, meeting the area.

Nuyani looked at him in surprise. With a deep breath, she then asked, "[Why?]"

"[Your strength. They want to know]," the man said. Nuyani recognized the word "strength" and pieced together the rest. She scoffed and looked at the others with irritation in her glare as Walgo kept the same mischievous smile. There was a small boy with copper-colored eyes who looked at Nuyani with a sense of wonder. Nuyani looked down at the boy and wondered if he was one of the so-called high-born despite his worn attire.

Walgo then called out, "[All of you. Come to the tent. We'll speak more in private.]"

After a sip of the wine, Nuyani's thrum was rejuvenated allowing her to have more control. Nuyani then felt the pulse of her thrum deepen, making her wonder how much stronger it had gotten. *Great lord, what is she planning for me?* Nuyani questioned as they started toward the tent.

Once the tent flaps were closed, the idol's light extended and covered the room with a faded glow. The openings at the top, sides, and entrance were all lined with a blue tint and remained rigid. Nuyani sat next to Zonqua with her spear in her lap. She had already returned the nimcha to its crystal. The cloaked men sat on the sides, pouring drinks from their cups. It was both odd and distracting to Nuyani, witnessing the figures using their magic to make the cups phase through the shawls, releasing a soft thrum each time that radiated through the room. Walgo sat on the opposite end, looking down at the table as she did.

Zonqua looked at the two. Nuyani continued to eye her spear, thinking about her loss while Walgo put up a front. Though each of her jewelry had magic, Zonqua knew most of them were wards to keep magic from affecting her or the other gems for more offensive use. The man wondered if she would have won if the two were alone. Zonqua then scratched a faded scar running along his cheek, remembering his own bout with her.

Walgo then looked at him with a glare. "[You have a plan, now?]" Zonqua asked.

"[Yes. I will need you and the others to start clearing the roads]," Walgo said.

Zonqua blinked for a moment before trying to speak once more, "[Clearing roads? What do you mean?]"

Walgo stated. "[Well, while you were out on your own, roads have been getting cluttered with the worms. They'll need to be removed.]" She then turned to Nuyani. "[The best way to do that is to remove them with their weakness.]"

Zonqua glanced at Nuyani for a moment only to get her looking at him quizzically. "[What makes her the answer?]" *Nuyani, what did you show?* the man wondered. His heart started to race. With all Nuyani could do, there were both suitors and slavers that would buy her for enough coins to outfit a battalion or make a bandit group stronger than most.

"[Your interesting friend here can power the shards of cities]," Walgo said. The others all stopped and looked at both Zonqua and Nuyani. One of them coughed as his eyes bulged at the priestess. "[Well, she showed me how far her strength could reach. I hope few people know her strength. It would be troublesome if anyone knew too much about her.]" Another mischievous smile rose on the woman's face.

"[Why would you need our help? You have plenty of weapons and men to face the nokragga]," Zonqua asked.

"[Not without exposing myself to the other bandits in the area]," Walgo said. "[It wouldn't do me any good if my exhausted "resources" were preyed on by another group.]" Emphasizing resources, Zonqua felt as if she were both accusing him, insulting her men or if she were alluding to another source.

"[You're losing ground? Don't wrap us up in a turf war. There are more pressing matters than that]," Zonqua snapped.

"[I saw, and I agree]," Walgo said. "[But the cities will die if the routes aren't taken care of]," Walgo said as she started to look at Nuyani warily. "[Your company seems to have a lot more going on than I could imagine, and I don't need her bringing trouble here.]"

"[What do you mean?]" Zonqua asked.

"[You didn't see?]" Walgo asked and looked at Zonqua. "[She encountered one of the cultists during Giode's infestation. She was knocked down from the top of the wall. I'm surprised she can still stand. That, and you don't like them weak.]"

Zonqua opened his mouth, ready to protest as he narrowed his eyes but, instead, cleared his throat as he crossed his arms. "[You're saying a cultist was there? Why are you worried about them coming here or giving you trouble?]"

"[I don't need to deal with plague runners. I need goods. So far, she'll be the best target for them if another city fails to fall]," Walgo said. "[Besides, I will give you all supplies so long as you get rid of the worms. The best chance to do what you need and for me to get what I need. That sounds fair?]"

"[What makes you so sure we need anything?]" Zonqua asked. "[Is that really all you need?]"

The bandit leader rolled her eyes. "[Zonqua, she's already shown me enough to make her worth selling to every kingdom in Tuikon. Don't act like I can't just find that simple solution. I just want to make this a fair trade instead, or did you forget that you are still considered a traitor in both kingdoms?]" Her brow furrowed, and her calm demeanor shifted to managed rage. "[Honestly, I don't know why you stayed if you were done.]"

"[You play coy now? You gave me enough to get food for me and Lugna for a day. You charged me for the rest in leaving]," Zonqua said.

"[Well, that spear of yours wasn't cheap. Not as if you couldn't sell that]," Walgo said.

Zonqua released a sigh. He then looked at Walgo with a scrutinizing look. He then asked, "[You're waiting until now to start clearing the trade routes? You never wait if you have a solution.]"

"[No. I just happened to get an opportunity to make the greatest results]," Walgo started. "[We are going to burn them out.]"

"[To the sands, what do you mean burn them out?]" Zonqua said.

"[These, Zonqua,]" one of the other men said as he pulled out a water skin and placed it on the floor. He then emptied his cup once more before placing the cup beside the water skin. Once he undid the stopper, he poured a strange brown liquid into the bowl. It smelt as if wood sap was mixed with lard. He then conjured a small flame on the tip of his finger, colored orange. He then placed it in the liquid, and the flame grew. The growing flame changed color with a sapphire glow in the middle and emerald along the edges. Another of the men then removed a clay pot with a sealed top from his sleeve.

Nuyani looked at the pot, feeling the faint pressure emerging from it. Hidden in the cloak of the man, she could not sense it before. The man holding the small clay pot looked at Nuyani, noticing her glare.

"[Hard to get anything by her]," the man said as he hooked a finger around a horn-like protrusion too small for a decent handle. The man then sat up and turned away from the others before pulling hard enough for the clay seal to break. With a release of his thrum, the seal was pushed down with his power. The man then turned around to the others with both hands firmly on the clay pot. The other man pushed the bowl of flame closer. When the clay pot was up-turned, the man took away the lid and allowed a smaller worm to fall inside. Nuyani looked ready to attack, but only for the third man to raise a hand before Nuyani did anything. The worm fell into the flame and started to blacken even in its descent.

The creature was charred once it reached the bottom of the bowl. The man who presented the oil then took a piece of paper that held no power or influence and waved its edges through the flame a few times before waving his hand as well. Nuyani stared with eyes growing wider. The man used a simple flame, yet the pattern of its thrum changed to something safer. Her curiosity compelled her as she moved toward the bowl and held it in her hand. She did not feel the heat.

"We can save them," Nuyani said. A gleeful look came over her as she looked back at the table where a few of the worms remained in the cities. "[We stop nokragga.]"

Walgo's eyebrows climbed high. "[She seems ready]," the bandit leader said. "[So, what about you?]"
Zonqua was looking at the cool flame as well, his mouth agape with wonder. "[Do you have enough for a nest?]" Zonqua asked.

"[We don't know yet. I think we should try it out]," Walgo said as she gave a wry smile.

Ch. 10 Burning the Plague

The stars all seemed brighter than usual as Nuyani fidgeted in her bedroll. At sunrise, they planned to attack a nest for the first time. She gripped the cover in her arms, wondering how the battle would be fair with the strange oils that were made. The clawing and clattering of the creatures could end. The fallen cities could end. There was now a better chance to answer the worms and their infestation. As she heard her heart pound in her chest, Nuyani released a thrum to try and soothe her nerves. The coaxing did little to settle her mind. Fingers tracing her new rings, given by Walgo, Nuyani wondered how well things could go on their test trial. She looked over to the others and saw Zonqua sleeping in his own roll but wearing a similar attire as the other casters she fought with.

The other three had accompanied them as well. Two of them were asleep, with the last one on guard, watching and tending to the flame. Annoyed that even in the past few days, the men were unwilling to share their names, Nuyani took to giving them nicknames based on their actions. It even helped to pass the time. She named the current caster on guard "Caution." She did not like to name him so but, compared to most of their actions and refusal to speak with her less it be about magic or different tactics, he always checked beneath things twice and sent thrum of edria outward to make sure there were no spirits or other animals that lingered about. Though she had to be careful to survive, she often grew annoyed and aware of his presence with the constant use of magic. If not for his own edragaurio enhancing his magic, she wondered if he would be tired within the day's first hour.

A soft thrum then passed through; the radiating from the same direction as Caution. Nuyani sighed, knowing that if she were asleep, it could wake her. Her attention was then turned to the others she called "Murmur" and "Rude." Both seemed to be asleep but often ignored Nuyani in different ways. The first man would dismiss her for his personal work but did so to everyone as the other would more or less direct her in working his items. Though Nuyani was there for assurance, the man thought of her as the camp hand as a woman. Nuyani challenged him on his attempt to dominate her actions, only for him to back off.

It was a troubling few days, but there were several things to learn about the bandits and the lands. Many tunnel networks ran through the desert, carved mostly by underground rivers where few worms were ever noted or seen. This was also the best place for most animals to reside, bringing game as the forest also remained. Most of the people knew of the caverns from the previous war, and Nuyani wondered why the other races had left if they knew there were places to hide. In her attempts to converse with Zonqua, she learned that humans would keep entering with armies to drive them out until they sealed the paths to the outside, at least paths that no human could reach on their own. There were constant worms as well, but none of them were able to crawl to that level. What disgusted Nuyani was that there were other women in the bandit camps who performed the same service to her men as others did in the cities. Before she could question Walgo's choices in leadership, she also knew that many of the people there were refugees. Going from a city condition to a worse one did not leave a lot of choices for many people. It also shocked her to see a girl entering womanhood already in service as the others were. It was just another reason to Nuyani for the group to leave as soon as possible.

Nuyani held her medallions in her hand, praying for her people and the success of their goal. It annoyed her to no end that the constant need to move on was a constant rush during the morning. Zonqua knew Nuyani prayed as well but seemed to agree. As she recited her prayer to Kelvert, pretending to sleep, she released her portion of her spirit. She did wonder if her own wishes would reach the haflaj. Contemplating her own spirit's travel, she then wondered about the effects of the desert. In entering, Nuyani could feel her strength lessen from the presence of prutosa swirling about. Now, it felt like the pressure weighing on her core was gone. The feeling of a present chill had lessened to the night breeze on her skin.

Great Lord, I do not hear the others but, I wish you well, Nuyani thought.

With the night still young, Nuyani turned over in her bed roll and looked out into the open desert. In the distance, a small circle of silver lights danced to an unheard melody. Nuyani watched the display as their haunting lights released soft thrums. Trying to keep her mind off sleep itself, she focused on the circle until she dozed off. Daytime soon arrived, and Nuyani had awoken with the group breaking down the camp and eating a little on the way to their destination. This time, Nuyani had her own mount, a nogowesa with light khaki feathers and red spots dotting her pelt. She called it Caluu. With a lighter frame, the animal often outran the others, but

Nuyani managed to slow the nogowesa to run along with the others.

Crossing through the desert, they eventually made their way to a series of sand dunes out in the open. The nearest outcrop of rocks or a town were several days away. However, Nuyani did ride ahead, letting her thrum warn them of any swarms moving toward them. It did not take long for her to feel the entire area teeming with worms. Just as they met the first dune, the group stopped, and Nuyani connected her thrum with the others, allowing them all to sense the same threat as she did. They then separated into two different groups. All dismounting and slowly stocking toward the epicenter of the spiritual surge, the thrill she once felt disappeared. Only her heart's nervous, rapid beating remained as they stocked a predator's nest. Whether it was her heightened senses or the pus she expected saturated the ground, Nuyani noticed every step met a firm surface. Even the grains of the dune seemed sturdier than usual. It became apparent as she looked down and found that some of her steps did not leave prints in the dirt. Zonqua took notice as well but waved so they could keep moving.

If the flame kept burning, Nuyani wondered how much of the ground would also catch fire. Once the parties made their way through the dunes, they saw a cavern open to them and a gradual slope entering it. Nuyani looked closely at the entire area in front. At least two acres of the surface were a porous surface of solidified pus with random smaller worms slinking in and out. Nuyani scowled as the faint stench of rot met her nose. The cavern itself was not naturally formed as the same sick porous surface of yellow also covered the underside of the cavern top. At the front were a few larger human-sized parasites guarding heaps of bodies, whether whole or in parts. What Nuyani was certain was that they were all dead. She kept scrutinizing the area as she remained hidden behind the dune. The energy was concentrated in several spots around the area.

She looked on, wondering what was holding so much energy, but little seemed different. On the other side, however, the other casters began to work. One of the men pulled out several small crystals from their sleeve. Each one had a metal band molded and wrapped around them. He then dropped one onto the dune. With a quick thrum, the sand then shifted and collected beneath the crystal, forming a snake that became animated as if it were living. The sand figure then slithered to the man's feet before another of the casters took out an urn and placed it atop the snake. The snake slithered toward the cavern entrance with another thrum radiating from one of the casters. The snake moved quickly, passing over the network of small tunnels. They all watched closely, hoping the nests would be as easy as the pit. Nuyani's breathing halted as she gripped her spear. When the snake was at least a dozen paces away from the entrance, Nuyani could feel the prutosa beginning to surge. A ripple in the power rose and washed over the sand snake, making the construct fall apart and causing the crystal to enter one of the tunnels.

The caster then struck his leg as he reared his head back and turned. Nuyani was almost certain he was cursing under his breath as they looked on. Toward the opening, it seemed that the worms were now more alert as two human-sized parasites made their way toward the same location as the sand snake. Their widened legs danced across the surface of tunnels with ease, seeming to remain unhindered. Their pincers stayed low to the ground as they found the urn and started to push at it. It moved from side to side, but there seemed to be no issue. When the worms were done testing the foreign object, a smaller worm rose and tried to use its pincers to grab it as the larger counterparts returned to the dead they collected. As they did so, another worm exited the cavern and began to drag one of the bodies inside. Nuyani felt enraged as she watched the strange creatures work.

Nuyani then saw one of the casters waving toward them and saw the man create a simple sphere of fire. They then pointed to Nuyani to create a sphere of edria.

"[Why apart?]" Nuyani wondered as she looked at Zonqua.

"[We weren't expecting that part, but your stronger thrum can break the pot, and they will light the oil. Keep us all hidden]," Zonqua answered. Nuyani understood for the most part as she then created a simple sphere of edria, keeping the thrum shallow so the worms would not expect it. One of the casters, sitting further in their position, then raised his hand as if ready to signal for them to fire. Nuyani sat up, looking at the small urn, and prepared the spell. With a swipe of the caster's descending hand, Nuyani released the sphere with a flash of light trailing toward the urn and shattering it. The flame came at a slower rate but connected with the liquid inside, causing it to ignite. Nearly every drop turned into a flame mid-air as they showered the pus and three worms. The larger creatures began to twist and turn about, attempting to rid themselves of the flames in their panicked dance, only to spread more onto the pus. The smaller worm continued to try to collect the shards even as its shell blackened.

Nuyani's eyes widened as she looked at the growing flame in a blue and green glow across the surface. The urge to cheer grew until the ground started to shift. A misshaped ring of sand started to spill onto the top as the pus around the growing flames receded from the area. Even the smaller worm, now broken into charred pieces, was pushed out of the tunnel with a rising pile of sand to follow. The area was aware of its dangers. The two other worms stopped moving as more began to exit the cavern and go to the same area for investigation. They were smart enough to remain at the perimeter until the fire burned out. Both Nuyani's side and the casters looked at one another, trying to think of what they should do next.

The flames soon died out, but the party of worms had grown outside. Nuyani then motioned with her hands as if she were reaching into her sleeve and removing an urn.

"[What are you planning?]" Zonqua asked. He looked at her as if she were about to do something crazy. The part he was starting to dread was that he would be right.

"[I run]," Nuyani said. The man's face froze for a moment as he looked at her.

"[Get the urn, and I will stop; hold the worms back. You will light it in the cavern, and we will follow to keep you safe]," Zonqua said. Nuyani nodded and repeated the action, waiting for the others to agree.

The other caster looked at Zonqua. Nuyani did not know the others' talents or gifts, but if none of the others had a way to do it, then she needed to act. The caster holding the urns then took another two out and rose. Understanding Nuyani's speed, he peered around the corner at the group of worms starting to spread out. He held out the urn as if he were ready to toss it a short distance. Nuyani kept herself in a low crouch. Their thrums started to race again, growing stronger by the second and sending ripples through the currents of prutosa. The signs of an enemy were clear to the worms now. The man tossed the urn across the space, sending it a quarter of the way between them. Nuyani darted for the container as Zonqua leaped up from the dust rising around him and released two spheres of condensed lightning clouds toward the worms.

Nuyani caught the urn in its lower arch as the two spheres of lighting met with the worms and expanded, covering the entire party. Flashes of light danced amongst the branching electric tendrils. Nuyani made her way toward the cavern, running with some difficulty on the spongelike ground but outrunning any surfacing worm. Just at the mouth of the cavern, a stream of prutosa rippled through the air descending from the ceiling. Nuyani leaned to the side as she felt her very core dull from the energy, and a chill ran through her body. A beam of light brighter than any construct struck the ground where she would have been, leaving a scorched crater in the dirt. Nuyani looked up with wide eyes another worm was taking form from the pus. A worm with a larger, flattened head like an angled shield was looking at her. Its four dark red eyes were placed together just below another opening above. Time slowed as she saw the whirling vortex of prutosa within the fifth eye. Spinning tendrils of blue and violet flame were contained within a thrum.

Magic? They have magic, Nuyani thought as she turned to the side to dodge another beam followed by a light radiating thrum. The energy struck the dirt once more and

Nuyani's speed proved her best asset as more of the strange worms formed from the walls and ceiling. Another thrum radiated toward them as lightning struck the worms, sending them into spasms, but still standing. Nuyani's heart raced. Scowling, she buried the panic threatening to rise and ran further into the cavern. Whether she found the right spot to start the fire no longer mattered. She had to try the flame or normal fire instead. Waves of prutosa washed over her as she went in. More worms appeared, forcing Nuyani to improvise with single-handed spear thrusts, shattering their shells.

As did the others, Zonqua whistled outside the cavern for Lugna to join him. With the nest stirred, countless worms appeared. The casters attacked with ice and lightning, hoping to keep worms from burning around them. Zonqua rode closer to the cavern entrance and encountered their new foes. There were only four, but he could feel the currents of prutosa flowing to them. As they did before, the creatures released streams of spirit toward the caster. Zonqua erected a barrier using both the synchronization with the others and his ring for power. The streams struck the barrier and danced over the surface like flames licking stone. Lugna was forced to circle about on the ground, releasing angry caws as she lashed at any parasites that rose. Before Zonqua could retaliate, an urn flew toward the four worms and was struck out of the air by one of the worms. It mattered little as it was followed by a flame sphere igniting the oil. The worms acted scurrying to the sides as they tried to evade the coming inferno.

To their misfortune, the flames caught on the ground and climbed, rapidly engulfing two of the worms. The others tried to attack once more, but spears of ice sailed forth and pierced their heads. Stronger or not, they went down. Zonqua gave a small sigh of relief only to realize that there were more, and Nuyani was alone. As he tried to steer Lugna toward the cavern entrance, half of the ceiling collapsed atop the flame, putting it out.

Zonqua raced forward and moved to the other side of the opening to create a barrier. He was not certain but knew that the worms had to feed the area with spirit. Expanding the defense to cover the ceiling surface, he kept the energy flow to a minimum, allowing only enough to keep the pus from changing form. Just outside of his reach, he saw the ground mold and rise once more. He expected another worm that could fire prutosa. What surprised him was instead a parasite nearly twice the length and size and arms that looked like maces were at the end of scorpion claws. The enormous worm slithered forth faster than any man could outrun and struck with both arms. A sharp cramp resonated through Zonqua. The barrier still held but Zonqua wondered how Nuyani would fair against both foes.

Nuyani had stopped already and was now fighting several worms in the area. With crystals all around, she often employed them to erect barriers, pushing away the worms and shattering their bodies when she had the chance. It was harder for her to ignore many of the remaining bodies, only for her to realize that they were kept to convert into smaller worms. The smell of rot was heavier than ever, making her head spin. Only the light of her magic-imbuing spear lit the crevices. Her breathing grew shallow, and her body became heavy. Every swing became an effort, and the clatter of legs and pincers echoed around her.

"Great lord, please guide me," Nuyani said as she swung once more.

Even with magic, she struck into the hide of a larger worm. The blade barely pierced the shell. The worm twisted to strike, knocking away the spear as it descended upon her. Desperate, Nuyani created a barrier between her and the flailing beast. She felt the wet splatter of pus stain her clothes as blue light highlighted the corners of pincers, claws, and shells. The barrier rippled from the strike of the creature. Nuyani stared on, feeling that this was all she could manage. Her heart pounded, nearly drowning out the noise surrounding her. As the creature's body rose to gain greater height and descend for another strike, Nuyani focused on her thrum, putting her entire being into her magic.

By the great lords light... Her mind echoed, and her magic responded.

Converted into ethereal spikes of light, they pierced through the larger creature and radiated through the area, skewering all the worms within a dozen paces. The other parasites stayed a distance away from the gleam. Nuyani breathed rapidly as she looked around. With a moment to think, she sat up, plunging her hands into the wet muck that covered her back and legs. All the pain was gone, and her mind felt clear.

The ground is wet. It's not hard like the other parts, Nuyani thought.

She then broke the urn and used another ring to ignite the oil. With the chance to flee, Nuyani grabbed her spear and raced toward the entrance as what first sounded like a distant crackle became a roar as the cavern was engulfed in the fire. Only a few of the parasites bothered with Nuyani, and most seemed interested in taking the bodies with them. Prutosa drained from the area as portions of sand began to fall from the ceiling. Nuyani continued to think at a faster pace than her body moved. She felt a sense of calm. Despite any parasite that approached, the lights acted as spears, skewering the weaker ones and lessening the flows of prutosa to the stronger versions in her stead.

This must be a spell. I don't know this one, though, Nuyani thought as she ran on. *Maybe… if there are storm spells for Do'alm and Do'alc, then I… made one. I made one for Lord Kelvert. Yes. A light spell for Kelvert.* Nuyani studied her situation. If her spell was good enough for the attacks on the worms, then maybe there were two methods to rid them of the worms.

Zonqua was nearing his end as the others battled surfacing worms, too preoccupied to fight against the growing number of parasites beating away at the man's defense. Zonqua kept himself steady as beads of sweat rolled down his brow. He then looked deeper into the cavern's darkness, hoping they did not risk their only chance. As a bright light began to rise from the depths, he wondered if it was the flame. With Nuyani's speed, she raced past them in a blinding eruption as her new spell killed and diced apart the worms in her wake. Zonqua looked back, seeing the blinding white light do the same to those in the open area. More sand fell, catching the caster's attention before he led Lugna away from the mouth of the cavern. The others did not wait as they raced toward the sides of the sand dunes where none of the flames bursting from the ground could reach them.

Even as emerald and sapphire flames surged meters into the air, the ground ahead caved in, forming a trench that deepened by a full story and stretched for several miles. Nuyani fell to the floor as she watched their work take place. Her body was wracked with pain as fatigue threatened to make her collapse. Even then, she grinned. Even a few worms who escaped at first seemed to die as they ceased to move before they too lit up from the flame.

"We've done it," Nuyani whispered as she laid on the ground breathing heavily. Her mind grew clouded as the thrum faded between them. Despite her new spell, Nuyani wondered if she could have created it on her own or if the thrum is so strong that she will make it. Just another question for her to ask when she could.

The party returned to a safe point where they knew they could recuperate with little trouble from spirits, animals, or worms. Nuyani fell asleep on her mount as Zonqua took up the reins. She was not the only one who felt exhausted as the others remained silent on the journey. They made their way toward an outcrop of stones protruding from the sand. Dismounting from their nogowesa, they kept their camp simple, only downing the saddles and bedrolls while keeping everything else packed away. Nuyani, once awoken, unraveled her bedroll and sat on the surface for a moment studying her edria. The thrum was stable and continuous, but her thoughts dwelled on the final spell. Her attention then turned to the center as a different lantern she had seen before was placed in the center by one of the casters. With a thrum, it created a light without a flame. Nuyani sighed, feeling relieved that they had managed to escape the worms.

"[We've managed a great deal. Bless the goddess, the oil works]," said the caster Nuyani knew as *Cautious*.

"[True. But now we know there are worse things to come]," said *Rude*. The man then lifted another gem with an iron ring around it. "Those worms now have their own magic and are growing resilient."

"[Resilient being the key word]," Zonqua interjected. "[Didn't know you picked up puppetry. They didn't seem to notice the snake.]"

"[That being said, perhaps another gem to solidify its forms or push against the worms, and we can send it further]," the last caster added.

"[Wet ground]," Nuyani said, getting the other's attention. "[Just wet ground.]"

Zonqua, who was closest to her, then asked, "[What do you mean "wet ground?"]" Nuyani looked at the man then wore a grim look on her face as she pointed to her brow. [*You don't know what you should share or not with them around,*] the man thought. [*Well, they aren't Walgo, but they are just as clever in many ways.*] Considering the option to share their thoughts, Zonqua nodded his head and allowed Nuyani to place her hand on his brow. The men already knew she was strong, but there was more to the situation. Nuyani rose, nearly stumbling on her footing before moving toward him and placing two fingers on his brow. The others watched as they saw both of their eyes light up and their expressions go blank. A thrum radiated between the two.

Nuyani's memories came forth, sharing her experience in the cavern. The firm press of the ground beneath her feet told her that the pus was covering most of the floor. Soon, the worms were attacking in such a large number that Nuyani could not press on them. "[Do'alc bless you, Nuyani]," Zonqua said as the sensations of fear lingered. Anxiety continued to climb as she went on fighting the worms. When Nuyani fell to the floor, and pus covered her clothing from the fall, she burst with a new light. Zonqua's eyes blinked at the sudden attack, skewering the larger worm with ease. [*That is something else we must discuss,*] Zonqua thought. Nuyani then looked to the ground, seeing that it was wetter than the other areas. A sense of calm had her as she remained in the light. Her thoughts became clear and set the nest aflame then and there. Nuyani ended the memory and backed away from Zonqua.

The man blinked, following her as it seemed that she did not want to share more. Only a glimpse into her mind revealed that she was as frightened as anyone else. [*I don't blame you, Nuyani. We must create another solution*], the man thought. Zonqua then turned to the others. "[She means that further inside, the pus isn't solid. The nests look like they're weaker closer to the center]," Zonqua added.

The other remained silent for a moment. Rude, then cut in, "[You two seem to have your own tricks. Is this woman a sage of Do'alc and Do'alm as well?]"

"[No]," Zonqua said dryly.

Murmur then said, "[What we need is a better way to get to that weakness. If we have to run into the caverns to get there, first, we'd need to ride into the very pit and back out. Speed is the essence for now, or we dig.]"

"[They just shared their thoughts without a word, and you still won't take a moment...]" Rude started but was interrupted.

"[A plague before us can be burned, and the girl has given us two options. Perfect the method is my only concern. Don't bother me with their relationship]," Murmur scoffed.

Nuyani blinked as the few words she understood told her that Murmur may have seen her in just as little light as Rude. Her thoughts on the matter were outweighed by the fact that he did have a point. They had barely accomplished their goal, but improvements were needed.

Caution then added, "[Send the flames with spheres of magic. Dig through the ground and pour it through the top. Get the hounds and control their minds to carry it with a timed spell.]"

The others looked at the man with mixed expressions. Rude leered at him as if ready to berate his colleague. Murmur stared maddeningly as he started to murmur once more. His thoughts spilled out in a low tone. Zonqua started to chuckle, which caught Nuyani off guard.

"[Great ideas. Better plans in minutes]," Zonqua said. "[What do we do to prevent the edria from being distorted? Do you have anything that could aid us in accomplishing that?]"

"[No]," Caution answered. He then looked at Zonqua with a gleam in his eye that gave a warning. "[We will have to report this to Walgo. She will want to know that spell of hers.]" Nuyani blinked and looked at the man quizzically as his tone held a sense of dread.

"[Wasn't that the idea to begin with?]" Zonqua said. "[We prove that the oil works…]"

"[Yes. In time]," Caution said bluntly. Zonqua and Nuyani looked at the man with curious glares. "[Right now, only a few rival groups have the strength and power to move about the desert and trade. This hands every abandoned route, due to the worms, to her and more control of the eastern side.]"

"[This could be the only way to keep the cities safe. Even the cavern is filled with refugees. Why would she wait…]" Zonqua stopped as he leaned forward. The anger slowly drained as he realized their purpose. Their fair trade did not come with any time measure but action. "[To the sands. She almost as bad as the court.]" Zonqua rubbed his brow as the others looked at him with curious glances.

"[What next?]" Nuyani asked. She had a simple understanding of their situation. They were not saving anyone. They were not helping the others. The oil was meant for the bandits to move unhindered.

"[We use the oils on the nests and routes that she deems worthy and report with each success or loss]," Rude said. There was a fatality or regret in his voice. Something to Nuyani that seemed strange for the actions of a man who was going to keep still despite knowing his actions could save others.

"[Cowards]," Nuyani mumbled as she looked to the side, trying to keep her expression neutral and the anger out of her tone. The others looked at her, wondering what she said, but none were wiser.

Nuyani gave a sigh and narrowed her eyes in an irritated fashion. She turned to look at Zonqua. "[I rest soon]," she said before leaving for Caluu and taking a tarp to change. Their leaving did not allow much time for grooming.

"[Rest sounds like a good idea]," Zonqua said as he turned over and lay down on his bed roll.

Caution shook his head before uttering, "[She's planning something.]"

"[Are you sure?]" Rude asked.

"[You know our plans are to stop the worms and the storms. Will you stop us?]" Zonqua said.

"[Mm. Perhaps not]," Rude said. "[No. I won't be.]"

"[I need to perfect more methods]," Murmur replied. Caution remained silent.

Zonqua was not surprised, as he never heard the man speak unless there was a real need or danger. Strangely enough, that trait of his character made him trust the man more than the others. He turned in his bedroll and went to sleep, as did the others.

After washing off the dried pus and changing into her own black tunic and robe like the others, Nuyani walked back, fighting the urge to spit as the smell of rot still lingered from her tarnished clothing. Making her way toward the group, she tried to keep her anger in check. Once she let her mount rest and climbed into her bed roll, Nuyani thought to herself, *The oil is for her little routes, but I'm not hers. I'm a priestess, and I will help the others.* Nuyani's thrum raced at a rapid beat, changing slightly to become a new rhythm. Then, she created a small spark of light floating in the palm of her hand. Pride rose in Nuyani as the light burned bright.

Ch. 11 Stirring the Spirit

Twenty days had passed since the initial attack of the first nest. During that time, Nuyani and the others had burned down three more with better luck. With the speed of the nogowesa and Nuyani's spell, they barged into each, killing most of the worms in contact with the shield. Once they reached low enough, they set the oil ablaze and fled once more. Nuyani rode with Zonqua on Lugna the second time, allowing the caster a firsthand view of the spell's action. His mouth was nearly agape; it surprised him that the swaths of parasites burned away like paper, and the walls covered in pus remained stagnant, unable to shift in the presence of her power. He leaned to one side and nearly hurled at the sight of a few worms eating the carcasses of a few victims Nuyani was certain came from a lone village. Even in the calming sensation of the spell, Nuyani felt her own stomach might give way. They both had seen death, but nothing could prepare someone for such a sight filled with a place of rot and death. After leaving the cavern and letting it burn, they went over different spells. Nuyani wore a look of panic as she understood that even in magic, there were different categories and glyphs far more complicated than she knew. Never thinking much of the embroidery in their tunics, she did not notice the intricate symbols and shapes that were stitched into the sleeves.

After each nest they destroyed on the hidden routes, the group returned to Walgo to report their efforts, and Nuyani would try to argue for more oil to give to villages. Each time, the priestess was ignored. Walgo compared her haste to being the fastest prey in the desert.

"You can evade most, but you will be sought for by all," she repeated the first few times until she started to ready herself for another fight with Nuyani in their conversation.

The others looked to the sides. Zonqua shook his head, knowing that there was no reason to keep trying to argue for either side, forcing Nuyani to relent at the end. When they were done, the other casters were supplied with more of the oil under watch before the group left. Leaving the bandit camp was often a tedious ordeal as Nuyani learned of low thrums and illusions playing a greater role in keeping to the correct path. Other areas had animals that Nuyani had not seen before and were quite venomous. Though she felt confident in learning how to survive the desert, she did not want to take any chances with other creatures. Her thoughts told her that any place a bandit would not go is a good place to hide any hord of shards she collects. She just wondered where else she could go. The cavern with the others did little to give her privacy, whether with other women or guards standing by.

Nuyani sat up against her bedroll and watched the fire flicker in the pit. Everyone had already eaten figs and dried kurru. She had finished trying to study both languages and the spells but held a look of panic when she was told that there were different categories to magic. Each requires different gods, drawn patterns, and power sources to match the demand. It was what she needed to create her seal, to begin with, but she found the task too steep even to understand. Triangles with symbols were meant to destroy, but circles were basic, and squares were built upon meaning. No longer was your will the only guiding force, but the contract to the gods was binding and lasting as long as there was compensation from a source. It made Nuyani's head spin, but she started to see more of the rules and designs as she recalled the embroidered tunics of the men or the slaves in the cities.

Beside her, Zonqua sat against his saddle and took a whetstone to his spear. Caution and Murmur were caring for their own eating utensils as Rude started engraving symbols into another crystal with a new band of metal around it. From what Nuyani understood of the different types of magic, not only was he making an edragaurio, but his magic was also transference. He had the ability to create his dolls of sand, all drawn in metal. All are powered by the crystal. Nuyani turned to the open desert, looking at the stars dancing over the horizon as if it were a clear blue-covered land from Buello's moon. Tonight, Gemorei's was gone. Nuyani sighed as she thought about the sun, moon, and stars. Before, she believed them all to be various forms of light given to the people by Kelvert before and after their deity had left, only staying to ensure their people's survival. Now she knew the world was vast, and her deity was just another part of it, yet still bigger than her. Nuyani clutched one of the medallions beneath her tunic, feeling the swirls of prutosa that came from the villagers, sending wishes, prayers, and guilts all the same. The waves of spirit lessened the longer she stayed in Tuikon, making her wonder if it was the thick presence of the false devourer's spirit or just dwindling faith as her presence was forgotten. Nuyani looked at the ground for a moment as she retrieved the other medallion to look at.

She looked at the misshapen, hastily carved line running through the width of the medallion and cutting through the neck of the woman engraved so elegantly in a side view. The guard who fired it at her, or near, yelled as she left. Nuyani was certain that it was near. A sense of mournful pride came over her, certain her people would not miss with a bow and arrow in hand. A weak smile rose as she wondered if that was better or worse.

You are making great progress. Just rest, though, Zonqua thought as he glanced at Nuyani. His thoughts trailed back to his own passed training the others and seeing himself in training to be a mage. What he had in a grand academy paid for by his father and a decade to learn, he was condensing to her in only a few dozen days. He was certain that there was more she could learn from him but, learning and mastery were two different things all together.

Putting away his spear, he then pulled out a smaller map. Keeping track of their movements meant that there were places that Walgo was not interested in or aware of. Zonqua studied Nuyani's spell and tried to use his own ring to replicate the shield. He only sighed, aware that its basic form was too high for him to create with ease. The thrum was far stronger in its rhythm, making it something only a Kelvertian might be able to do. Curious about the spell, Zonqua then retrieved one of the shards and started feeding his thrum into it. He expected the shard to break even further but was surprised to see that it maintained its form. He rolled the piece in his hand, feeling the pressure push against the stubborn, dull thrum. Nothing gave. As if placing an object in loose clothing, there was a lot more give to the shard's thrum.

These things are changing. Is this one a bit stronger, Zonqua asked himself as he considered the possibilities. He turned to Nuyani, prepared to ask her to use her magic, only to find her asleep. *Better to wait in the morning then,* the man thought. Their plan was to attack another pit sitting in a crossroads of sorts where more petrified soldiers of varying races collected into groups as markings. Many thought the matter disrespectful at first, but considering the bodies prevented the worms from rising, no one complained. He continued to study the map. The city closest to them was Moic, just a day or so to the east, while Cihun and Johwa were further west by two or three days. Within the area between the three cities, there were more worm sightings than ever, and a lot of goods were lost. Zonqua wondered how safe they were, however, since they had hidden from a unit and had left Moic only a couple of days ago. Using illusions to make themselves out to be stones far off the beaten path, the soldiers did not bother to check their own maps for misplaced boulders. The area also had the fewest villages around, but each one was still standing somehow despite the growing swarms.

Putting away the map, Zonqua went to his own bedroll and went to sleep. The others soon followed. The barrier created by the fire pit remained wide enough to cover the group and the nogowesa. It had an edragaurio, a figurine of Do'alc, suspended in the air above and blocking the embers from escaping. Nuyani felt something pressing on her core. Her memories fluttered to the same night as when she first encountered the banshee searching her home so long ago. The pressure continued to bore into her core, causing sleep to become elusive.

[This is not a dream], Nuyani thought as she opened her eyes. The orange ember glow shown on her bedroll. Nuyani sat up and looked out toward the open desert. The pressure was coming from that direction. The problem was that there seemed to be many faint sources of pressure. *[How am I able to sense this?]* Nuyani questioned as she wondered. She concentrated

on the racing thrum of her core. Her breathing hastened as she felt some of the pressures disperse. Immediately rising to her feet, she knew what the matter was. There were spirits attacking people. Nuyani grabbed her spear and ran for the source. The sudden steps awoke the nogowesa. Lugna and Caluu cawed in worry of Nuyani's departure. Zonqua then awoke, looking first at the animals and then at the cloud of dust that stirred just beside them.

He blinked twice before looking at Nuyani's bedroll and seeing that she was gone. "Nuyani. Why…" the man groaned as he, too, rose in a rush but then checked with his ring for anything strange radiating against his core. Surely enough, the faint pressure of spirit lingered on his senses. He then threw his saddle atop Lugna, quickly fastening it before getting into the saddle and taking off after her. Outside the barrier, he even felt her thrum radiating through the area. The cold air brought a chill to his face and throat as he held onto the reins. Zonqua wondered what was out there for Nuyani to run toward until he remembered that there was a village only a little ways away from them.

His heart pounded as he felt the weight of pressure increase rapidly. He ended his thrum only to feel a cold burrowing into his core. Even Lugna let out a wary caw, either for herself or Zonqua. They continued toward the source for only a brief wait. As the small huts and farms came into view, Zonqua could see the fleeting lights of blue and green dancing against the night sky. Banshees and heganirri attacked not only villagers but also each other. The weight of pressure made his body feel weak. His breathing labored as though the air had grown thin.

As two of the heganirri raced forth toward a fleeing woman, a barrier erected between her and the apparitions stopping them in place before changing shape and stabbing through both with magic javelins exiting the back of their heads. Emerald sparks erupted from their forms. The javelins stayed in place before turning upward and firing into another banshee just overheard. The first severed its right arm before the second hit mid-chest. A second rain of embers fell. Nuyani then came forth and helped the woman to stand. Lugna and Zonqua soon arrived. Nuyani turned with a shocked look on her face. It quickly turned into a smile, but her attention soon returned to the battle as six more of the banshees remained, and three heganirri fought them or clawed at people.

Zonqua did not wait as he rode toward the fleeing crowd, firing spheres of edria at the specters. Two of the spheres struck the malformed figures, only stunning them as they remained adrift in the air. Worry covered his face as he realized the specters were stronger than before. He scowled, seeing that the false devourer was creating solutions as much as they were. Two more men wielding spears fastened with gems fired into their chests, with each blast batting away the specters but not breaking them. Zonqua then created a barrier keeping the banshees in place as they fired once more. After a series of strikes, sapphire embers then fell. The men nodded their heads before running to join the other villagers. Neither seemed like seasoned warriors but station soldiers who seldom saw action, if any at all. The ground then shook, making Lugna widen her stance. The thought of another colossal worm rose on all their minds.

Nuyani whipped around her spear filled with edria and caught one of the heganirri on the side off their head. The creature froze in place as if it were a statue; its construct rippled sporadically. She spun the spear and chambered it to her side before stabbing forward and striking the specter in its chest. The creature moved for a moment only to pause as the blade was buried halfway. With magic radiating from the weapon, Nuyani could feel the flows of prutosa repelling the weapon, slowly pushing her back. Nuyani bared her teeth as her thrum raced. The new rhythm soon took place, and the spear's gem glowed with a white star engulfing it. The light expanded to the size of her head. The heganirri whaled as its body burst. Looking through the emerald flames, she saw the last beast specter being clawed apart by one of the banshees as another two held its arms to the sides. The hound man broke apart in each slash until it burst as well, only for the energy making up its body to feed into the banshees.

When the specters looked at her, she felt the growing surge of their presence. What she expected were the same cold howls that could freeze one's spirit. Her eyes widened, and her mouth gaped as she saw their shriveled forms condense into brightened lights before firing at her in streams of prutosa. Nuyani had raced her thrum, prepared to brush off the screams, but with three specters concentrating on her core, they struck the ethereal drum, nearly stilling her magic as cold enwrapped every limb. Nuyani's head snapped to the sky as she screamed in pain. Her body grew unresponsive for a moment as she fell to her knees. Her teeth clattered with only her grip on her spear, keeping her from lying in the dirt. Her body shook as the specters continued to beat at her core, trying to pierce it. Nuyani focused and released a chaotic pulse to her ring, amplifying the thrum to purge the violent spirits.

Glowing blue vapors rose from her body as her desperate thrum rang out, pushing them away little by little. The specters swiped and cried, trying to reach her as their energy remained too sparse to damage Nuyani. They seemed to understand the situation just as well and retreated a short distance to reform. Nuyani felt the surge of power weighing on her core. The specters were preparing to repeat their assault. With her teeth still clattering, Nuyani did not see any means to escape.

Another beam of blue then fired through the strongest specter, creating a spiraling wisp of blue mist in the air. Nuyani could not gather the strength even to look surprised as the vapors collected into another banshee with a healthier figure compared to the starved, near-skeletal forms of her counterparts. The claws of the new banshee then tore into another, turning them into embers before the last attempted a desperate howl. The new specter's form partially stretched backward like clothing caught in the wind, only for a final swipe to tear through the other banshee. The distant whale did not last long as the embers it released were absorbed by the other.

The specter then looked toward Nuyani. The priestess's heart raced as tears started streaming down her cheeks. The cold she felt still clung to her muscles, but she still mouthed the word.

"[Mother]," Nuyani said in her own language.

Zonqua soon arrived atop Lugna and fired a sphere of edria. The specter whipped about dodging the projectile before releasing a wave of prutosa, giving them a sense of ease.

Zonqua resisted the influence, thinking it was only a trick until he noticed the woman was more of a normal spirit than the vengeful banshee. He gawked at the spirit, thinking at first it to be a copy of Nuyani's, only to see portions of her arms and legs withered with less atrophy than the other spirits.

"By the goddess, Nuyani, is this her?" Zonqua asked.

Nuyani's answer only came with the release of her spear, dropping to the side as she held her arms out to the specter. Nuyani's tears grew into a sob as the specter lowered to the ground and sat on her knees as if her body were real. The man said nothing as he watched the two embrace and press their brows together. Nuyani's core was stable as the soft thrum radiated forth. She could feel the familiar currents of her mother's and father's spirit flowing through the apparition's construct along with hers. Even other people in the village were held within the spirit's making.

[They all prayed for her], Nuyani thought as she felt more tears welling.

"[Be at ease, my Little Flower. There is more to be done. There is still danger]," Huloat said. Nuyani's eyes widened as questions piled in her head, only to be shut down by the few answers she cared for. Huloat's spirit then sank into the second medallion with the image of the priestess. The passing currents of prutosa washed over her mind as she saw the thoughts and memories in visions. More worms were on the move. More towns and cities were being attacked. The false devourer had hastened their actions to combat the others. With the tremble of the earth beneath her, Nuyani was certain that another attack was heading toward the city.

Nuyani turned desperately, struggling to right herself as her strength returned. Terror covered her face as she looked at Zonqua. "Moic! Moic is going to be attacked!" she shouted as she reached out to the mage. Already off Lugna, he moved to keep her standing.

"How do you know?" Zonqua asked.

"She showed me. We have to go." Zonqua gave a nod and whistled for Lugna to approach. When the nogowesa slithered to their side, Zonqua helped Nuyani to climb on and retrieved their spears before racing off into the distance. The villagers who remained watched on as the two faded into the distance.

To Be Continued

Appendix

A) Timeline
B) Maps
C) Country
D) Races/ Species
E) Animals
F) Gods
G) The Arcane

A) <u>Time Line</u>

- o <u>912(-) Before The Grand Incursion/Age of Rule</u>

Tuikon is now embroiled in a war between the six kingdoms while facing the nokragga. The latest storm had shifted the tides of power as resources became scarce and the nokragga grew wiser.

During this time, most countries and continents dealt with their personal feuds as minor gods fought, schemed, and crawled to relevancy in their cults.

The age of the High Pantheon's growing might as they ruled Olcagon before being contested by the Incursor.

- o <u>920(-) Before The Grand Incursion/Age of Rule</u>

The Emperor of Tuikon dies leaving his vessel states to fight amongst one another without a proper heir. With each region's king seeing themselves as rightful rulers, the warfare began even as the nokragga continued to plague the land.

- o <u>1070(-) Before The Grand Incursion/Age of Rule</u>

Humans had won the war against the forces of the Vorjecoudya, Kymacs, Dwarves, and Denbonquo both due to the higher populating numbers of humans and the infighting of the kymacs turning against the denbonquo and vorjecoudya.

- o <u>1198(-) Before The Grand Incursion/Age of Rule</u>

The satellite territory for the kingdom of Do'nirri was attacked by one of the nine generals of the Incursor felling the settlement and killing one of the forms of Do'alm and Do'alc.

The people of the fallen Kingdom, "Do'nirri", fled from the city established to stretch their territory to another continent. They traveled with nearly twelve thousand people by ship into the larger caverns leading from the northeastern coast of Moleshde further inland. Surrounded and unprepared for another attack, the mountain-dwelling races of man took advantage of their turmoil capturing the people as slaves.

B) <u>Maps</u>

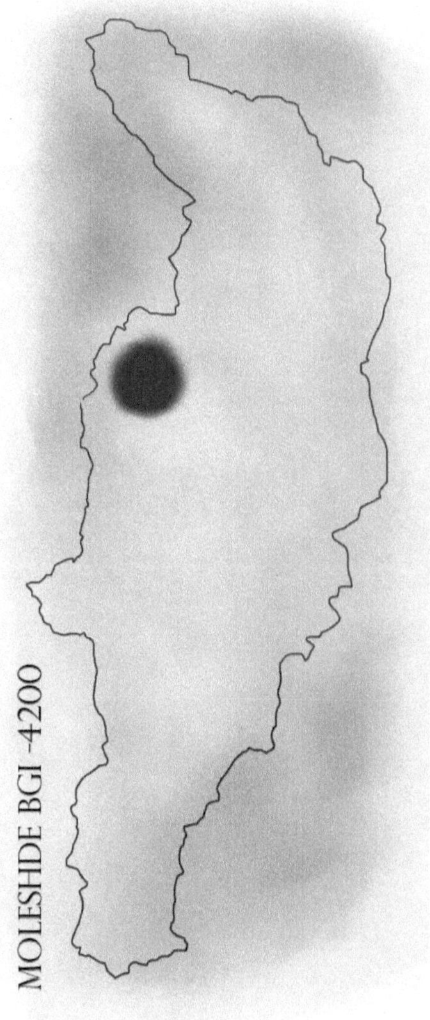

TUIKON -912 BGI
KELVERT DRYLANDS
LAYOYEM
DAIBOT
ULAH
WAHOP
ALSAC
NAYMO

C) <u>**Country: Tuikon**</u>

- Tuikon is a country formed on the borders of the desert and neighboring plateaus around it. The fourth largest desert in Olcagon, the area was formed due to a battle long ago pinning a powerful unflam (demon) in the center, the blast creating a crater and shaking the stones around it to house several networks of caverns before water flowed and the mountain races could shape them as well. Life is sustained both by the different bodies of water within the desert and also by the gods Do'alm and Do'alc who supply what rain they can. Their strength weakened by the Incursor general left them too weak to combat the threat of the caged unflom directly. Most life and resources of the desert come from the mountains but, the annual storms crossing the land cause several issues as the forces often collapse weaker caverns and form new ones. The lack of crystal shards, available in the open desert, does not protect from the waves of prutosa coursing through the stones. Few areas or settlements can withstand the storm and keep those dwelling inside safe.

- ***Kymacs***: Often called lizard people, kymacs across Olcagon are mostly known for their want for battle. As is their nature, they seek to prove themselves and often employ themselves to other races during warring times. The individual kymac often prays to the gods Gemorei, Homaig, Yasvenge, Elemus, or Melpobroech; each of the deities is of battle or hunting. The kymac women do not share the same shorter stature as their male counterparts but, stand with twice the height and strength. The kymacs fail to flourish with more settlements as their warring nature prevents stable settlements larger than a few hundred on their own. Kymac women often ventured out to find trophy towers of male bands to attract them. Most towers are made of stones with animal skulls, weapons, and armor fitted into the mortar with gleaming lights stretching for miles. The average kymac lives for twenty to twenty-five years, reaching adulthood at the age of fifteen, but few know how long the kymacs could live rarely seeing any living into their thirties. If a female visits a settlement and is impressed, she often finds a mate and has a clutch of eggs within a month. With two or three eggs, all the size of a man's head, the kymac woman will leave their eggs in a nursery with others relinquishing her claim of them. The nurseries are formed from stone, metal, and bone, with a few fireplaces to keep the area warm and several guards to protect them. Most eggs hatch within a few weeks and rapid growth occurs allowing them to reach the strength to defend themselves within a month. The women stay until they either feel the urge to leave once more, or the settlement seems to weaken.

- ***Dwarves (Udrog):*** a mountain-dwelling people, the dwarves are one of the oldest living races since the primordial state of Olcagon. Vast in their cultures, and even in the gods they worship, what remains true of the dwarves is their drive to innovate, create, and battle. Living up to three hundred years, it is common for dwarves to find themselves as full masters of different subjects from magic to smithing, medicine to battle, and even in combinations. The dwarven races are not far different from any other mortal race aside from their shorter statures remaining closer to four feet. It is unknown who or what created the first dwarves on Olcagon. All the same, different cults and factions are worshipping not just deities for battle or crafting, but even those of growth and nurturing. With long lives, there have even been individuals who have lived to see their kingdoms change rulers and countries. Their strength is slightly greater than those of humans but, their prowess in the arcane is on par.

- ***Humans (nolsaf):*** One of the longest-living mortal races, humans are an embodiment of the tenacity, survival, and weakness of mortal beings. For all of the beings that live on Olcagon, what a human man or woman may not have compared to others, they often and several traits over others. Only living up to a century, a human civilization could still stand for centuries to a millennium. As vast as the lands around them, different cultures can rise from humans as their fates are not tied to one god. Most, however, do favor the man gods, such as Aczuriv or Do'alm and Do'alc

as examples. Symbols of those who strove to reach
deification from mortal limitations were often praised
by most. Humans are capable of learning and crafting
as the dwarves and warring continuously like many
others. The greatest strength of humans is their
reasoning as their populations can grow larger and
spread throughout lands faster than most. Despite their
middling abilities and weaknesses, many other mortal
races, and monsters, were created from humans. As a
regular base, many gods find that creating their own
humans is preferential for their flexibility.

- *Vorjecoudya*: A single-gendered race, the first
vorjecoudya was a woman blessed by the god Vorjeo
with the skills and abilities of serpents. Their bodies
are covered in soft scales of varying colors and patterns
and have the top half as humans but the bottom half of
long apposable tails triple their height in human form.
In this shorter form, they only possess the strength
comparable to human women, and the scales are fused
into skin of the same colors and hue. Their eyes
contain the same diamond-shaped eyes. The
vorjecoudya can live up to two centuries and give birth
only to women while only taking six months. Due to
their singular sex, most covens are made of only two
thousand or so women who hide within mountains or
underground tunnels only to surface when they look to
capture men of various mortal races. However, if the
vorjecoudya were to attempt to mate with another
monosexual race as denbonquo or minators, only a
stillborn would be produced. With bodies of scale, the
harder material compared to skin allows, more magic
and spirit to dwell within them. Because of this trait as

well, their eyes which can instill fear have a natural curse to petrify the bodies of men, less their true interests differ. From the flux of energy through Olcagon over the centuries, this curse has grown stronger causing it to make its victims turn to stone throughout the generations. This has caused a limitation in their population but, their ingenuity allowed the vorjecoudya to will their deadly stare as a one-time gift allowing immunity to the men they choose. This gift can only be offered once per lifetime and has been used by many kingdoms to create relations between them and other mortal races. Though most tie their faith to Vorjeo, many still look to other gods. This is a byproduct of their uniform search to create a male vorjecoudya. This is a blessing the god will not honor.

-    ***Denbonquo***: A single-gendered race, the denbonquo are reliant on others. They are often employed as guards for mortal races. A cursed man for his rage, he was cursed by the god Volsba into a form that only grew in pain after killing a worshipper in regard. With blue bark-like skin, and three horns pointing backward, the hand transformed into thicker fingers with only three on each hand and retractable claws. His legs bent in a digitigrade form and his feet transformed into hooves. With his body marked by the god, and left for the people to see his crimes, he was captured and used to guard the secrets of the kingdom dedicated to the deity of pain. The denbonquo have great speed, strength, and endurance as their tough hides allow them to take damage. Though the first man was used to create others with unwilling victims, the

denbonquo eventually broke away from their initial
shackles seen as the perfect guards for other kingdoms.
Their fate is still determined by the people they protect,
the denbonquo in the world number less than one
hundred- thousand. Most only live to the age of thirty
due to the growing pain within them.

-       ***Edricoudya (people of magic)***: A single-gendered
race, edricoudya are women with immense magical
prowess as the eight jewel-like eyes encircling their
brow allow them to wield more magic than most races
are born with. The edricoudya have blue skin which
becomes darker and violet for those closer to or at the
equator Seeing the world through a mixture of waves
and colors, the edricoudya can see the very souls,
spirit, and magic of those around them. Possessing
such power, many others considered them demigods,
for their unmatched strengths compared to most others.
Created through the shared interests of Buello and
Ellamay, the edricoudya are often named scholars of
the moon. Their lives often reached two centuries.
Many believe their lives were so short only due to their
abilities to propagate on their own sacrificing the
magic within some of their jewel-like eyes in turn for
the gods to bless them. This is not their only means to
populate as many civilizations with the women were
known to have their own brothels and pleasure houses
as they looked to explore the pleasures of life instead
of shunning others. Many would prefer male partners
but, they too will only produce daughters. This even
allows them to keep the full strength of magic without
sacrifice. Many seek arts more than warfare but can be
as deadly as others. The areas of their eyes are covered

in skin, they are slowly filled. Many of the edricoudya
are captured however for purposes many unfortunate
women face, and the harvesting of their eyes. One of
the naturally formed concentrations of magic outside of
larger beasts in the wild.

E) <u>Animals:</u>

- *Nogowesa (Owl lizards)*: Used as mounts, these animals are found in the wilds of Moleshde and Elethyil in harsh environments with mountains and or caverns. Nogowesa have the heads of owls and their bodies are shaped like lizards but, covered in both feathers and scales. Depending on the region, their pelts are colored dark red and brown, white with light-khaki spots, or slightly darker khaki with subtle red spots. The males are often larger. The darker nogowesa are often shorter in body length only four men's height in length and have more muscle. The others are both longer and faster but are usually chosen for scouting parties as the others are for war. Any variation still is quick and capable of reaching fifty miles per hour both for long distances and across walls. The strength of their sharp talons can puncture plate armor and their intelligence allows them to understand most commands and some portions of conversations. In the wilds, they are territorial with herds of up to twenty containing at least four males as the rest are females. Though the animals fight for space and often choose to hunt wild dogs (hega) or kurru, they prefer to fight and defend with feats of ability such as group competitions instead of battles. As though a greater sense of preservation, it's often heard that the beasts would compete with one another leaving scores of worms or wild dogs dead in hunts and the larger number produced the winner. The animals rarely deal with the arcane, but their intelligence often allows them to both hide their presence and strengthen their bodies to do more.

- ***Kurru (Cows/bull-like animals)***: Stout and sturdy, the kurru are some of the only animals that can withstand the blasts of the sandstorms directly. They lie and hurdle together in the lower sections of stone platforms. The animals in the wild seek solid ground away from worms. Despite their slow and unimpressive natures they are strong enough to crush worms with their wide protruding horns but do not have great defense and mobility as being flanked will almost always guarantee a kill from the parasites. The kurru live long and with what little vegetation remains in the desert can contain several pounds of fat needing only a third of its daily intake to sustain itself. Their docile nature makes them the best animals for farming for both meat and cultivating farms. The animals often travel to the water pools to drink, then return to the hardened grounds for safety.

- *Hega (hounds):* Even known as wild dogs, the hega are very dangerous predators in the desert. With a large pack containing thirty or more these animals are a threat even to Nogowesa when caught unaware. The ambushers can mask their presence with magic to appear in smaller numbers. No single hega would try to face a nogowesa alone, but fifteen disguised as one can prove fatal. The animals are burrowers keeping their young in litters of eight hidden in the hardened dirt closer to the watering holes or underground sources. With a mutual hatred for the worms, some see the hega as a good sign of protection as their strong bites can shatter a worm's shell. This, however, does not mean they are immune to the parasites. The animals tend to hammer the cores of their magic during attacks to try and dissipate any lingering portion of the curse. Though they stay away from humans, larger bands can raid villages for cattle and sometimes the farmers themselves. With so much reliance on magic and spirit, those who die after killing a man can have the wills converged onto one another and the magic containing a new violent spirit, in a result creating the heganirri. Despite their nature, the hega prefer to stay away from settlements unless an opportunity is too good to pass up.

- *Noggujo (Snakes):* Within Tuikon, most serpents grow to the height of a man and stay in burrows or small cracks in rocks to hunt tcere (small rodents). Aside from the curious, and medicine men, few want anything to do with snakes of any kind. All are venomous within Tuikon, making them another reminder of the deadly touch the Nokragga have. Some do take the snakes for extraction of their venom both for medicine and other purposes. Noggujo come in a short variety of scales and patterns. Red, black, white, or golden like the morning sands are the most common ones. The snakes often have diamond-shaped patterns on their back that tend to change depending on the animal's age. The hatchlings rise from cracks with dark brown or red scales to blend into the rocks, while the black or golden rise at night, or day, to hunt during their respective times before returning to their burrows for the day. A useful function of their venom, they often secret it onto the walls of their burrows to create fixed tunnels.

- *Do'mirre (falcon):* Resourceful pets, do'mirre are some of the scouts' favorite animals to train. The animals have razor-sharp talons and wing spans as wide as a human arm's length. With a unique light blue torso and beige on the back and top of the head. The falcons live up to twenty years and choose to nest in high crevices in the plateaus. With keen eyes, the animals can locate even the snakes as their main source of food. Not picky eaters, the falcons will eat nearly anything they can pick up. With a stronger sense of magic, that even includes the smaller worms. Often falconers will create traps with fake snakes to snare the animals and layer them with an adhesive to capture them. Most falconers send the birds to fly about their space to scout for danger or game and will hover over the threat to mark them. The sound does vary between a caw for a game or fighting.

- ***Nogelm (Rock spiders):*** Beige arachnids with white lined underbellies from the mouths to the spinnerets. They produce silk not just from the end, but along the line. For other prey like tcere or marudek, they fire an entire net from this white line to capture them. Aside from the threads being a good source of adhesives, they also have a paralyzing chemical many collect and concentrate for other affairs. The nogelm are not worth keeping as pets. Many owners had been found with webs created over their mouths at night seemingly too thin and wide to suffocate anyone, but the venom paralyzing their lungs and egg sacks laid inside. With a place filled with moisture, their instinct is that it should also attack insects. The creatures roam for their prey and do not ambush making their threat more likely.

- ***Tcere (unique small mouse used for finding nuts):*** Foraging critters, these small mice have a brown fur coat with wide ears and thin tails. They are numerous in the desert and can be the bane of farmers as they can ruin crops. Many people like to use them to gather nuts from vegetation. Their fast reproductive numbers allow hundreds to be born and reach adulthood within eight months. With many animals preying on them, it's their only option to remain alive. Though some have tried to train their nests to look for more shards, it tends to only lead other animals or worms to come and prey on them instead, even leading them back to the homes of their owners.

- ***Buwamo (sheep):*** Docile creatures, the buwamo are small animals that only reach hip height with wide snouts and gray noses. Their bodies are covered with thick layers of fur that are sheared off to make clothing. In the desert, the animals are sheared three times a year. Most stay near the water holes furthest away from the desert center and have large herd populations. Nogowesa, hega, and blood manes often hunt the animals. They are short, thin-legged with hooved feet and are socially dependent on large groups to survive.

- ***Marudek (deadly beetle mixed between a Hercules beetle and wasp):*** Marudek are palm-sized beetles with sharp singular horns pointed forward and a carapace as hard as bark. The males have larger horns and greater wingspans than the females, but both have flexing abdomens with stingers at the ends capable of injecting enough venom to kill a man or paralyze nogowesa. The animals are only sought after by healers or assassins as they do not have much use for others. The creatures themselves only hunt for other insects, tcere or smaller noggujo. Similar to dragonflies, they lay their eggs at watering holes and often don't come out until fully grown. Once they can fly, they can travel for miles across the desert. Despite their location, each one is fully capable of withstanding the storms and worms as their hard shells give them a lot more resistance. Often in ten-month cycles, the insects repopulate with little hindering them. Not even the nogelm can dent their numbers.

- ***Nokragga (worms):*** The bane of Tuikon, these creatures are not truly living but are the remnant copies of the caged demon, classified as mortal-demons. Beings transformed by the Do'alc Kaddap's energy lose their minds, souls, and will as their bodies are transformed into large worms with dark brown shells, wide stub-like legs only good for burrowing through the loose sands, and four pincers and eyes surrounding the mouth at the heads center, lacking a clear description of which side to orientate as upright. Those are at least the variations created through the energies exposed to mortals, the others are smaller worms, formed through raw energy saturating the land or physical matter to form the copies. Though they share the same shape, the smaller nokragga usually burrow through the sands and into flesh until they either reach a mortal's magic core and tear it apart to form several smaller cores within. Then the pus of the worm rots the insides separating flesh to collect around these false cores and propagate more worms. For most only a few days will due to kill and transform someone, often extended into ten or more if one were to wear a talisman or was well trained in both magic or spirit. The scratches of the larger nokragga are able to cause the same effects. Aside from direct, contact with the spirit of the demon, most worms grow to man-size from prolonged consumption of flesh or saturation in the pus forming their nests. With the sudden change in tactics, the worms have now reached larger sizes rivaling buildings, and are more resistant to magic while forms are slightly different; one being larger than the man-size worms and having scorpion-like features, and the other sporting a sort of face with another opening that contains magic used to fire out beams of prutosa. Though the worms have changed, they are still susceptible to mortal wounds and cannot regenerate.

F) <u>**Gods**</u>

- *Do'alc:* As a storm goddess of the Do'nirri, she represents the outlet of power from destruction to creation. Often shown as a beautiful woman with large assets, she is looked upon both as a standard of beauty and a goddess of fertility. She had three different stages of storms, from the natural calm to its destructive out, and finally its lull. She is often depicted representing the control of wind, lightning, rain, and magic in flux and to breath life into the lands around her. This is known due to the widespread of their faith and even their survival within the desert. Both she and Do'alc were granted godhood through ritual sacrifices of strong enemies to the other storm gods in the higher pantheon during the age of Open Reign. Their rule expanded across both Moleshde and Elethyl's coast only to dissolve further from the onslaught of the Incursor's generals to the people in Tuikon.

- *Do'alm:* As a storm god of the Do'nirri, he represents the destructive force of storms to their fine point and embodies the strength of man to concentrate them into weapons. Often depicted as a man of war, never without a weapon, he is always ready to destroy the obstacles hindering his path. Do'alm is often depicted in three stages, from the storm calm before the storm with a hand on his weapon (usually a dagger), the destructive force of lightning concentrated like a spear and sword, to their sheathing after drawing blood or the down pore of rain. Both he and Do'alc were granted godhood through ritual sacrifices of strong enemies to the other storm gods in the higher pantheon during the age of Open Reign.

- ***Kelvert:*** An angel (halfaj) of immense power, Kelvert was brought down to a tenth of its power after being repelled by the Do'alm Kaddap and sent to the drylands. Though weakened, Kelvert still had enough strength to guard the lands against most of the caged demon's (unflom) attacks. When the band of Do'nirri arrived, the angel was given his name after a late hero who saved them. The people then changed their faiths to fit even their existence to Kelvert's strength. The angel was seen as a beacon of light tied to the sun because Kelvert floated above the newly formed settlement of the survivors for the first century as the stronger storms swept over the lands. Each storm took more power from the angel and forced it to dive into the land itself, where the angel fed its magic blocking as much of the Do'alm Kaddap's influence as it could. The feeding of his energy into the living creatures of the drylands gave more abilities to the Kelvertians, but without their god's presence, personal situations soon took to a culling of those with greater abilities weakening the people and leaving them vulnerable to storms.

- ***Do'alm Kaddap:*** Though only a cult follows any belief related to the false devourer, the knowledge of this being is never truly known. The worms it creates are mere weakened demonic copies formed by the influence of its lingering power and will, shaping reality around it. To the cultists, there is reason to follow such power. Before the Do'nirri fled to the desert they were captured by people who were resistant to Do'alm Kaddap's influence. Yet, it was here before them. Though the humans proved to overtake the desert, they still succumbed to wounds from the kaddap. Despite the power of the gods they worshipped, the storms created in the Do'alm Kaddap's wake were never contested. To the people, they questioned whether the power could be greater than Do'alm and Do'alc.

G) <u>The Arcane</u>

- ***Edria (Magic)*** is the fusion of spirit and matter
  forming this ethereal energy. With qualities of both, it
  can interact with the mortal realm with ease, but
  remains an energy capable of controlling the elements
  with enough knowledge and will. The third element to
  life, it is essential to living and makes up the veil that
  separates the mortal realm and soul realm. Even in all
  mortal creatures, it plays much of the same role and
  has been referenced as the internal drum or ethereal
  drum. One's magic core is formed in the womb, egg, or
  seed during gestation before a soul is summoned from
  the soul realm or guided by the haflaj to the new
  vessel. This becomes a barrier that keeps the soul
  within the mortal realm until it is broken as the soul
  draws spirit from the other realm into the body. As
  beings of matter, this was used by the gods to create
  aging in mortals. The soul within the core creates
  waves through the spirit (prutosa) which beat against
  the confines of the magic barrier forming a unique beat
  to the individual vessel, though depending on the gods,
  the beat will still match rhythmically with their
  creators making different magic sources remain distinct

and even conflict. Magic can strengthen with use but breaks apart depending on the source. Magic converted from the body is still strong but can be torn apart easily compared to magic converted from steel or stone. These differences remain as traits of their densities though this can be overcome as the stagnant natures of a converted blade won't resonate faster than one's own core unless the wielder is able to use their core to influence an external source as well. The vibrance or rhythmic patterns of the core are what allows one to use spells though this can be blocked if the waves are too weak. Most animals merely rely on strengthening their core's pulse or hastening the beat to strengthen their bodies, while man uses this to create barriers outside their bodies and influence the world around them in conjuring or blocking spirit and other arcane attacks. Being an ethereal force, it can be collected almost infinitely within objects, or concentrated on its own into crystals or gems.

-       ***Spirit/ Spiritual energy (prutosa)*** is the first ethereal force needed for the creation of life. Without this force, not even the demons would be created. As matter floats about in the soul realm, it eventually becomes saturated with prutosa to create magic, thus creating vessels for souls to become trapped in. Once a soul is stuck in any floating stone or debris, it draws in more spirit creating a denser spot and transforming the matter into demons. With more complex steps, this is a similar production for both the angels and mortals. Spirit flows land burns, requiring quantity over quality to fuel spells. Spirit is often the fuel for energy-based attacks for fire or lightning and often for afflicting curses or spells to manipulate the mind, body, and stone instead. What effort it takes magic to cast a spell for water, is three times the equal effort and energy for spirit. While practiced casters can reduce the requirements with the amount of magic needed, the same cannot be said for prutosa. One's spirit (soul shadow) is merely the repeated flow and pattern making up a vessel's conscience. Apparitions are completely formed on this same flow to create their forms, though without constantly feeding on others, or in an area to retain their flow as false vessels, spirits will eventually burn out. The energy without a host will return to the soul realm or be taken by another source. For mortals too much spirit can rapidly age them or cause strange changes while too little spirit will force their souls to leave their bodies and return to the soul realm as well. This can cause severe changes, and mutations before death as life and will could transform the vessel into ghouls (womteg) or other monsters associated with their creators.

\-   ***Souls/Seeds of Life (Prajial)*** are the constructs fused of both spirit and magic intertwined. All vessels contain them, from a blade of grass or small insect to the towering gods that dwarf mountains. Their constant need to be around spirit is what creates life. With the collection of souls comes the collection of more spirit. This is why many demons, gods, and casters seek to steal or bargain with such treasures. Though different souls only depend on how much energy they draw from the other realm, all souls have the same function. One of the main abilities of gods that distinguish their might is their ability to create souls mastering the amount of matter magic and spirit to concentrate into one point and forge life. The Titans can destroy and separate these forces from one another. Souls are only destroyed based on either a god or titan's influence and are effectively immortal. With the souls remaining the same, there are times when the souls fail to return to the soul realm but, just to another vessel as a form of reincarnation. Sometimes the same remnant energy of spirit can linger with a passing life adding to ghostly thoughts or memories of previous lives.

-        ***Spells:*** There are different variations of spells from the natural, such as barriers or constitution to one's body, to the scripted, such as conjuring lightning due to a god's name. Magic and spiritual energy can fuel this call but differ in various ways. Spheres of edria, javelins of energy, and beams of prutosa are all categorically spells, but the spells for conjuring are in the domains of the pantheon. One may be able to conjure a flame but, the purpose of the flame can be denied if the god finds you unworthy. All spells from mortals cost spirit, whether edria or prutosa in quantity, spirit will be given to the deities who power the spells that are used. This is the conscription the high pantheon has over the mortal world of Olcagon. The mortals normally do not have the strength to use the arcane but, were shown symbols to resonate their cores to manipulate reality. These circumstances make mortals dependent on the high pantheon to allow anything to happen but, this is also why some mortals seek to create their own sources of power or contract with demons and deities outside the pantheon. The power granted may be enough to move mountains but, most of the gods will not bother with pagan faiths as they have their own affairs to attend to. With the levels of power between different deities, this system is both a gift and a curse for mortals. The mortals know who to answer to, and who they will cross. The answers to nature are even written into the natural world around them. Even the vibrations of matter can give the names of gods to call upon.

-        ***Magic Items:*** (edrabisrak) are items infused with magic or made of magic to perform different tasks, spells, or curses inscribed on them or in them. This allows them to strengthen, maintain, or lessen and sever power from others:

o   Forte items of magic (tegria bisrak edria): amplifies the power given to double per source

o   Retainer items of magic (gaurioxash bisrak edria): items using magic with written orders or spells from the source. The items have their own fixed source that can be activated under set conditions and will first channel the energy received into performing the set spell.

o   Severance item of magic (pojlif bisrak edria): similar to the retainers, and the opposite of the forte, these items can rebound energy received and send energy into something or someone to disrupt magic.

-    ***High pantheon:*** Once the first eight gods banned together, they fought in heated battles and formed Olcagon out of the bodies of the slain gods and titans that looked to challenge their might. After the onslaught, the eight deities formed the planet, the sun, the twin moons, and other worlds as their individual domains. The remaining fifty-six deities all were created, captured, or crowned as worthy champions to the gods expanding concepts of life and will from the people. As the deities rule over Olcagon, their strength grows. With each rotation of the planet. To keep themselves protected from other rival gods, they often allow other deities to find worshippers to strengthen themselves as well. A separate faith can be a revealing beacon to the deities of Olcagon and measured allowing a better chance to strike down or capture.

9 781735 948225